We Are the Ghosts

———

This is an undesigned advance proof.

WE ARE THE GHOSTS

Vicky Skinner

SWOON READS

NEW YORK

A SWOON READS BOOK

An imprint of Feiwel and Friends and Macmillan Publishing Group, LLC

175 Fifth Avenue, New York, NY 10010

Our books may be purchased in bulk for promotional, educational, or business use.
Please contact your local bookseller or the
Macmillan Corporate and Premium Sales Department at (800) 221-7945 ext. 5442
or by email at MacmillanSpecialMarkets@macmillan.com.

Library of Congress Cataloging-in-Publication Data is available.
ISBN 978-1-250-19535-7 (hardcover) / ISBN 978-1-250-19536-4 (ebook)

Book design by Liz Dresner

First edition, 2019

1 3 5 7 9 10 8 6 4 2

swoonreads.com

For Alice

"Their love and their hatred and their envy have already perished; neither have they any more a share in anything that is done under the sun."

—Ecclesiastes 9:6 (AMP)

"When my time comes, forget the wrong that I've done."

—Linkin Park

Chapter One

I have a sex dream about James Dean the night I find out my brother is dead. I watched *Rebel Without a Cause* before bed, hours before my mother woke me in a panic, and it's all I can think about while she tells me Luke's Mazda slid on an icy road, taking him right off the side of a bridge somewhere in Michigan.

I stare down at the dining room table, unsure of what to do. I want to tell my parents that they can't be saying this to me right now because it's the middle of the night and I have to work in the morning. Instead of telling them this, I think about James Dean. I think of him in my mind yelling, "You're tearing me apart!" instead of my mother telling me that someone from the police station in Ann Arbor called her an hour ago, after they found Luke's car upside down in the Huron River.

"Ellie? Are you okay?"

Later, when I think back on this moment, I'll focus on the fact that neither of my parents is crying. Shouldn't they be blubbering? Shouldn't they be crawling over each other to get to me, the only child they have left? It feels like it should be that way, like pictures of parents when they've found out their children went away to war and never came back. But my parents aren't crying. My father is staring down at the table, his eyes wide and unfocused, like he's not actually seeing anything, and my mother is just staring at me. What is she waiting for? They're not touching each other. My mother sits with her hands in her lap while my father keeps his arms on the tabletop. Neither of them reaches for me.

"Ellie?"

I know my mother is asking me a question, but I can't see her anymore. Or hear her. My world goes fuzzy, and I stand up from the table, holding my stomach because I suddenly feel like all my insides are going to come spilling out, until I'm nothing but a lumpy mess on the carpet.

My brother's body is lying on a slab in a morgue in Ann Arbor. I imagine it as I walk away from the table, his skin cold and pale the way that they always portray it on TV, his chest cut open down the middle so that someone can do an autopsy. Maybe this is really how it is. Maybe it isn't. I don't really know.

According to my mother, it's pretty clear that his tires slipped on the icy road, so I don't think they'd even do an autopsy. Luke never drove on ice. After that time he skidded on his way to school and ended up facing oncoming traffic, he did everything he could to avoid it. I want to tell her she's mistaken. That he slid off that bridge but that some kind bystander dove in after him, pulling him free and performing mouth-to-mouth on the edge of the highway.

But that isn't what happened. No one saved Luke. Luke is gone.

Luke is dead.

I'm chanting it over and over in my head as I move down the hallway toward the bathroom. I don't make it all the way there. I throw up on the carpet outside of my parents' bedroom.

———

I don't want to go to the funeral. It's more than just everyone staring at me. They've been staring for the last week, making my skin crawl, making me feel like I should walk around with a black veil over my face or something, like I'm on display.

And it's more than seeing everyone I know in the church. I know everyone from Eaton High will be there. They'll be there because everyone loved Luke and everyone knew him and now he's gone. To them, he'll be the track star, the debate champion, the golden boy forever, a smiling face in the yearbook. What it must be like to be able to shed a tear at a funeral and then move on with your life.

But it's more than the fact that it's Luke's funeral. To me, funerals are some kind of social ritual, something you do so that you can put your grief on display, but experts (apparently) say that not going to a funeral can stunt your grieving process.

Grieving process. Like it's a science experiment.

I always thought of funerals happening on cold, cloudy days, people holding umbrellas or pulling their thick coats tight around them. But on the day of Luke's funeral, the sun is shining. It's a sweltering Texas summer day as we walk into the church with everyone's eyes on us—my father, my mother, and me, trailing behind because I'd rather be the one going in the ground than the one witnessing it.

When we get to the front of the room, my mother goes into the pew first, but my father gestures for me to scoot in before him. They're going to trap me between them like a child at a movie theater so that I can't make a run for it while their attention is diverted.

I keep my eyes away from the casket the whole time. It's closed, thank God, even though no one explained to me why. I can't bring myself to ask any questions. Too many graphic possibilities cross my mind. My hands tremble slightly, and I'm not positive if it's because of the attention, eyes hot on my skin, or the huge picture of Luke sitting on a stand at the front of the room. I keep my eyes off it, too, the picture from his graduation, even though knowing it's there is enough to make something heavy settle right at the base of my throat. I think I can handle being watched by the whole city of Eaton today; I can't take being watched by Luke, too.

I don't sing the hymns. I don't listen to scripture being quoted. My family isn't religious, but this is Texas and funerals happen in churches. I didn't go with my parents when they met with this priest for the service, but I imagine them picking out his eulogy like someone picking out a cool design at a tattoo parlor. The words are cold and generic. I'm sure the speaker plugged Luke's name into the empty blanks on his handy-dandy eulogy form like Eulogy Mad Libs, though I'm sure they're supposed to be comforting.

He died too young. He was so loved by everyone. He was a good kid.

He was a good kid who walked out of our lives a year ago and never came back.

For one uncomfortable second, a picture flashes in my mind, the one that always flashes in my mind when I think about Luke, about the last time we were together. The two of us driving home from the Nova concert the night before he left, laughing, singing, acting normal. He was acting normal, even though he knew what he was going to do.

I rub my forehead, like I can force the image out, and look around the church. Family from out of town; business associates of my father's; professors who teach at Tate University with my mother, the school that sits in the center of Eaton; and in the back half of the room, people from Eaton High School, some of them in my grade and some of them people who graduated with Luke. Most of them are now Eaton High School alumni and current Tate students.

I scan the faces for Wes, but I don't see him, which makes something in my chest ache. At the very least, I thought I would see Wes.

I don't see him, but I do see Gwen Garcia. I almost miss her, invisible in the corner of the room, standing behind two guys from the football team who are almost twice her size. She doesn't seem to have a problem with them blocking her view because she's not watching the service. Her eyes are squeezed shut behind her glasses, and she's crying quietly, her face puffed and wet, her hands clenching a pack of tissues that she's not even using.

I look away from her before I can get caught up in her sadness, my eyes continuing to travel until they land on Cade Matthews, standing with his back against the closed doors, his eyes on the floor and his hands stuffed in the pockets of his black slacks. His jaw is firm with solemnity and respect, ever the perfect gentleman.

While I'm still watching him, his eyes lift from their spot on the floor and find mine. The entire room is between us, but when his focus lands on me, I feel it like a shock to my nervous system.

My mother's hand lands on my knee, bare because she made me wear a dress, and I spin around.

"Can you pay attention, please?" she hisses in my ear.

I grit my teeth against the things I want to say and stare at the hymnal in the shelf on the back of the pew in front of me. I can't look up at the rent-a-priest or the casket or the bouquet of gardenias that's overflowing onto the podium. It all feels like a circus. Why should his funeral be perfect when nothing else was?

———

The guy my mother is speaking to looks familiar. I think he might work at Tate, and based on the conversation that my mother is having with him, she's still trying to sell him on Luke being a good student, like he's going to show up at any moment, ready to enroll.

"Luke was so assertive and intelligent," she says, putting her hand out as if she can demonstrate. "You know, he was on the debate team. I was surprised when he chose to join on top of all the work he was doing as class president, not to mention the track team, but he really enjoyed it. Cleaned house at competition." She sounds like a commercial for Luke's accomplishments, and she looks like one, too, her eyes bright, her mouth smiling, her hands poised just so. I'm almost able to believe that she actually liked Luke. But I have too much evidence to prove otherwise. The sound of their constant shouting back and forth plays on repeat in my brain all the time.

Controlling.

Ungrateful.

Obnoxious.

Childish.

Tyrant.

I've maneuvered myself into a corner of the living room, half-hidden behind my father, watching my mother through the unobstructed doorway and trying to be invisible to all the people floating around my house.

They're looking at our pictures and picking apart the little pieces of Luke that still remain: his high school diploma framed on the wall, his old pair of running shoes tucked under the entry table, the stupid video-game console he begged my parents for, taking up one shelf of the entertainment unit.

They approach my father, one-by-one, shaking his hand or pulling him into a hug and offering him condolences, only to smile at me sadly without a word before walking away. No one feels the need to tell me they're sorry, and I'm thankful for it. I just want to stay in this corner and try to disconnect, try to pretend this isn't all for Luke. My hands are fisted in my skirt, sweaty and achy. My father's eyes are glassy. He's a zombie, shaking hands with people while barely making eye contact.

"Ellie?"

I don't even realize that Cade is standing right next to me until he's saying my name, and I'm immediately caught off guard by how close he is to me, so close I'm worried he can hear my heart hammering in my chest. Can he see that every muscle in my body is tense, ready to detonate?

"Oh. Cade. Hi." Cade and I have been something like friends for years, always partnering up for projects, always hanging out in the halls after school. I've known him half my life, until that night I ruined everything. But I've never seen him like this, his green eyes uneasy, full of concern. He says something, his mouth moving slowly, but I can't make out the words. All I can hear is my mother's voice in the kitchen.

"He was special, you know? That way that some people just are. They walk into a room and command the attention of every person in it." Her eyes go starry, like she's imagining Luke walking into this room right now. I don't even know where this is all coming from. I've never heard her talk about Luke like this. If she wasn't fighting with him, she was complaining about him. Always the Luke-induced sigh.

Luke never picks up after himself. Always expecting me to be his maid.

Would it kill Luke to show up to one family dinner on time?

Why can't Luke ever meet deadlines? I'm sick of having to do things for him.

Sigh.

The man, looking down into his coffee cup, nods solemnly. "I know the type."

"I'm sorry, but I have to go," I say to Cade and walk away from him without another glance. I rush upstairs and into my room, shutting the door behind me and leaning against it. I gasp in a breath and wait to wake up from whatever this is, this dream I'm floating around in, someone else's life. Not mine.

I sit on the edge of my bed and take off my heels. My mother bought them, a size too small, and I spread my toes the second they're off. I scrub my hands over my face, through my hair, down my neck. The heat is stifling, even sitting directly under the air-conditioner vent, and I'm starting to think that maybe it has nothing to do with the thermostat and more to do with listening to my mother spout those lies downstairs. There was affection in her voice. Stiff, artificial affection.

Something becomes unsettled in my stomach, and I have to lie down, wrapping my arms around myself and curling in tight. My hands ball into fists and my jaw clenches and I think maybe I'll live like this forever, my entire body tensed, braced for a life I don't recognize anymore.

I fall asleep like that, my body finally giving up the fight, and I wake up at sunset to the sound of a car door slamming. The house is quiet, and I push myself up on my bed to look out my window in time to see my dad's boss get into his car and drive away. There are no more cars in the driveway or against the curb. Everyone is gone.

I hear footsteps on the stairs. Without thinking, I drop back down on my bed, turning my back to my door and pretending to be asleep. My mother knocks softly and then the door opens. I squeeze my eyes shut, even though I know she can't see.

After a pause, the door closes again, and I listen to the sound of her heels moving back down the stairs.

And then it starts, quiet at first, like she's trying not to wake me, and then worse, louder with every second.

"You barely spoke to anyone," I hear her say. The house is so quiet that I feel like I can hear the breaths she takes between sentences. "You just stood there. You barely even *looked* at anyone." I know she's talking to my dad. This is always how she talks to my dad. It's how she talks to everyone.

It's how she talked to Luke.

"You think the world is any better outside of Eaton?" she would say to him. "You think you're going to find fame and success and happiness if you leave? You won't. It's misery everywhere else, too, Lucas, just different misery."

"We're supposed to be doing this together," she says now. "We're supposed to do everything together, but every time I turned around, you weren't there. How am I supposed to do this by myself?"

I listen hard, but I don't hear my father answer her, and when she speaks again, her words are shrill, so loud, my heart pounds and my blood goes cold. "Say something!" she yells, and I'm on my feet before she can shout anything else, feeling the same chill crawl up my back the way it does every time she yells. It's a kind of fear, even though the anger is never directed at me. I move to the window.

Luke and I perfected the art of climbing down the trellis that separates my window from his years ago. We never did anything too terrible, mostly just went to parties at Tate or met up with Luke's friends to go for late-night drives or play drunk pool in someone's basement. Sometimes he snuck out without me to meet Gwen in the middle of the night.

The only difference between then and now is that I've never actually scaled the trellis in a dress and pantyhose, and the wood is slippery beneath the nylon. But I make it to the bottom, where the grass feels nice under my feet, and make a run for my car.

I stand outside Wes's house and stare at the metal knocker on the door. It's shaped like an elephant, and as well as I can remember, I've never seen it before. But it's been over a year since the last time I stood on this welcome mat.

I lift my hand to knock when the door flies open and Wes appears in the doorway, shirtless and holding a cordless game controller. I focus on his face instead of his long, dark torso. That's a lot of bare skin.

"Ellie?" His eyebrows come together in confusion, and I don't miss the way his eyes glance over my shoulder quickly, like he's expecting someone else, before meeting mine again. "I saw your car pull up. What are you doing here?" I look down at my feet, and I guess he does, too, because he says, "And why aren't you wearing shoes?"

I shrug but don't tell him that I left my shoes at home in my hurry to get out. I'm second-guessing my decision to come here, even though it was the only thing that made sense when I made it to my car. It wasn't until I pulled up to his curb that the nerves set in. But this is Wes, and I know I shouldn't be so nervous. "Can't be at home right now." There are more reasons why I'm here, standing in front of Luke's ex-best friend when we haven't spoken in over a year, but his front porch just doesn't seem like the best place for that kind of explanation. "Could I come in?"

He watches me, his thumb moving over the buttons on the controller absently, and then moves to let me in. When I step into his living room, I'm hit with a wave of nostalgia for this place where I spent more time than I spent at my own house. It smells like dinner and fresh laundry and scented candles, and I breathe in the scent of it, thinking of all the times Luke and I came here because we couldn't stand to be at home. So many hours spent watching TV, playing video games, having burping contests, carving our names on the underside of all the beds. I've wished I could move in here and never go back home more times than I can count. I wish it right now. Somehow I miss it, even as I'm standing here.

"Give me a second," Wes mutters, and I wait in the hallway as he disappears into his bedroom and comes back wearing a T-shirt. EATON HIGH TRACK AND FIELD. My heart stutters when I see it. That was Luke's shirt, probably transferred to Wes the way so many clothes were, their entire wardrobes moving back and forth between the two with perfect ease.

I can hear Wes's mother in the kitchen, but she doesn't seem to know I'm here, so she continues what she's doing, the sound of pans clacking together streaming from the open doorway. She was at the funeral, but I don't remember seeing her in our house after. Or maybe she was there, but my brain was too fuzzy to notice.

I know her well enough to know that if she knew I'd just walked into her house on the day of Luke's funeral, she'd smother me with affection and sympathy. Wes seems to know it, too, and he ushers me quickly toward the dining room, where a door leads down to the basement.

This, at least, hasn't changed. The recliners, the huge TV, the shelves and shelves of Cowboys fan memorabilia. The basement is usually Wes's dad's haven, but when he's at work, Wes gets to use it. I settle into one of the recliners. The only light in the room is coming from the TV, where something is paused. A video game, I'm presuming. The curtains are pulled over the window. Music plays from a stereo at a mostly reasonable volume, a soft rock ballad, something I don't recognize.

"It's really good to see you," Wes says after a moment, his eyes on the TV.

I consider not saying anything. I pull my feet up onto the chair with me and wrap my arms around them. It would be easier to say nothing, to stay silent like I have at home, to clamp my lips shut and not risk crying or screaming or something else unimaginable. "I'm sorry I haven't been around."

Wes shrugs. "Just because I was Luke's best friend doesn't mean you have any obligation to come around."

"I'm still sorry." This much is true. There were days growing up when Wes felt just as much of a brother to me as Luke did. They'd been friends for as long as I can remember, and when Luke left, I was the one who had to tell Wes that he disappeared in the middle of the night without a word to anyone. Wes was just as confused as I was. And then Wes went to Tate, and I went back to high school, and we forgot we knew each other.

I watch his hands squeeze and unclench around the controller. "How have things been?"

I know what he's asking. How're Mom and Dad holding up? Is our world still the same as it was a year ago? Have our lives gone completely off-kilter since we got the call from the police? I shrug. "I don't know." What I mean is, I don't know how to say what I need to. I don't know how to juggle everything I'm feeling and not feeling all at the same time. I don't know how to feel anything without feeling too much.

This makes his fingers stop fiddling with the controller. I can feel his eyes on me, but I can't look at him. I haven't spoken to anyone about Luke leaving, and I definitely haven't spoken to anyone about him dying, and right here, in Wes's basement that smells like Febreze and the subtle lingering scent of BBQ, I can't tell him that something inside me is on fire, an animal that waits patiently for its moment to strike, a moment when it can rip free from my chest and raze the whole universe, and that to cage that animal, I've chosen to be numb instead. Being numb, being hollow, it's easier than anything else.

He opens his mouth to say something, but at that moment, the music changes, and a familiar song plays low from the speakers. And like a golden retriever, my ears perk up at the well-known guitar notes. I'm rushing to the stereo before I'm aware my brain has sent my limbs any messages. I can't find the button to change it to the next song or the power button or anything, so I reach down and rip the cord from the outlet, and the room plummets into silence.

I stare down at the speaker system as my pulse slowly goes back to normal. I'm breathing heavy, like I just sprinted a mile, and embarrassed heat spreads across my skin. I've become so good at not reacting, when my mother says something cruel, when my father says nothing at all, when I find one of Luke's shirts in the laundry or a pack of his gum in my glovebox or a pair of his shoes in my closet, when anyone says Luke's name or tells me they're sorry or asks me how I am. I should have been able to hear that song without snapping. I'm slipping.

Wes is standing now, his arms crossed, looking tentative. "I'm sorry, Ellie." He says it so carefully, like somehow this is all his fault, and if he says just the wrong thing, I might attack. I don't have the energy to attack.

I take a step forward and sit down on the recliner gently. This thing between us is so fragile, and I'm not ready for it to shatter just yet.

Wes settles back onto his seat. He scrubs his fingers through his curly hair, cut short against his scalp.

"You didn't come to the funeral." I didn't even realize until just now that it's bothering me, that his not being there somehow made everything *more*, more empty, more confusing, more unreal, more alone. If he'd been there, he would have sat with me and maybe I wouldn't have had to face everyone alone.

His hands fall open by his sides. "I couldn't handle it. I'm sorry, but I just couldn't sit there and listen to the songs and see all the flowers—"

"But you're his best friend! And I needed you there!" I don't mean to yell, but it doesn't matter. I'm terrified that I've just broken the spell. I curl my lips in between my teeth, like holding them there will be able to hold in everything that's threatening to crawl to the surface. I have to force it down, keep it in.

"I *was* his best friend," Wes says quietly. "He didn't want to be my friend anymore, remember?"

The room is so quiet that I can hear Wes's mom talking to someone on the phone. She laughs, and I envy her.

"Was it bad?"

I shrug. "Everyone kept saying how tragic it was that he died so young. Like it didn't matter that he died, just that he died when he was twenty. It was bullshit." I cross my arms hard over my stomach, holding myself together. "Way too many flowers."

Wes rolls his eyes. "The worst."

All the things we want to ask each other lie on the floor between us. We have a year's worth of crap to talk about, but I don't want to talk about any of it.

"Can I play?"

He looks over at me slowly, and I see his mouth twitch, like he wants to smile, but then his eyes widen, his mouth going firm again. Maybe he thinks he's not allowed to smile. Maybe he's right.

He doesn't say a word as he passes me a controller, but before he can start the game, his mom is calling down the stairs to him. "Wes! Baby, dinner is ready! Come help your girlfriend set the table! I taught you better than this!"

I try not to seem shocked as I look over at Wes, but I can tell he didn't mean for me to hear about this from the way he can't meet my eye, from the blush I can see in his cheeks when he goes to turn on the light and turn off the TV.

"Sorry," he says. "Duty calls."

"Right. Yeah. That's fine."

"Did you want—"

"I should probably—"

We both stop talking, but as we move up the stairs to the dining room, Wes asks, "Do you want to stay for dinner? I'm sure there's enough for everyone."

I wave him off, but he doesn't see me with his back turned toward me as we emerge into the dining room, and I don't have a chance to answer before the door shuts behind us, and I'm met by Wes's mother. And his girlfriend.

Gwen.

"Ellie!" Wes's mom squeaks. "I had no clue you were here!"

She isn't the only one. With an empty plate in each hand, bent slightly over the table, Gwen stops, her eyes as wide as the dinner plates she's holding. "Ellie," she says, her quiet voice in perfect contrast to Wes's mother's.

All the nostalgia I had for this place just minutes ago vanishes, and I immediately feel out of place, like I just stepped into an episode of *The Twilight Zone.* I try to somehow reconcile how life has been for the last year for me with whatever I just stepped into here in Wes's kitchen. Wes's mom called Gwen Wes's *girlfriend.*

"I have to get home," I lie.

"I'll walk you out," Wes says. He doesn't even seem like the same person he was a minute ago, when we were in the basement. Now, he's a person who's dating Luke's ex-girlfriend and I feel like I don't know that person. Everyone is staring at me, and I'm starting to sweat.

"It's okay," I say, moving for the door before anyone else can try to persuade me to stay.

I feel like I don't recognize anything or anyone anymore, now that the world looks so different than it did a year ago. Just when I thought I knew what my new reality looked like, everything has changed, and I've lost track of where I fit in.

———————

It turns out that getting back up the trellis is way harder than getting down it in the first place. It also turns out I was wrong about my parents not knowing I was gone, and when I tumble into my bedroom through my window, my mother is already standing in the doorway, waiting for me.

"Where were you?" she asks. Her voice isn't angry, but there's enough anger written across her face to make up for it.

I stop in front of her, trying to concoct a lie in my head. I wasn't prepared for this, assuming she would just be asleep or completely clueless when I got here, and now that she's standing in front of me, anything I might want to say gets caught in my throat. I can't tell her the truth. My mother hasn't seen Wes in a year, either. I still remember the last time he came over, three days before Luke disappeared. Mom made lasagna, she and Luke argued about what he was going to major in at Tate, and then Wes and Luke sat in the living room, playing *Call of Duty* until my mother stumbled in and told Wes it was time to go home. I remember Luke storming out of the room before Wes was even gone. My mother never kicked Wes out of the house.

So, I can't tell her I was with Wes, even if I wanted to. And I don't. I can't even describe it, but I feel like I need to keep it a secret, especially since I'm pretty sure that was the end of it. Wes and Gwen have moved on without me, and it was stupid of me to think they wouldn't. But knowing it, having the evidence right in front of me in that dining room, feels like being untethered from anything that might have been left of my old life.

"Just went for a drive." I regret saying it as soon as it comes out of my mouth, but I regret it more when I see the way my mother's eyes go wide, the way her mouth takes on a horrified shape.

Just went for a drive. Luke used to say that all the time. He told me once that he would sometimes turn his music up loud and circle the entire town of Eaton twice. He said other times he would drive to Eaton High, park in the lot by the softball field, and listen to an entire Nova album with his eyes closed and his air conditioner running. Other times he would be gone for hours and never tell me where he went. He would come home quiet and pensive.

I can't blame my mother for looking at me like I just slapped her. Because it isn't my thing, *just went for a drive*; it's his. *Was* his.

"I'm tired," I say, hoping that will make her leave. It doesn't. I can't take her standing in the doorway anymore. I need a moment to breathe, to just *be*.

"There's dinner," she says instead, her voice uncharacteristically hesitant. "Rita Matthews left us a casserole. I didn't really expect to see her today. Don't think I've ever had a conversation with the woman—"

"I'm not hungry." She holds my eyes for a long moment, and I know she's surprised. I never talk back to my mother. I never argue with her authority. But I just want to do what I want *just once*. "Ellie, I haven't seen you eat in days."

"I said, I'm not hungry." I say it loud over her, since she didn't seem to get the hint the first time. I just want her to leave me alone. I want her to stop trying to play attentive mother, like she needs to take care of me. I don't need her to take care of me.

I'm ready for the argument. My mother's favorite thing to do is argue. She'll pick a fight with anyone standing too close, and picking fights with Luke used to be her favorite pastime.

For a second, I remember the argument they had last year, the one they don't know I heard, the one I still don't really understand.

My mother doesn't argue. Maybe she's cutting me some slack because of the funeral, maybe she's just too tired to be her normal, angry self. I don't care what the reason is. I'm just grateful for it when she finally turns and goes back downstairs, leaving me in peace.

I shut the door and immediately slip out of my clothes, ready to be rid of them. Instead of putting the dress in my hamper to be washed, I toss it into a bag in the back of my closet, full of clothes I intend to donate. I'm never wearing the thing again.

I take a shower because I still feel like I smell like gardenias and polyester, and while I sit on my bed, brushing my hair, I see it.

Among the books and miscellaneous junk on my desk is an envelope. I don't know if it was there before I went to see Wes, but I know it wasn't there this morning. At least, I don't think it was. I try to remember the last time I paid attention to anything in my room other than my bed. I pick it up and look at the return address, and my heart leaps into my throat.

There's no name, just an address. A Michigan address. It isn't in Ann Arbor. It's in a town called Dexter.

My hands tremble as I rip open the envelope and pull out the contents. I stare at the folded map in my hand, seeing just fragments of highways and state lines and blue bodies of water before I unfold it.

I recognize it immediately, and it's my first instinct to drop it, my heart beating loud in my ears. Because it's like having Luke's ghost in the room with me. I press my hands to my stomach and look down at it, lying sprawled open on my carpet. I can't really be looking at this map. That map can't really be on my floor. That map has been lost for ages.

"These are all the places we have to visit before we die," Luke said when he brought the map home. It was the summer before my freshman year of high school, before his junior year, and he spread the map across the dining room table like we were about to discuss war strategy. "If you want to add anything to it, just put X's over the places, but I've already got most of the big stuff. Grand Canyon, Mount Rushmore, Times Square . . ."

For months, we took turns researching new places to add to the map, and eventually we brought Wes into it. We picked big cities, ghost towns, weird attractions along the side of the highway. It was a whole summer of daydreaming about adventures in the mountains, relaxing on the beach, soaking up history and culture and sunshine.

I slowly reach down and pick it back up. All the X's, in different color marker, his and mine and Wes's, are so plentiful, I almost can't see the city names beneath them. Notes in the margins about gas mileage and hotels and entrance fees. It's been folded and refolded and laid out flat so many times that the original creases are gone. It was just a stupid thing he got excited about, the way he got excited about things and then didn't usually follow through on them. The map was our world for a few months and then it was forgotten about, and that was that.

That was three years ago. Three years ago, and here it is, in my hands, and I feel dizzy with confusion and disbelief and maybe even a little fear. Where the hell did it come from?

I turn the envelope over again, looking at the address it came from. My name is written as Ellie Johnston. Not from some stranger, then. A stranger wouldn't know I go by Ellie instead of Eloise. Someone who knows me personally?

But that can't be possible because other than Luke, I have never known anyone who lived in Michigan, and the idea that someone in Michigan knows my name and my address is enough to make me glance over my shoulder, like there might be someone behind me, watching me.

I look back at the map, at the places that are circled. All this time, we've never really been sure where Luke went when he disappeared. My mother called the cops, but very specific things were missing from his room: his computer, his backpack, his phone charger. And his car. That was gone, too. The police told my mother there was nothing they could do because Luke was eighteen, and it seemed pretty obvious that he just took off, not that anything bad happened.

I run my finger over the line that connects city-to-city, from Eaton to New Orleans to St. Louis to Indianapolis to Chicago. He had to have followed these roads, stopped at all of these places. In my hands I have evidence of where Luke spent the last year of his life, and the knowledge sends a shock through my bloodstream. How many hours did I spend wondering where he went, lying in bed, wishing he would just come back? I kept hoping he'd just be gone a few days, that he had gone off to Oklahoma for some kind of wilderness hike or something.

But one day turned into one weekend which turned into a month, and I guess a part of me was still waiting for him to come home when my parents told me about the accident. I cough around the solid thing that's settled in the base of my throat.

If I'm right and Luke used this map when he left, then who sent it to me? And why? Why would I need to know now, after Luke is gone, where he was this whole time?

The only answer this map seems to give me is this: Ann Arbor was never in the plan. Nevertheless, if that's where this map came from, that's where I have to go. Because suddenly, after almost a year of feeling lifeless, like a ghost walking through the halls at school and sitting at the dinner table and attempting to get on with my life, I buzz with urgency. What if, somewhere in Michigan, there's a person with answers? What if there's a person who can tell me *why* Luke left and where he's been and who he's been *with*?

And why he never called.

Whoever it is, I have to find them.

Chapter Two

I heard someone say once that if you suck enough water into your lungs that you'll die happy. If you get to the point of death, drowning somehow becomes euphoric. It's something that I've thought about a lot since I heard about Luke. I tried to imagine drowning turning quickly from terrifying to blissful. It just doesn't compute.

This is what I think about as I step into J-Mart the day after Luke's funeral. I don't imagine drowning as something exquisite. I imagine it like this, walking into a grocery store in a small town for the first time since you found out your brother died and having all eyes on you.

I know they're not all really looking. I know it just *feels* like they're all looking. But that feeling is so intense that I feel like I can't breathe. I live in a college town with a population of twenty thousand in theory, but Tate students make up so much of that. The rest of us, the permanent ones, we all know each other, see each other around the blurry faces of four-year Tate University residents who will pick up and leave when their time here is done. And I see so many of them now, the ones who live here every day of the year. Almost every single person I pass is someone who was at Luke's funeral or at my house afterward, and I feel like I can't hide from them like I used to. My business is on display for everyone, whether they're looking or not. I'm careful not to make eye contact, in case anyone is planning on sending me any sympathetic looks. I came here for toilet paper and milk, so I just need to get those things and go back home. Quickly.

I grab the first package of toilet paper my fingers find and am on my way to the cold-food aisle when I walk right into someone. I stumble back and two hands reach out to steady me.

"Whoa. Might help if you look up from the ground every once in a while."

At first, I think it's an insult, and I'm ready to argue with the person whose hands are still clutching my shoulders. But when I look up and see the smile aimed at me, all the fight dies.

Cade.

His hands fall away from me, and he tucks them into the pockets of his jeans. I can see the second he remembers that the last time we saw each other was at a funeral. Whatever easy joy there was on his face a moment ago is quickly replaced with a frown. Death ruins everything.

"Hey, Ellie."

I blush furiously, the way I have around Cade since freshman year, when he started to buzz his hair short and his jaw took on a very irresistibly square quality.

"Hey," I say, still looking at the ground, despite his teasing suggestion that I do the opposite.

I watch his feet shuffle around me, and I think maybe he's trying to escape the awkwardness of this encounter, but when I look up, I realize he's just moving out of the way of an older lady trying to get down the aisle. She glances over her shoulder at me as she reaches for a box of pasta, and I realize it's Mrs. Mori, my world history teacher.

She smiles at me, but I look back at Cade. A huge mistake. I almost forgot how handsome he is, and it's almost startling to have the full force of his attention on me again.

"Doing okay?" he asks, so gently that I'm not as frustrated with him asking me the question as I have been with anyone who's asked me in the last week. Because of course I'm not okay.

But there's something in his eyes that makes me think maybe he's not talking about Luke. Or, not Luke specifically, but just life in general.

It makes me want to tell him the truth: that I'm numb. That I'm empty. That I'm directionless. That I feel like the map in my bag may be the only way back to my sanity.

He watches me, and I almost say it. Cade has always been so easy to talk to.

But that was before. Before we went on that date. Before Luke left. Before I stopped answering Cade's calls and stopped flirting with him and stopped saying hi in the halls.

"I'm fine," I finally say.

"Look, if you need to talk—"

"Thanks," I say quick. "I have to go. I'll see you around."

"Yeah. I guess I'll see you around." My stomach twists when hurt flashes across his face. I've seen that hurt expression before, and seeing it again now makes me want to get away faster. I rush to the cold section and grab a gallon of milk and head back for the front of the store, carefully checking around each corner to ensure I don't run into Cade again.

It's my first high school lunch period, and my stomach is in knots. I know Luke isn't going to want to sit with me. Wes, either. They're high school boys, on the track team, and I know there's no way they're going to let me crash their lunch table when I'm just a freshman. There's some kind of high school law against that, I'm pretty sure.

I come out of the line with my head down, but before I've taken more than a step, there's a commotion, and when I look up, I realize that the entire track team is standing up on their chairs. I recognize most of them from meets and parties that Luke snuck me into.

Someone behind me shouts something I don't understand and then every member of the track team is saluting. I stand where I am, all of them in front of me, towering over me, while everyone else in the cafeteria laughs or takes pictures or catcalls.

And then Luke appears at my side. "Everyone, come say hi to my baby sister, Ellie! Welcome her to Eaton High School!"

The track boys immediately dismount their cafeteria stools, and next thing I know, someone whose name I can't even remember is carrying my tray of square-cut pizza and chocolate milk to my spot at their table, and they're all telling me hi and patting me on the back, and I feel like a celebrity or something.

Once I've been herded toward my seat, Luke drops down in the seat beside me and throws his arm around my shoulder. "Welcome to high school."

The bookstore/antique shop where I work is alive and full of people when I get there. It's a month until school starts, which means that half the people here are buying their books for school already and the other half are looking for something to do other than sneak into movies at the Cinemark.

When Laurie comes around the corner, pushing a cart piled high with books, her eyes go wide. "Ellie. What are you doing here?"

"It's Monday. I always work on Mondays." Especially since school starts in a month, and then my hours will be cut in half. I need these hours because my mother says I'll be responsible for all of my own expenses when I go to Tate, so I'm saving every penny. And more than that, without this job, I would be at home, with her and Dad, and I would lose my mind. This morning, I pressed my hands to my ears while Mom yelled at Dad for calling into work again. She's been on him all week about vegging on the couch. I'm pretty sure he's been sleeping there, too.

Laurie grips the handle on the cart and bites her lip. Laurie, my boss and the owner of the shop, is pushing fifty. She wears skintight jeans and enough jewelry that I'm surprised it doesn't knock her off balance, but somehow, right now, she looks like a little kid, wanting to speak but not sure if she should. Two girls I go to Eaton High with walk by us, and Laurie watches them go before leaning across the cart to speak to me quietly. "Ellie, if you need more time, it's okay, I promise. I can handle back-to-school rush on my own."

My heart rate picks up. If she asks me to go home, I don't know what I'll do. I can't be there anymore, with my mother who's home most of the day and my father who sits glassy-eyed on the couch. It's like a prison. "It's either this or be at home with my parents."

Laurie makes a weird shape with her mouth and nods. "Yeah, I guess you got me there."

I sigh, relieved, and stash my stuff behind the counter. Laurie pushes the cart she has with her in my direction. "Well, here, you can stock the Required Reading display."

The Required Reading display sits at the front of the shop, right by the front window, and I push the cart over to it and start stocking copies of *The Grapes of Wrath* and *The Great Gatsby* while Laurie rings up customers at the register.

Outside the window, I can see Main Street, running right in front of the strip mall, and at the end of the parking lot, the garage where Cade works. I can see him in there now, through the glass doors. He's talking to a customer, holding a large chunk of metal in his hand that I can't identify from this far away. Not that I would know what it was if I were able to see it better. I don't know anything about cars. My stomach does that uncomfortable, fluttering thing it does every time Cade is anywhere near me.

I've caught glimpses of him over at that shop so many times that it's almost become part of my work routine. Sometimes, I'll see him on his lunch break, leaned against the side of the building, his shoulders against the brick and his hips pitched forward, talking to one of the other guys that works there while he drinks from a coffee cup or munches on a bag of chips.

Cade hands the object to the customer, and I can only imagine that the part has left grease on his skin. Cade always has darkly stained fingers. He started working at the garage when he was fourteen, as young as he was allowed by law. He's always been so fascinated with the mechanics of things.

"Mostly just oil changes," he said to me once when I asked him what he did there when he was younger.

"You want to date a grease monkey?" Luke said, only weeks before that night I spent with Cade at the drive-in. I smacked him on the arm, and he swatted me away. "I don't know, Ellie. The kid is weird. Spends more time at that garage than he does with people."

We were driving home from school after Luke's track practice, passing by the garage in question, and I saw Cade inside, underneath a pickup truck on lifts.

"He works with people," I said when we stopped at the next traffic light, and Luke rolled his eyes.

"Coworkers don't count."

When I didn't answer, Luke glanced over at me. He always seemed to know exactly what I was thinking, and he sighed loudly. "If you think he's your knight in slightly greasy armor, then you have my blessing, Ellie."

Looking at Cade now, I regret all of it. I should have just let it be. Maybe then he wouldn't look so hurt every time I can't speak to him. He smiles, just a flash across his face, and then nods at something behind the guy he's talking to. The guy walks away, and Cade stands there for a beat longer, his eyes wandering until I swear he's looking straight into the bookstore's window, right at me.

On my break, I sit in the back office with the map spread out on the desk in front of me. My nerves seem to vibrate around inside me, like they're trying to get out, like they alone can propel me forward, out of Eaton and toward someplace I've never been before. I have my fingers pressed to my mouth, wondering if this is what it would have been like to see

Luke in an open coffin. I bite down on the tips of my fingers.

I've only figured out half the plan, how I'll leave on Friday, drive up to Michigan, see who sent me the map, and then drive right back. It'll take a day to get there and a day to get back, if the only stop I make is in Michigan. I think that's a short enough trip that my mother will only be mostly pissed off. She'll panic, but by the time she tries to do anything too rash, I'll be home and grounded forever, and she won't have to worry again. It's not like I'm ever leaving Eaton after this trip.

I just want to know who sent the map. I just want to see where Luke was when it happened. I calculated the miles between Eaton and Dexter. Over 1,200 miles. I can't even imagine Luke 1,200 miles away. It makes my throat burn.

I look down at the map, at all the things we added, all the lines and the stars and the notes, but our handwriting is faded slightly. It's Luke's red ink that's the easiest to see. He traced over the highways in red, like he might lose them if he didn't make them stand out.

New Orleans, St. Louis, Indianapolis, Chicago, New York, D.C. Miami. Those cities are connected in a red circle on one side of the map. Phoenix, San Diego, Los Angeles, Las Vegas, San Francisco, Seattle. A bigger circle, on the other side. It doesn't make much sense, and I can't even figure out where Ann Arbor would have fit in, much less the small town of Dexter, which I found out is a miniscule suburb outside of Ann Arbor.

"What's that?"

I jump and spin around in my seat to find Wes in the doorway, looking down at the map in front of me. I scramble to fold it up, but I suck at it, and I end up with a crumpled mess in my shaking hands. "It's nothing.

You shouldn't even be back here. Employees only."

Wes scowls at me. "Laurie said I could. Is that . . . ?"

I stop struggling with the map when Wes reaches for it, and I feel a weird sense of possessiveness when he takes it. It feels like mine. Whoever had it sent it to me, not Wes. But I know he has as much a right to it as I do. That note scribbled over Las Vegas that reads *nude girls* is one of Wes's classy contributions. I watch him examine it, like it's brand-new, like his handwriting isn't all over the margins. Like he didn't put an X over the salt flats in Nevada because his dad used to talk about taking his family there all the time, even though they never got around to it.

"God, where did you find this thing?" he asks, unfolding it. His green eyes run over the whole thing, and I wonder if he's thinking of the hours we spent with Luke, conspiring like criminals over a bank heist. Is he thinking about the way Luke always locked the map away so lovingly at the end of each meeting, like it was an antique, worth a fortune? That's all I've been thinking about since I opened that envelope, every memory of Luke touching that thing crossing my mind. None of it seems real anymore.

"This is our future," Luke said when he brought it home. "We will not be lifelong Eatonites. I don't care what it takes."

All this time, I assumed he forgot about it, the same way I did, dismissed it as a joke or a childhood pipe dream.

But it wasn't just a joke to him.

"Someone sent it to me." I just spit it out, and I'm not even sure why. I want this to be a secret, something I can hold inside myself, that I can protect. But if anyone deserves to know, it's Wes.

Wes's dark eyebrows curve in, and one corner of the map droops in his hand. "What do you mean, someone sent it to you?"

I slouch back in Laurie's office chair. I've only had this secret for two days, but I feel a weight lift off of me as soon as I tell Wes. Some of the pressure in my chest loosens, not yet ready to explode. "Someone sent it to me from a Michigan address. Just the map. Nothing else. No name, no letter." I realize too late that my voice is shaking. I take a deep breath and say the part I'm terrified to utter aloud. "I'm going to go to Michigan to find out who it was."

At this, Wes almost drops the map. "You're going to Michigan?"

"Yes." Doubt starts to creep into my chest when Wes doesn't say anything. His eyebrows are so high, they almost reach the line of his almost-black hair.

"Do you think this is the route he took when he left?" He folds the map and hands it back to me, but I already know I can't take it back. It's ours now, not just mine.

"Maybe. I don't know."

When I don't take the map, Wes smacks it against his open palm. "I want to come with you."

Doubt is replaced by something else. Dread maybe. Regret. I never meant for anyone to go with me. This is my trip. I have to go alone. "I don't think that's a great idea."

He's already shaking his head. "You shouldn't go alone. We'll go, all three of us. A trip around America."

Whoa. Things are getting way out of hand here. "America? No. I'm just going to Michigan. And who is the three of us? You, me, and—"

"Gwen."

I snatch the map from him. "Absolutely not. Luke's ex? No way."

Wes snatches the map back, and I grit my teeth. I never should have said anything. I want to go alone, to just be away from everyone's eyes and grief and sympathy for a few days. This is not how this is supposed to go.

"Look," Wes says, holding the map out of my reach as I get up from my chair to get it back. "I came here to apologize that you found out about us that way. I should have told you. It's just, we haven't talked in a while, and I didn't know how to . . . you know . . ."

I stop grabbing for the map. I'm definitely not going to tell him that it bothered me to find out. I don't want him to know that the first thought I had was a selfish one: that they left me behind, too. How could I demand they be unhappy just for my sake? "Why would I care if you're dating Gwen?"

He shrugs. "She's Luke's ex." His arm sags, and I rip the map out of his hand while he's distracted. "I wasn't sure if you'd care, but I mean, it's not like they were together or anything. When he died, I mean."

I have to block out what he's saying. I can't hear him say words like *died*. I hold the map to my chest, wishing this conversation could just be over. "Wes, you and Gwen can date whoever you want. I don't care. But she's not coming on the trip."

Wes crosses his arms over his chest. "I'm not going without her, and you're not going without me. Come on, Ellie. This was our trip. Let's take it. It'll be like honoring him."

I get a strange twisting sensation in my stomach. Honor Luke? What does that even mean? I picture the enlarged photo at the front of the church at his funeral. How can anyone really honor Luke? Did anyone even really know him? How many people know he ran away? How many people know how much we fell apart afterward?

It was a mistake to tell Wes. I know him well enough to know that he's not going to let this lie, and knowing that makes my skin crawl, like I'm trapped. I know Wes is trying to do what he thinks is right, but I don't really care what he thinks is right. I don't think I really care if Gwen feels left out or if Wes is lonely without her.

What about me? What about what I feel? I've been left out since Luke vanished in the middle of the night and everyone moved on with their lives like we didn't all orbit around him. I've been lonely since my best friend took the map in my hand and walked out the door.

I grip the map and look at him. He stares back, and I know I'll be the first to break, just like I always am, always the one to concede.

"Fine," I say because I can't bring myself to say no anymore.

Chapter Three

For the first time in almost a year, every single light is on in the house when I get home, and my mother is in the kitchen. It's ten in the evening, and it smells like my mother is making seafood. My father is planted in front of the TV, his eyes glazed over as he watches some show about a pawnshop. As my mother pulls something out of the oven, I see that her eyes are a little unfocused, too. It's like a cemetery in here, solemn and quiet. I thought it was bad when Luke left, when we all stopped talking and started avoiding one another. It's worse now.

When my mother sees me, her eyes go wide. "Ellie. Finally. I thought maybe dinner was going to get cold before you got home." Pink fillets of salmon sizzle on the pan she just pulled out of the oven.

"What are you doing?"

Her eyes stick to mine, like she's afraid that if she looks away, I'll run. And maybe I will. It's hard to know at this point.

"I know it's late, but I thought it might be nice if we started having dinner as a family again," she finally says, pulling the oven mitts off her hands.

"As a family?" My stomach tightens. "The three of us?" I can feel an ominous ripple in my blood as I look at my mother, like something swelling inside. Sure, we'll just have family dinner, the three of us, what's left of our family. Now that Luke is gone, we can pretend he never existed. We can move on with our lives. We can have dinner together the way Luke always hated. I grit my teeth and turn away from her. "I'm not hungry." It's never bothered me before that my mother feels the need to control everyone around her. Not the way it bothered Luke. I've always been willing to do exactly what she tells me to, never saw any reason to argue. She wanted me to take gymnastics, so I did. She wanted me to quit gymnastics, so I did. She wanted to me to get up ten minutes earlier, so I did. She wanted me to go to bed an hour earlier, so I did.

But Luke was always ready to defy her. They fought about school, about his future, about the girls he dated, the classes he took, what time he woke up in the morning, what he spent his money on. Always, always she micromanaged. She would tell him what time to get up in the morning, and he would *forget* to set his alarm clock. She wanted him to try out for the swim team, so he joined track. She told him to be home by eleven, so he snuck in at three.

She told him to stay, to go to Tate, to give Eaton a shot.

So he left and never came back.

It makes me sick just thinking about it.

Well, I'm not interested in backing down anymore. I'm not sitting next to an empty chair and pretending that we're still a family. We haven't been a family since Luke left. And now we'll never be one again.

I turn for the stairs, but my mother steps out of the kitchen. "Eloise, we're going to have dinner together." She's got her stern voice on now, the one she uses on her lecture classes at Tate. *This* is the mother I know: unmoving as granite. Why did I think for even a second that she might just let me be? "And tomorrow, I think you should tell your boss that you're not available to close up the shop anymore."

I grip the handrail beside me. It's my own fault, I guess. I've given her free rein of my life, I've always been the easy one, the malleable one. "I'm not a dog," I say, heading up the stairs, torn by both a bone-deep desire to please her and also a Luke-inspired desire to tell her off. "You can't just order me around."

"I can take your car away."

I freeze, surprised, even if it is her, that she's threatening me. She's never had to do that before. I twist my hands into fists and consider my options. Sure, no car means my mother giving me a ride to school every morning; it means taking the bus from school to work; it means not getting to leave home anytime I want to. But there are worse things.

"I'll take the bus," I say. I'm determined to win this one. My mother was the one who insisted I get a job in the first place. She wanted me to learn life skills. She wanted me to have something to keep me out of trouble. She wanted me to learn what it meant to be an adult. And now she wants to take it away. Because she can.

"Maybe it's time you quit the shop."

I bark out a laugh. I feel manic, like I'm going to rattle apart if I don't have something to grab onto. But there's nothing, no anchor. Just my mother, pushing and pushing and pushing.

When Luke was twelve, he asked for a scooter for his birthday. Everyone had scooters, including Wes, and Luke wanted one of his own, a little silver thing that he could ride around the neighborhood. Mom got him a brand-new bike instead.

"You'll like it better," she told him. "I promise."

He didn't like it better. He hated it so much that he mowed lawns all summer to save up for a scooter. And then he rode it around our house to rub it in our mom's face.

"Just leave me alone!" I shout, throwing open my bedroom door. "Please, for God's sake, leave me alone!"

The tightness in my chest gets worse, until I can't breathe, and even as I slide to the carpet, wrapping my arms around myself, trying to just make it stop for a minute, just a minute, I hear her voice on the stairs, then right outside my door.

"You're not the only one who lost someone, Eloise."

———————

Mom and Luke fighting is like the soundtrack of my life. It's turned into white noise, always going in the background when I'm trying to do homework, trying to do dishes, trying to live my life. I've learned to ignore it, learned to drown it out with a constant internal monologue of equations and lines of Shakespeare.

And yet somehow, the fight this time is happening in the hallway outside my bedroom door, and even though I'm plugging my ears as hard as I can and have my music playing loud, I can still hear them, every single word crystal clear.

"Lucas, if you'd like to run around in the middle of the night, doing God knows what, well I guess I can't stop you, but you are absolutely not getting your sister involved in all of your shenanigans."

I wait for Luke to growl at her not to call him Lucas, which he hates, but instead he latches onto something else. "God! Shenanigans? Really? Mom, she's sixteen! It's my senior year. I just want to spend a little quality time with the one member of this family who doesn't want to put a fucking leash on me."

Usually, I don't want to hear it. Mostly because they never seem to fight about anything real. It's always the same things: how Luke never does what he's told and Mom works so hard and why can't we just be a normal family? I almost never make an appearance in these fights, unless Mom is pleading with Luke to be a little more like me. I'll do what Mom tells me to. I'm obedient.

"Oh, give me a break, Luke," our mother sighs, like she's just so exhausted. "You act like you're so misunderstood, such a tragic case. Must be so awful to have a roof over your head and parents that love you and a future all planned out for you."

"I don't want a future all planned out for me!"

I flinch. Luke is always the first to raise his voice, to really get angry, and it's always enough to make me want to cringe. I'm used to the quiet Luke, the gentle Luke. That's who he is with me, all smiles and afternoon naps and goofy jokes whispered low where no one else can hear. I don't like the Luke that yells.

"Great," my mother says, sarcastic. "That's just wonderful. I guess my job here is done."

I hear her footsteps move down the hall, but Luke's stay put.

———

The next morning, my car won't start. I stare at my steering wheel. I'm exhausted down to my bones, and the idea that my mother may have sabotaged my car is just a little too much for me to handle this morning. I grind my teeth together, standing on the edge of rage. I will myself not to go over.

And then it starts to rain.

I get out of my car and stare at it, letting the rain drench my hair and my clothes. I know it's not the battery because I've had a dead one enough times to remember the sound it makes. This is something different.

I have two options. I can take the bus.

Or I can call Cade.

———

The hood of my car blocks Cade from the rain as he leans under it and messes with something in the mass of metal guts. He makes a humming noise and then a clucking noise and then leans back out.

"I think I need to look inside," he says, not meeting my eye.

I rush to open the door for him and then watch as he sits in my seat and pulls a panel free from the inside of my car. He examines it for a second and then nods.

"Yeah, it looks like your starter fuse is missing." He pops the panel back in and looks up at me, expectantly, like I have any clue what that means.

"So, I just need to replace it?" I back away from the car so he can get out and shut the door, and then we're both standing in the rain beside my house, pretending that we're not getting completely soaked. I'm trying not to show just how nervous I am, how the way he's standing so close to me is affecting me. I cross my arms like a barrier.

"Oh," he says, like he forgot something and then he pulls an item out of his pocket. It's a little piece of plastic with metal plugs sticking out of it. He offers it to me, and when I reach out to take it, I feel a surge of affection toward him, like he just put a blanket around me on a cold day.

"You just carry fuses around in your pocket?" I ask, a smile trying to creep up. I bite it back down. I shouldn't be flirting or whatever it is I'm doing. I should be getting in my car and going to work. I should be planning this trip to Michigan.

I shouldn't have called Cade. I shouldn't have asked him to come out here in the rain when we haven't really spoken in over a year.

He smiles down at his feet, where rain water is pooling around his shoes. "When you explained the problem, I narrowed it down, that's all. I brought one just in case I was right."

I grip the fuse so tight the metal spokes dig into my skin. "I can pay you for the fuse."

"They cost, like, four dollars. It's not a big deal." He reaches up and runs his fingertips along his scalp. Once upon a time, Cade had thick, dark hair. And then the summer before sophomore year, he buzzed it, and he's been wearing it short ever since. But I've noticed that he presses his fingers into his scalp like that, reaching up as if the hair might have grown back without him noticing.

"I should get to work," I say at the same time that he says my name, like a whisper beneath the sound of the rain hitting the roof, the metal gutters, the hood of my car.

He shuffles his feet and tries to put his hands in his pockets, but the denim is too wet so he lets them hang at his sides. "Would you maybe want to get dinner sometime soon? Maybe just to talk? Maybe we could even—"

"Cade." I brush the water droplets off my face. I tried to save Cade from me a year ago, when I was just beginning to fracture. Now that I'm completely broken, I can't let him any closer to me than he is right now, for both our sakes. "Now's just not a good time."

He nods, and specks of rain fly from the ends of his hair. "Right. Yeah. I'm sorry." He pushes away from my car and starts walking down my driveway, back to the bus stop at the end of my street, where the bus dropped him off.

I watch him go, and when I get in my car, my entire body is wet, my shirt heavy, my pants soaked all the way up to my knees. I do what Cade did, opening the fuse box and putting the one in my hand where there's an empty space. The car starts, and I pull out onto the road, whisking water off my windshield.

Cade stands there at the bus stop, the rain pouring down on him, and I feel that same tug toward him, an attachment that's somehow still there under the surface after all this time. I can't just let him stand in the rain for the bus.

I stop at the end of the street, pull up to the curb opposite the bus stop, and roll my window down.

Cade's head hangs low, and I say his name, trying to get him to look up at me. When he doesn't move, I realize sometime between my house and the bus stop, he put earbuds in his ears.

I take a deep breath and shout his name louder. His back straightens, and his head comes up. The rain has slowed down a little, but it still leaves tracks on his face. He sees me and glances at the (I hope, water-proof) watch on his wrist then back at me. Maybe he's afraid that if he comes to talk to me, he'll miss the bus, but he comes anyway.

"Get in the car," I say when he's close enough.

He looks over his shoulder at the bus stop. I don't know the schedule, but I know chances are good the bus that runs all the way around Tate is just around the corner. It doesn't matter, though. He came when I called him, and he brought me a fuse, and even after what happened between us last year, he still wants to take me out to dinner, so the least I can do is give him a ride to work.

"Just get in, Cade."

He hesitates, but he finally walks around to the passenger side of my car and opens the door. "It's no big deal," he says as he climbs in. "I wait for the bus in the rain all the time." He shuts the door, and I put the car in drive.

"Well, not today."

He smiles at me, unexpectedly. My foot slips off the brake pedal, and we jerk forward.

"Sorry," I whisper.

His white T-shirt is waterlogged and sticking to his skin, I see when we stop at a light on Main Street. I try not to notice the shape of his body through his wet T-shirt. Unfortunately, this means I can't look at him at all because his torso makes up such a large portion of his body that every time I look at him, all I can see is wet, peachy skin.

I focus on the road.

"So, you work at the garage, but you still don't have a car?" It's a stupid question, but I'm still a little distracted by how wet we are, not to mention the fact that this is the first time Cade has ever been in my car.

He looks over at me, eyebrows raised. "And exactly how many antique lamps do you own?"

I smile out the windshield. "Touché. Although I have about a million books, so that argument doesn't quite hold up."

When I sneak a look at him again, he's laughing quietly, moving his fingers over each other in a way that says he might be as nervous as I am. "So, out of curiosity, how exactly did you just *lose* a starter fuse?"

I grip the steering wheel and try not to growl in frustration. "My mother. She's trying to get me to quit my job, so that I can be home all the time, and we can pretend we're a perfect family." By the time it's all slipped out, my eyes have gone wide. I can't believe I just said all that to him. "Sorry. I didn't mean to——"

"It's okay," he says over me. "I know your mom can be a bit of a control freak."

I scoff. *Control freak* seems like too forgiving a term. "Yeah. I forgot that I told you all that."

"Yeah, before we——"

"Right."

The car falls into silence. We're almost to the strip mall where we both work, but we're sitting at the worst light in Eaton, watching cars fly through the intersection.

"What's that?" Cade nods his head in a gesturing motion, and I realize I left Luke's map sitting on the dashboard, tucked against the glass of the windshield. My eyes go wide, my thoughts immediately spinning in an attempt to come up with a lie. I didn't even realize I left it up there, and from where I'm sitting, I can see Luke's handwriting along the edge of the paper. There's a crackle of panic under my skin.

"Oh, it's just a map." I try to play it off like it's unimportant so that he won't ask to see it, but my casual answer has him reaching for it instead. I fight the urge to get to it before him. Instead, I watch him open it, watch his eyes fly over the marks all over it. It's not a big deal. I don't have to tell him about Luke. I don't have to tell him that someone sent that to me just a few days ago. To him, it'll just be a map. I can almost breathe again.

"Are you going on a road trip?" he asks, still looking down at it, and I pull into the parking lot by the mechanic shop and stop the car.

"Yeah, maybe. It's just a little thing. Me and some friends." It sounds weird coming out of my mouth, and I think Cade understands that I'm trying to make it sound like something it isn't by the way he looks over at me carefully before folding up the map and putting it back where it was.

"Looks like a lot of fun," he says. "Have a nice time."

I start to thank him, but he's already opened the door, and the sound of the rain drowns out anything I try to say.

Chapter Four

On Friday morning, the house is so quiet, it feels like the silence is crawling along my skin as I pack my things.

Before Luke left, there was always noise in the house. My father was throwing an office Super Bowl party or my mother was hosting book club or Luke was holding a Call of Duty tournament in the living room. It was almost never me. Even when I had friends over, we mostly camped out in my room, watching movies and eating junk food. But our house was always like Grand Central. The front door was often left open because someone was always on their way in or out. "They're right behind me," my mother was so fond of saying. Wes and Gwen came in without knocking because they practically lived here, and sometimes my father's office buddies were mingling with the track team in the kitchen because if you came over, chances were good you were going to bump into someone you didn't even know.

But when Luke left, our need for social interaction went with him. First, the holiday parties stopped, then the book-club meetings, then, of course, my friends stopped coming around because I stopped asking them to. And now, our house is so quiet, all the time. Even now, I can hear the ice maker all the way downstairs, the tree limbs brushing against the window of the guest room, the soft ticking of the clock above the TV in the living room.

I shove clothes into a duffel bag as fast I can. My mother is at a meeting at Tate, my father at work, and I don't know how long I have before one of them comes home.

And I intend to be gone by that point.

———————

A knock at my window wakes me up with a pounding heart and an uncertainty that it wasn't just a dream. I reach out, stretching as far as I can manage and push my curtains aside to see Luke hanging from the trellis.

I groan and get up to push open the window. Luke stumbles in and crashes onto my bed, laughing.

"Why didn't you go to your own room?" I ask when I glace at my clock and it tells me it's almost four in the morning. Tomorrow is the first day of junior year for Luke, and he's out partying.

"Tried," Luke sighs. "Mom locked it. Must have checked on me and found me gone."

I climb onto the bed with him. He smells like sweat and heat, like he's been out in the sun, which is impossible. Then I lean forward and turn on my lamp. In its light, I spot the difference. "Did you get a tan?" I ask incredulously.

Luke smiles, but his eyes are closed, his fingers laced across his chest. "Did you know Marcie Clements has a tanning bed?"

"How would I know that?"

He chuckles. "Well, I just told you."

I roll my eyes and turn off the lamp. He's obviously not going anywhere. I crawl under the covers, shoving him aside. He's still on top of the blanket, and that's probably for the best. He still smells like tanning lotion.

"*I thought you didn't like Marcie Clements,*" *I say into the dark.*

Luke shrugs. "*I like what she does for me.*" *In the dark, I can hear the suggestion in his voice.*

"*Oh, gross. Shut up.*"

Luke laughs. "*Calm down. I don't mean that. We just make out a lot.*"

That's still a little too much for me, but I don't say so. Luke turns. I can see in the dark that he has his back to me now. I shift, too, pressing against him, my face buried between his shoulder blades.

I hear a car pull into the driveway, and then someone honks.

Go time.

I pick up the duffle bag I packed and shut my bedroom door behind me, feeling something akin to joy and satisfaction that at some point, maybe tonight, maybe not until tomorrow, my mother will open this door, and she'll find my room empty. She's built up this sense of security, thinking I won't take any risks like Luke did, but if Luke can disappear, so can I. The idea makes me stop, my shoes halting on the carpet, my confidence dimming. Can I really do this? Can I really leave like Luke did?

I've got one foot on the stairs when I glance back and see Luke's bedroom door. It's cracked, like someone has been in there recently, and I pause, one hand on the banister. I know Wes and Gwen are downstairs, waiting for me, but without hesitating, I turn around and slip into Luke's room. My breath catches in my throat once I'm in there.

It's ridiculous really that after a year of Luke's absence, his room still smells like him, like the cologne he wore and the way his skin smelled when he woke up in the morning. My eyes travel around the room, taking in trophies, posters, shelves piled high with CDs and vinyl.

For some unexplainable, unquenchable reason, everything in here feels like it's not real, like I've walked onto a stage, where all the props of Luke's life are littered around like evidence. It feels like the real stuff, the stuff that Luke touched and left his fingerprints on, should have vanished overnight. How can it still exist in this world when he doesn't?

I step across the room and place a hand on the bed. It's cold. The AC vent blows directly on the bed, a fact that Luke was always fine with. He loved it when the house was cold at night. He loved sleeping under layers of blankets. I pull back the blankets and settle onto the sheets. I burrow my face into them. They smell like dust and dryer sheets. My chest constricts, and I clamp my lips together to hold in a sob, press my face against the cotton harder until I have to gasp for breath.

For just a second, I close my eyes and pretend like he's still here. I pretend that any second now, he'll come into the room and tell me to get my smelly feet off his sheets. Or he'll let me lie here while he turns on a Nova CD and surfs around on the internet. Or he'll tell me to scoot over and climb in beside me to read a book or take a nap.

Why did he do this to me? Why did he throw away everything we went through? Was living out his adventure more important than the life he built here? I fist my hands in the blanket and beg, silently, for it all to not be real. I beg for our life back.

I open my eyes and sit up quickly. There's no going back. Luke did what he did, and now he's gone, and I have somewhere to be.

I step over to his desk. There's an empty space on top where his computer used to sit. When he left, he deleted all of his social media accounts, and even though, in those first few weeks, I tried to get in touch with him via his e-mail account, I never got anything in return.

Beside the empty spot is a stack of CDs. None of them are Nova because there's no way Luke would leave those behind, but I recognize some others, bands that we've listened to together over the years and some mixes that Luke put together for road trips and study sessions. I pick one off the top and pop open the case. And something falls out.

It's a sticky note, no longer sticky. I recognize my own handwriting immediately.

#1, 3, 7, and 15 are the best. Please mix accordingly.

I stare down at the note. Luke used to beg me to tell him which songs were my favorites when he lent me CDs. It was imperative for him to know. "For future musical experiences," he would say. I bend down and pick up the sticky note and stuff it back in the case, a little shaken that he kept it. It's an old CD, and I remember him lending it to me years ago when he first bought it.

My hands start to tremble, and I put the CD down before I drop it. It's like this room is sitting here, untouched, just waiting for him to come back to it. I turn to leave, slamming the door behind me, like it can hold in all the monsters, if I close it tight enough.

In my front driveway, Gwen and Wes are moving things around in the trunk, and it feels surreal, just looking at them, my dead brother's ex-girlfriend and his ex-best friend. I feel like I stepped into a dream, the world clear and bright and strange. My legs are numb as I walk around the back of the car and join them. I can't believe we're really doing this.

They both look at me and straighten away from their task, and even though I just saw Gwen a few days ago, I feel like I'm seeing her for the first time in years.

When we met two years ago, Gwen was already so thin and slight. But now, all that's left of her is the points of her bones, her clavicles and her elbows, sticking out awkwardly beneath her brown skin, her clothes swallowing her. She looks so sallow, I almost can't even see the Gwen I used to know anymore.

Gwen and Luke dated for a year, the year before he left. Two years ago, she walked into my life with her head held high, always the life of the party, always prepared for an adventure. She was fearless. That's why Luke loved her. What I could never figure out was why he didn't love her enough to stay.

"Hi, Ellie," she says, and I can almost see her hesitation as she decides whether it's more polite to smile or not smile.

"Hey, Gwen." I might not have seen Wes over the last year, but I haven't gone out of my way not to see him. Gwen, on the other hand. . . . Well, it's different with your sibling's ex. I took her off all of my social media, ducked for cover if I saw her at J-Mart, pretty much did my best to avoid her at all costs, and now I feel guilty for it. I don't even know how to begin to talk to her after a year of radio silence.

"Thanks for letting me come with you guys," she says, putting her bag in the trunk and reaching out to take mine from my hands. "A road trip out of Eaton sounds . . ." She trails off and then turns from me to stuff my bag in the trunk. "Perfect," she finishes, coming back to face me. This time, she does smile at me, and I know immediately that something is off, like hearing a siren in the distance.

I catch Wes's eye, and I know without him telling me, just from the way his eyes widen and his mouth stretches into a stressed line, that he hasn't told her about the map. He hasn't told her that this trip is about Luke or the person in Michigan who might have known him. And now he's asking me not to tell her, too.

I shoot him a glare and wait for Gwen to go around to the front seat before I say, "What the hell? You didn't tell her?"

He glances around the open trunk at her, sends her a little wave in the side mirror before turning back to me. "No, okay? I didn't tell her. I want her to come with us, and I wasn't sure she would if she knew. She's . . . upset, okay? She needs this as much as we do."

No, I want to say, she needs something completely different. Because this isn't a vacation to me, and if that's what she needs, then our needs are not the same. "This isn't some fun road trip," I say, trying to keep my voice down. "This is important." I can't even say for sure that this is true. Sure, it's important to me. But I don't know what we're going to find in Michigan. Was Luke important to whoever sent this map? Is it really important for me to know who sent the map in the first place?

Wes grasps my shoulders, surprising me. "I know. And that's why I want her to come. I'll figure out a way to tell her."

I sigh, unease twisting inside me. Secrets are never a good idea, and this seems likes a particularly bad one, but he's the one who wanted to bring Gwen, so he'll have to be the one to figure out how to tell her. "Okay."

The side of his mouth quirks up, and he tips my chin with his finger. "She wants to spend time with you. I think it'll be good for all of us."

"Right." Anxiety creeps along my back. In the trunk, I can see the map sticking out of the pocket of my bag, and I reach out and shove it back in, zipping the compartment so that it won't slip out again. I take the bag back out of the trunk. It should sit in the back seat with me, where I can keep an eye on it.

"I got snacks for the road," Wes says, "and all of our stops plugged into my GPS. I can pay for hotels and shit, and we can figure out financials as soon as we get back."

I nod, trying to hold up my end of the conversation, but I'm stuck on the words *as soon as we get back*. I haven't thought that far ahead. I haven't thought about what will happen when we pull right back into Eaton and the world goes back to exactly how it is right now. I shove the thought away.

He reaches out to close the trunk just as someone calls out, "Wait!"

We spin around, and I realize that I know the figure that's jogging toward us from the end of the street. I know his slanted shoulders, his long legs, his short hair, and watching him now, it's like I'm dreaming.

"Wait up!" Cade says, and it's now that I realize he has a bag slung over his shoulder. Oh my God. What the hell is he doing? He stops in front of me, a little out of breath, and then he smiles wide. "Hey," he says and then sends Wes a meager wave. Behind me, I hear the car door open, and then Gwen comes to stand beside me.

"What are *you* doing here?" Wes asks, and I'm relieved because I want to ask, but I can't make my mouth move. But the way he asks it, of course, is different than the way I would have. Because he asks it as if he's more interested in why Cade, himself, is here. If I was the one to ask, I would be more interested in why Cade is *here*, of all places, at this time.

Cade takes a deep breath, and then he settles his eyes on me, as if I was the one to ask the question after all. And in one long huff, he says, "I want to come with you."

Of all the millions of things Cade could have said in this moment, this particular combination of words is not something I ever could have prepared myself for.

"What?" Wes and I say at the same time.

Cade holds up his hands, already prepared for us to reject him. "I know this has nothing to do with me." At this, Wes glances over at Gwen, probably afraid that the whole thing is about to come crashing down before we've even gotten in the car. "But I need to get out of here. Out of Eaton. Just for a little while. And I can offer you a place to sleep in Indianapolis."

I scowl at him. I feel a little like someone is asking me a very complex math question. "Indianapolis?"

Cade nods. "My family lives there." He runs his fingers along his scalp. "I just, I really need to be away from here." Something in his voice breaks, and I have to hide my surprise.

"Did something happen?" I've never seen Cade like this, desperate and something else, something urgent. Despite my dedication to trying *not* to care about Cade, worry blooms in my chest.

Cade shakes his head, forcing a smile, but I can tell it's a lie. "No. I've just, uh, you know other than Indianapolis, I've never been outside of Texas."

"Never?" I'm surprised when Gwen jumps into the conversation, but her eyes are wide, and Cade nods in her direction.

"Never." His eyes come back to me, and I'm surprised to see desperation there. I feel like any second now, he's going to drop to his knees and beg me.

"Me neither," Gwen says, and I see their eyes connect, and I'm appalled at the jealousy that stings at me at the knowledge that they have something in common. It's not jealousy because Gwen is so much prettier than me or because I think Cade might like her. But jealousy that it's so easy for them to find a connection, that I haven't had anything to share with Cade in so long.

"It's a long trip," I tell him, not sure who I'm trying to convince, him or myself.

He's already nodding. "I know." His eyes meet mine, and he looks embarrassed, his cheeks going a little pink. "You wrote all the dates down on that map. That's how I knew you guys were leaving today. I came here hoping I had the right place."

"What map?" Gwen asks.

"The map we used to plan out the trip," Wes says easily, and I guess he's not actually lying. I don't have a second to dwell on this before Wes steps up close to Cade, his hand already out, like he's going to shove Cade back. I immediately become defensive, reaching out to latch onto Wes's arm.

"Wes, what are you doing?"

Wes glances at me and then narrows his eyes at Cade. "Look, man. We don't even know you."

I open my mouth to tell Wes that I, in fact, do know Cade and that since it's *my* trip, I should be the one to decide, but before I even have a chance, Cade has spoken up for himself.

"Sure you do. We had Spanish together, two years ago." It's amusing to me that this is the detail Cade chooses to point out, not the times he came to my house to work on homework with me while Wes was there, not the times we all ate lunch together. Just that one class, like it matters.

Wes makes a noncommittal noise beneath his breath. "That doesn't mean I *know* you. I'm not just going to let some stranger get in my car and ride with us across the country, okay? This isn't your business."

"It's not your decision," I hiss at him, but Gwen has already stepped forward, and I see some of the tension melt from Wes's shoulders immediately.

"I know you," Gwen says, and Cade looks at her. "We had world history together. You always screwed up the grading curve." Cade's eyes are a little wide, but Gwen smiles at him, and we all fall silent. Again, that tiny sting of jealousy that they're discovering each other this way. I shove it down. Ridiculous.

I know there's no way Wes will argue with Gwen if she wants Cade to come. With me, sure, but with Gwen? He's looking at her like she just brought the sun out after a rainstorm.

Gwen considers Cade, her brown eyes sweeping over every inch of him like she can judge his sincerity by the way he stands, the way one of his hands grips the strap of his backpack, the way his eyes are sweeping over her in turn.

"I'd like to come," he says to her instead of us. "I want to be part of this." His eyes go to his shoes, and I see the way he nervously picks at the strap of his backpack. "I guess it's been a while since I felt like I was part of anything."

I get a shock at hearing him say this, something I've felt but didn't know how to describe. I see him in the darkness of his grandmother's car, turning to me and smiling, the light from the movie screen casting shadows along his face. I take a step toward him, not even really meaning to. My body just propels me forward, like he has his own gravity that I'm being pulled toward.

"You can come with us."

Wes's head whips around, and his eyes are so wide, I'm afraid they might just fall out of his head. "It's my car."

"And the whole trip was my idea."

Wes's mouth snaps shut.

"I vote yes, too," Gwen says, and Wes's angry eyes shoot to her next.

"This isn't a vote. It's not a fucking democracy. He has nothing to do with this." Wes jabs his finger in Cade's direction.

"What's your problem?" I ask, ready to argue with whatever he's going to throw at me, ready to fight for this boy who I'm not even sure I want to come, either. But he just shakes his head, like it's not worth fighting over. And then he throws his hands in the air and climbs into the driver's seat, and I can't tell for certain, but I think that means Cade is coming with us.

Chapter Five

The first hour is the most awkward. I didn't really take into account that it would be difficult to find something to talk about with a group of people as splintered as we all are, and even though I know Wes and I have similar taste in music, I'm not sure how to ask him to turn on the radio or put in a CD or something, so we're driving down 281 with nothing but the blowing of the air conditioner to break the silence.

Cade has been staring out the window the entire time, and I've been staring at him. I can't believe he's really here. After the way things went down between us, I assumed that was it. Cade would become another face in the hallway, one more thing in my life that got turned upside down, something I couldn't seem to control, and now here he is, and having the familiar shape of him beside me makes some of this tension inside me uncoil, like I can let some of it go.

But I still feel the fizz of anxiety about what we're doing, what I just did, leaving home without a word to my parents to find some mystery person who may or may not be able to tell me why Luke left, why he never called, why he was in Ann Arbor in the first place. There's a burning in my throat at the idea that I just did to them what Luke did to all of us, instead of the triumph I thought I would feel. Instead, I think about my mom telling me Luke is gone.

My vision goes blurry, the way it does every time I start to think about that night, and I have to look out the window to focus again, to make the world right itself before I can look at Cade, feel that same comfort, let it take away the edge of panic inside.

Cade turns, and his eye catches mine, and he smiles. He smiles like he knows me, like the last year never happened.

———

Cade drives me an hour out of Eaton, to the drive-in theater in Berryton. He just got his license this week, and he said he wanted our date to be the first place he drove without his grandmother in the car. My stomach has been in tight, excited knots all day.

"I've never been here before," I tell him, and he smiles while he waits for the lady at the box office to get his change.

"I know. You told me."

I laugh nervously. "Oh. I don't remember."

Cade pulls his grandmother's car into a spot and turns the radio to the station for the movie. "There's mini golf, too, if you're into that sort of thing," he says, gesturing toward a little course by the highway, where a group of people I recognize from Eaton are laughing over a game.

"Totally my sort of thing." I smile at him, and he smiles back, and my heart is pounding so loud I can't hear the cheesy old-fashioned concession stand advertisement over it.

"I've been wanting to ask you out since, like, eighth grade, you know."

I barely knew Cade was alive before freshman year, but I'm definitely not telling him that, especially since hearing him say he's liked me that long just makes my heart race faster.

"So, why didn't you?"

He shrugs. "Talking to pretty girls isn't really something I'm good at, if you haven't noticed."

I blush, but I have noticed. Like me, Cade doesn't seem to have too many friends, and I've never seen him with a girl.

"Why is that?"

He glances sideways at me. "People think I'm weird."

I think back to Luke's comments, those very words, and feel embarrassed for all of us. Luke barely knows Cade, knows no more than anyone else at school, and I hate that he judged Cade this way, and that Cade knows it.

"I don't think you're weird. You're smart and you work hard and you're interested in things no one else is. I mean, who is going to be able to tell me how many countries there are in the world?" I raise my eyebrows at him, and he smiles slowly.

"One hundred ninety-five."

I smile and reach for his hand, loving that it's a little stained around his fingernails. "See, interesting. Not weird."

We've made it all the way to Louisiana before the sound of Wes's voice wakes me up. I sit upright in my seat and find Gwen leaning over the console between her and Wes, studying something on the dashboard.

"Shit," Wes mutters. "Shit, shit, shit." Wes swerves to the side of the highway and puts the car in park, but I can already feel it, even before Cade gets out and throws open the hood, steam pouring out into the open air like a fountain. I know something is seriously wrong, and I know, whatever it is, that there's probably no way to fix it here, on the side of the road.

Long moments pass as Cade does something under the hood, and I rap my fingers on the window as I watch cars fly by us on the highway. This is just great. Less than twelve hours into the road trip, and we've already hit a road block. My eyes go to the side pocket of my bag, to the map that I know is there but I can't see. I should have just insisted we go straight to Michigan, no lies, no pretense. I want to be on our way there, not here, in Louisiana. Stuck.

After a few minutes, Cade pokes his head inside my open window, draping his arms along the car door. "It's the radiator. It's shot. There's nothing I can do from here. We'll, uh, we'll have to have it towed."

In the front, Wes lets out a humorless laugh. "Well that's just fucking amazing." I can't help but agree.

Cade gets back into the car, and Gwen starts to look up tow trucks on her phone. We can't even turn on the air conditioner, so we sit with the windows rolled down and the doors open.

"God, everything is going to take hours and cost a fortune," Gwen says, hanging up on another call.

"I could fix it easily," Cade says, "but I'd have to be able to get a radiator, and I don't even know where we are." He picks at the black specks of grease on his skin. It's amazing how five minutes under a car's hood can do so much damage.

"We're almost to Shreveport," Gwen says, tipping her head back to look at us over her headrest.

"Maybe if we—" Cade doesn't get the chance to finish his sentence before a pickup truck rattles by us on the highway and then slows as it swerves onto the shoulder in front of us. It's an old red GMC, and with all of our windows down, we can hear the country music playing loud inside the truck.

"What the—" Wes says, and then the music stops, the truck turns off, and a very tall guy in jeans and a western shirt climbs down out of the truck. While the four of us watch in silence, he comes to Wes's window and bends down to look in.

"Need some help?" he asks, his eyes moving over all us and, I notice a little uncomfortably, lingering on me. Cade glances over at me, and I do my best not to make eye contact with anyone.

"Just a shot radiator," Wes says casually, but he doesn't really sound like he knows what he's talking about. "We're just waiting for a tow."

"Oh, I got you," the guys says, smiling in at us. "I've got tow straps in the back. Gonna be a hell of a lot cheaper than whoever you got coming out here. Where y'all headed?"

The four of us exchange glances because, of course, this is a complicated question.

"Do you think you could tow us to Shreveport?" Gwen asks. "We can get what we need there."

The guy leans even farther down, raises an eyebrow in Gwen's direction, and smiles. "Yeah. Sure."

Gwen grins at him, always the first to be kind to anyone who's kind to her, and the guy heads back to his truck, opening the tailgate and pulling out some kind of straps. "Are you sure we should—" Wes looks over at Gwen, his face uneasy, but Gwen is already halfway out of the car.

The guy is standing on the edge of the highway, bent slightly at the waist to see something under the front of our car, his hands planted on his hips while Gwen speaks to him, her mouth moving quick. She claps her hands together and smiles at him, and I see Wes's hands grip the steering wheel.

Cade leans over in the seat beside me, and when he speaks into my ear, it sends a chill down my spine. "Are Gwen and Wes, uh . . .?"

He never actually finishes the question, but he doesn't have to. "Yes," I whisper back.

He nods and goes back to his side of the car, and I do my best to focus again on what's going on with Gwen and the guy outside. She smiles big, and then she races back to the car, sticking her head in through the open window and letting her dark hair cascade inside.

"He's going to tow us to a garage in Shreveport," she says, like she's telling us we just won the lottery.

"Yippee," Wes says sarcastically.

She leans all the way into the car just to smack him on the arm. "His name is Kevin, and you're going to be nice to him because he's doing us a favor."

Cade leans up between the seats, and the three of them are all so close together that I feel like I'm being left out of some secret meeting. I lean back in my seat and watch them.

"We don't need to go to a garage," Cade says. "Just an auto-parts store. I can fix the radiator."

"This'll be faster," Gwen says, but she says it so gently that Cade couldn't get mad, even if he wanted to. Cade nods in agreement.

Only it turns out that it takes a long time to hook something up with tow straps and then you can't drive very fast, so by the time we actually make it to the garage in Shreveport, we've spent an hour baking in the sun, since all three of us wouldn't fit in Kevin's truck, and we all stubbornly refused to take advantage of Kevin's air-conditioning if all three of us couldn't.

It's a quiet and slow ride, and by the time we've made it all the way to Shreveport, I'm ready to pull my hair out.

"Yeah, we can take care of it," the mechanic says when we're finally parked in the garage. "But it's gonna take a few hours. We're pretty backed up today."

The mechanic in front of me waves at Kevin, who takes off in his truck, and next thing I know, we're carless at a mechanic's shop in Shreveport.

"What do we do now?" Gwen asks, her question so innocently spoken, and her eyes on me, like I can somehow fix the situation we're in.

"Shit," I whisper. We have nowhere to go, nothing to do, and we're still more than five hours away from New Orleans. It's already late in the afternoon, since we didn't really get an early start, so now we have to make the choice to either stay in Shreveport overnight or drive into New Orleans in the dead of night. Everything starts to spin in my brain.

"Maybe this is a sign. Maybe we shouldn't have left." I say it to myself, and I don't even really mean for anyone to hear me, but I hear shoes slip over the gravel to me, and then Cade is beside me. "Ellie, no. Come on. This isn't a sign, okay? It's not anything. It happens. Cars break down." He puts his hands on my shoulders, and even though I know he's trying to comfort me, it's my first instinct to pull away from him, until his hands fall to his sides. He watches me for a second, and I have to look away because he always looks like a kicked puppy, and I already feel bad enough.

"Look, we'll just have to take a detour." I hear him pull out his phone and start typing.

"What are you doing?" Wes asks. I almost forgot they were with us, Gwen and Wes.

"Calling us an Uber."

———————

"Is this a joke?"

I'm not usually inclined to agree with Wes, but at this particular moment, I can kind of see his point. Cade has taken us to an old theater in downtown Shreveport with a statue of Elvis in the front, and the doors are locked.

Cade presses his face to the doors, which are actually just giant metal gates looking onto another set of doors. The building looks like it was built about the time the Roman Empire came down.

"Not a joke," Cade says, "but they're closed. It looks like we're going to have to get creative." I have no idea what he means, but a second later, Cade looks over his shoulder and waves our Uber driver away.

As tires scrape across the concrete, Wes turns to Cade. "Why'd you do that? How are we going to get back to the garage?"

Cade smiles over at me. "We don't need any witnesses," he says, casually, and my heart starts to pound at his words, and it ratchets even higher when he starts to rattle the doors and examine the lock on one of them. He looks around, and next thing I know, he's taking something out of his pocket and sticking it in the lock.

"What the hell are you doing?" Gwen hisses at him, and surprisingly, that's enough to get him to stop. His hand drops down at his side.

"Look, this theater is the first real stage Elvis ever performed on. Aretha Franklin. Johnny Cash. I'm not letting this stop be a total wash. We're going in there." With that, as if we've all agreed just with our silence, he starts to wiggle something in the lock again, and I glance around quick to make sure no one is watching because even though I'm not sure I'm down with breaking and entering, I'm also not sure I'm *not* down with it.

"How do you even know all this shit?" Wes asks Cade.

Cade grunts, struggling with the door, and I watch someone across the street walk out of a building there and into their car before driving away without a glance in our direction.

"Read about it in a book last week," Cade says, all of his focus on the door.

"Cade's into . . . research," I say because I can't really figure out another way to put it.

Wes sends me a look, and I know exactly what he's thinking. *Weird.*

Something pops, and then the gate opens slightly in Cade's hand. "Your party awaits, my lady," he whispers to me, and I give one more look around before I slip inside.

Cade repeats the process with the front doors, and then we're in.

With all the lights off, I can't see anything, but I can make out the shadows of a lobby as I hear everyone come inside behind me. The door shuts behind us with a *slam.*

Cade steps up beside me. I gasp when his fingers brush against mine, but then he's pulling me along, his hand in mine, and the rhythm of my heart matches the rhythm of our footsteps.

Behind me, I hear Wes's voice. "Been away from home for six hours, and we're already going to get arrested."

I look at him over my shoulder, contemplating the possibility of security guards a little too late, when Cade stops, and I run into him.

"Sorry," I whisper, but he doesn't answer me because we've reached a set of doors. I'm not sure exactly what that book Cade read said about this place, but he seems to know exactly where he's going.

He reaches out and opens a door. "Wait here," he tells me. I wait, holding the door open with the side of my body, until suddenly the lights come on, and I'm staring out at the stage. We're at the stage entrance, looking at it from the side, and Cade appears again to pull me into the room.

When we're standing in the center of it, looking at the empty auditorium, there's a weird tingling in my stomach that I can't quite put a name to, and for the first time, I'm aware of how far from home we are, and I get a rush in my veins. Six hours from Eaton, in a completely different state from my parents.

"This is amazing," Gwen says, taking a seat on the edge of the stage and throwing her hands up. "Elvis stood here, on this very floor." She slaps her hands against the stage beneath her and grins.

Wes comes up behind her, sticking his hands in his pockets and looking up at the catwalk above us. "I doubt it. It's probably been renovated. Maybe even more than once."

And that's when I realize that Cade is still holding my hand. And I realize it because he's trying to sit down without letting go, and I'm being tugged to the floor beside him. Cade lets my hand go once we're seated.

I watch Gwen and Wes move away from the stage, out into the seats. Wes says something, and Gwen laughs. There's that twist in my stomach again, and I can't even figure out why. Her smile is so bright, I can see the white of her teeth from across the huge room.

"You told me you really liked music."

I pull my knees up and wrap my arms around my legs, watching as Gwen and Wes move down the aisles and then out the door and into the hallway, talking as they go.

Once they're gone, the auditorium is completely silent. The door bangs shut behind them.

"I did?"

He nods.

"It was Luke." The words are out of my mouth before I can stop them, and I don't know if it's because we're so far from home or because we're sitting in this auditorium, but it feels okay to say it here, like anything I say here won't follow us when we leave.

Cade looks over at me. "What?"

"It was Luke that loved music. I mean, it's not like I don't like music. I do. But he was the one who was always discovering new bands, making me playlists, walking around with his headphones on all the time. He got a job at J-Mart just so he could afford concert tickets when my parents wouldn't buy them anymore. He always took me to the concerts with him."

"You'd just gone to a Nova concert."

I blink up at the lights until my eyes start to burn.

"You said you'd just gone to a Nova concert. At the drive-in. I remember because you had a sunburn."

At the drive-in. I scrub my hands over my face, rub my eyes, do anything I can not to look at him. I'm scared if I do, he'll have that look on his face again, the one that tells me that night changed everything.

I press my head to my knee and turn my face away from him. Why are we doing this? Why are we rehashing what happened that night, like it matters? I get that flutter in my stomach again, the one that never really went away, and I'm frustrated with myself for still feeling this way, for feeling anything.

"Hey, Ellie, I'm sorry I didn't mean to—" I hear him slide closer to me, feel his hand on my arm, and this time, I don't flinch away. I just feel the heat of his palm on me. "I'm so sorry," he says, and it's not like when other people say it. Everyone has been telling me they're sorry for the last two weeks, telling me how sad, how devastated, how heartbroken they are, but this is the first time I believe it.

I open my mouth to say something, my face still turned away, but the door to the auditorium slams open. "We have to get out of here!" Wes says, trying to keep his voice low, but he and Gwen are rushing toward the stage. And just before the door shuts behind them, I see lights turn on in the hallway. I scramble to my feet, and the four of us make a run for the stage door.

"What are you doing in here?" a voice shouts right before we throw open the door.

"We'll never make it to the front door before them," Gwen says as we stand in the hallway, unsure which way to go. "There are two of them."

We all look at each other, and then Cade grabs my hand. This time his palm is sweating. "Emergency exit," he says and takes off down the hallway, pulling me along behind him.

Unfortunately, emergency exit also means that an alarm goes off as soon as we throw open the door, and next thing I know, we're all racing out of the building with the screeching of the alarms following us as we run down the street.

Behind us, I can hear a security guard shouting, but we keep running until we've reached a shopping strip nearby, round a corner, and crash into a coffee shop. We're all trying to catch our breaths, and once we have, Cade navigates us to a booth, where we all slouch down into our seats, waiting for something terrible to happen.

Nothing happens.

Except the barista behind the counter sending us strange looks. Cade taps his fingers on the table, and then he starts to snicker. And then we all start to laugh quietly. And then we're all laughing loudly and the barista is sending us even stranger looks.

"You know, man," Wes says. "I never took you as the breaking-and-entering and run-from-security type."

Cade smirks and shrugs. "There's a first time for everything."

I sit back in the booth, unsure if we're actually going to get coffee or if we're just going to sit here, huffing, and my eyes catch on the three of them. Smiling.

There's the twist in my stomach again. It feels like someone just strapped a belt around my chest, pulling it as tight as it'll go, and I think I'm going to puke. I push out of my seat and rush to the door. Maybe security is still looking for us, but I don't care. I can't breathe in here.

The air outside is better, the sky pink with the sunset, and I gasp, trying to make sense of what just happened. I scrub my hands over my face and try to ground myself.

"Ellie?" I open my eyes and look at Gwen. She's standing in front of me, her hands stretched out toward me, and I jolt when they touch my elbows. She looks concerned, but I can't wipe away the way she looked moments ago or back in the auditorium, smiling and laughing.

Inside my pocket, my phone vibrates, and I take it out, just to have something to do, just so that I don't have to look at Gwen and try to decipher my feelings about what just happened inside the coffee shop. But my phone doesn't make me feel any better.

I have several missed calls and text messages from my mother, and when I scroll through the messages, they're all anger or disappointment or worry. I'm supposed to be home by now, especially since I wasn't really expected to leave the house in the first place, and since my car is still in the driveway, I'm sure it's just a matter of time before my mother loses her shit. And then tomorrow, she'll understand that I'm not just at work or off somewhere she doesn't know about. Eventually, she'll figure out that I'm gone, really gone. How long will it take her to put two and two together?

I turn my phone off and put it back in my pocket.

"Can I ask you a question?" Her fingertips graze my arm, and I fight not to pull away. I don't want to upset her. She doesn't wait for me to say yes or no, but she bites her lip like she's afraid I might reject her anyway. "Do your parents know you're here?"

I think about lying, but I know she already knows the truth. My eyes find hers, and her shoulders sag, like she was hoping for a different answer. "Are you sure this is a good idea?"

I'm not sure how to answer that. I don't think I'm qualified to say what's a good idea or a bad idea anymore, but with my body still feeling like I've just run a marathon and my head cloudy, there's no way I want to see messages from my mother.

On the quiet street in front of us, a familiar pickup truck comes to a stop, and the passenger-side window rolls down. For a minute, I'm afraid I've lost my grasp on reality because I find myself looking at Kevin, the same Kevin who brought us here in the first place.

"You ladies want to go to a party?"

Chapter Six

"You want us to just let you take off with some strange guy so that you can go to a party?"

Gwen sighs and crosses her arms. "You make it sound so dramatic. Kevin is going to give us a ride, you're going to pick up the car from the mechanic, and then we're all going to meet up at the party."

I stand behind Gwen and let her talk, but over her shoulder, I glance at Cade. He's watching me, and I can tell by the look on his face that he's feeling about as confident in our plan as Wes is. The only reason I'm even agreeing to this is because we're stuck in Shreveport either way. It's too late now to try and get to New Orleans, so even though all I can think about is getting back on the road, about how if I had taken my own car I'd be halfway to Michigan by now, I agreed to let Gwen go to this party because what else are we going to do here?

Wes sends Kevin a lethal look, but Kevin just smiles back politely.

"I'll make sure they're safe," he says, pressing his back to his truck, parked against the curb in front of the coffee shop. "It's just a party with some college friends. A bunch of them are renting this huge house, so they throw a lot of parties."

None of us really asked Kevin anything about himself, so I don't know if this means he's in college or if he just likes to hang out with people in college. Either way, the decision has been made, and Gwen and Wes kiss goodbye as I climb into the truck next to Kevin. There's just one seat in the front, so I'm sitting between him and Gwen, squished up against her to avoid Kevin's hand as he shifts gears.

"So, you're in college?"

Kevin smiles over at Gwen when she asks the question, and I feel like maybe I'm supposed to be attracted to him, maybe he thinks I am, because he's supermodel attractive, and when I look at him, he looks a little two-dimensional, like he can't possibly exist in the real world.

"Yep. Louisiana State." He says it with so much pride that I'm almost jealous. Will I be able to answer with that much pride when I tell people I go to Tate? I remember Luke telling me that he got his acceptance letter, how defeated he looked. My chest starts to tighten, the same way it did back in the café, and I try to subtly gasp for breath so that Gwen won't notice and try to comfort me.

Gwen glances over at me, oblivious, a little smile on her face, and I think maybe it's because of the way he said Louisiana. Loos-ee-anna, instead of Lou-ee-see-anna. Gwen smiles at me and then asks another question. She's much braver than I am. I'm still having trouble making my mouth move.

"And this party is a Louisiana State party?"

Kevin pulls in front of a house, not more than a few miles from the coffee shop where we were, and the three of us climb out. I'm thankful for the fresh air, even if it's so humid that it's like trying to take water into my lungs.

I had my first drink when I was fourteen. One of Luke's friends had "cool parents" who provided beer and then went out for the night. We sat in the basement with Wes and Luke's friends, and even though I didn't want to taste it, I took a sip of Luke's beer because everyone said I should. It tasted like dog piss and smelled worse.

This is just one of a million reasons I never enjoyed parties, not the way Luke and Gwen and Wes did. They liked going to parties and drinking and playing games and kissing people because what else is there to do in Eaton anyway? I always tried to play along, but by midnight or so, the party is always a little less fun for the only sober one in the room.

But when we're standing in the living room of a huge house, with bodies writhing around us and the music thumping so loud, for once, I don't want to be the person in the corner, observing, pretending to have fun. That was the old Ellie, and I left her back in Eaton. I shove down the girl who just freaked out in the café and the girl who freaked out in the truck. I want to be different now; I want to be as brave as Luke, as fearless as Gwen, as tough as Wes.

"Where can I get a drink?" I say to Kevin, who's standing beside me, his hands in the pockets of his tight jeans. I see him exchange a glance with Gwen, and I have no idea what it means or why they've decided to be coconspirators in this moment, but it has the immediate effect of pissing me off. "I thought we came here to party!" I shout up at him. In the truck, it was almost too easy to forget how he towers over me, but now I have to crane my neck to look up at him.

"Yeah, okay," he says, and then he takes my hand, and I think of Cade, pulling me along through the concert hall, holding my hand at the drive-in. I'm about to pull away, I don't even really know why, when Gwen takes my other hand. When I glance back at her, her eyes are darting around the room, like any second someone is going to jump out at her wearing a Halloween mask. It was her idea to come to the party. "To get the most of our experience," she said, like random college parties are crucial to life. But other than that moment as she huddled over the trunk of Wes's car, deciding whether to smile at me, this is the first time I've seen her look like this, hesitant and unsure.

My mind travels back to Luke's funeral, to her in the corner, crying.

We push through the room. It's still early, barely after eight, so the party hasn't gotten particularly rowdy. Perhaps the worst thing is a few couples grinding on the dance floor to a remixed version of "Summertime Sadness."

Other than the intense smell of pot, the house in itself is much tidier than I imagined in my head. With the exception of party debris, the furniture is nice and the kitchen counters clear of rotting food or other oddities. When I hear that a bunch of college boys are renting a house together, I imagine the worst.

Inside the kitchen, coolers are spread across the floor, plus a keg, which I recognize from TV shows, having never actually seen one in real life. People are pushed up against counters, laughing as they do shots or drink beer out of plastic cups.

"Pick your poison," Kevin says, gesturing at the coolers that are halfway closed at our feet. I open a few of them and see only cans of beer and wine coolers. Kevin and Gwen watch me until I stand and cross my arms. I motion at the bottles of liquor lined along the cabinet beside us, conjuring every ounce of courage I can.

"You got anything harder than beer?"

Gwen glances at me warily but doesn't say anything.

Kevin grins and steps over to the counter. "Tequila and rum, if you're that kind of girl." Gwen sends him a blank look. She's constantly scanning the space around me like I'm the president and she's the head of my security detail.

"I'll have a shot of tequila."

He nods and smiles like he's been waiting all night to hear me say this. "Mixed with . . . ?"

"Mixed with oxygen."

His smile falters a little. "You sure?"

His words grate on my nerves, especially since Gwen is still standing so close to me, like she might have to take a bullet for me at any moment. What is it about me that makes people feel like they need to treat me like I'm twelve, like I need to be protected? "Give me the damn shot."

His eyebrows shoot up, and he tips some tequila into a plastic shot glass. I throw it back. Luke taught me how to do shots. He taught me to tip my head back fast so that as little liquid as possible touches my tongue on the way down. Luke was good at drinking. He could down more shots than anyone and not show any signs of being wasted. Once, at a party someone on the track team threw, I caught Luke throwing up in the bathroom and asked him if he wanted to go home. But he just rinsed his mouth out, rejoined the party, and went right back to drinking. Wes had to drag him home that night.

"Want some?" Kevin asks Gwen.

"No, thanks," she says and then bends over to grab a can of beer from one of the open coolers. She immediately pops it open and takes a few gulps while we watch her.

I take the shot Kevin's already poured. I knock it back and squeeze my eyes tight as the liquid burns a path down my throat. I shudder. It's awful for a second, but then my body goes warm, the music starts to sound better, the conversation becomes a little more interesting.

"I gotta say hi to some people," Kevin says in my ear. "I'll catch up with you ladies later." I get a chill when he does this, but I can't tell if it's a good thing or not. Mostly, I just feel a little unsteady, a little overheated.

As soon as Kevin's gone, I reach for the tequila bottle he set on the counter and pour myself another shot that I grip in my fist for later. "Let's find somewhere to go," I say to Gwen, and we press back through the party. The lights are dim and mostly everyone is starting to slip closer to slightly hammered, judging by the sloppy way they move. Some people are dancing to the loud music while others are just making out in corners.

We see some people heading for what looks like a door to the basement, and we follow them down. The basement is just a collection of recliners and a couch surrounding a TV, where Call of Duty is flashing on the screen. The people watching the game are passing a joint from person to person, their eyelids heavy.

"God, I thought Wes's dad's Cowboys obsession was bad."

I hesitate, reminded again that all this time, Gwen and Wes have been hanging out together while I tried to move on alone, but I can't let myself dwell on it. My eyes catch on a framed jersey on the wall, and the room starts to explode in black and gold, Saints memorabilia covering shelves high above our heads and scattered across multiple display cases. My eyes are so distracted by the sight when I finally start moving again that I trip on the last step going down into the basement, and some of the clear liquid in my shot glass splashes out onto my hand as Gwen reaches out to steady me.

"Are you okay?" Gwen asks, but I don't answer. I know she's asking because I almost just faceplanted in some stranger's basement, but all I can hear is the question over and over in my head from everyone: my boss, the cashier at the gas station, the guy stocking produce at J-Mart.

My head spins, and I think the shots are starting to kick in, but I toss back what's left of the one in my hand anyway because I don't want to waste it.

In the corner of the room, two boys argue over a foosball table, and when I've gotten my footing, I realize that one of them is looking right at us. He starts to twist the handles on the table, and I can hear the little plastic ball roll from one side of the table to the other. He smiles up at me. "Want to play?"

I hand Gwen my empty shot glass, walk over to the foosball table, and grip the handles of the side opposite the guy. Wes's dad has a foosball table. Or at least he used to. Now I can't remember seeing it when I was down there last week. I stood at that table so many times, beating Luke until he was a bad sport and didn't want to play anymore, playing with Wes until he became a different kind of bad sport and started rubbing it in my face that I would never be as good as him, strategically rolling the ball back and forth with one set of players while Wes and Luke played video games or watched horror movies.

"Okay, but I should warn you that I'm pretty freaking good."

The boy's smile gets bigger, his eyes scrunching up in the corners. "Put your money where your mouth is," he says and drops the ball into the table, among our little plastic men.

I plan to dominate, but when the little ball moves toward my row, a perfect shot for me to take, I spin the handle, slip off of it, and stumble right into Gwen.

"That wasn't how that was supposed to go," I mumble as the room tips back in the other direction, righting itself. The boy's face swims in my field of vision, but Gwen is already pulling me in the other direction, away from the foosball table.

"Let's just have a seat," she says. "You went through those shots a little too fast, I think." We turn in a circle, looking for a place to sit, but all the seats are taken, so Gwen deposits me on the floor between the two re-cliners, sitting down across from me, with her back to the other chair.

I watch the game play out on the screen, but it starts to make me dizzy, so I look away, at Gwen. Her eyes are on the TV, her beer grasped in her half-open hand. She doesn't look like she's having fun, even though she's the one that wanted to come.

"I don't really get games like this," she says. "Wes likes them, but it all just seems a little sad."

I shrug, stretching my leg out and then moving it back in when I acci-dentally kick Gwen. "Sorry," I mutter and then close my eyes, leaning my head against the vinyl behind me, feeling a little more stable even as the chair shakes with the enthusiasm of the guy sitting in it.

"It's mindless," I say. "Comforting." When Luke left, I spent hours playing Call of Duty in the living room when my parents weren't home. My mother hated the game, didn't really like that Luke played it and wouldn't openly allow me to play at all, but I liked the way it kept me from thinking, kept me focused on what was on the screen, kept my hands busy.

"I can think of about a million things in the world more comforting than this," Gwen says. She shifts, and her leg presses against mine, warm through our clothes, and I agree with her. There are more comforting things.

"Hey," Gwen says, nudging me lightly until I open my eyes to look at her. "Are you sure you're okay?"

I'm not really sure if she's referring to the fact that I just tossed back three shots of tequila or the fact that my brother just died, but either way, I feel sick to my stomach. The tequila is in charge of my mouth now, and I can't seem to stay quiet.

"No," I say honestly. "Are you?"

This seems to catch her off guard. She watches me, and when I glance down at the beer can in her hand, I see that she's shaking, just the tips of her fingers, just slightly.

She presses her head back against the seat behind her. "The guys should be here already," she says, instead of answering. Apparently I'm not the only one trying to pretend I'm fine. "Let's go back upstairs."

I want to protest since sitting right here on the cold linoleum feels just right, but she's already hauling me to my feet and guiding me in the direction of the stairs, which might as well be Mount Everest. She wraps an arm around my waist, and we stumble up the stairs and back into the throng of people. There are almost twice as many as there were before, but I still catch sight of Wes in the crowd, coming toward us with a relieved smile on his face.

"Here you are!" he shouts. "We couldn't find you."

Instinctively, I look over his shoulder to find the other half of his *we*, but he's not with Wes. My eyes travel over the room, searching, and then I see him. He comes into the room from somewhere beyond the kitchen with a girl attached to his side like a barnacle. She's smiling up at him, and when they stop in the living room doorway, he leans down to say something in her ear.

I've never felt anything like jealousy over a guy before in my life, but when I see him lean down to her, see the way she tilts her face up toward his just enough for the movement to be intimate, it feels like having something ripped out of my hands. Which is utterly ridiculous. We went on one date a year ago, and now because he's here with me, that means we're soul mates?

Beside me, Wes and Gwen are chatting, but the music is loud enough that I can't hear what they're talking about. I sneak a glance at them and am immediately struck by the way they seem to curve around each other, their bodies slanted like parentheses, their cups the comments between them. Gwen smiles, and I see the anxiety melt away from her, but just as soon as her easy demeanor appears, it vanishes because the music changes and Nova blasts out over the speakers. My skin burns, and I wish I could do something to change the song, to make it stop, but short of tackling the radio in the living room, there's not much I can do.

I watch as Gwen's eyes change, see her straighten away from Wes and tug at her shirt like it's too tight. "I'm going to go outside," she says loudly, loud enough for me to hear and loud enough for Wes to look disappointed. She turns and heads for the front door while Wes watches her go.

"This is lame," he says after a moment. "I'm going to get some air, too."

I don't think the party is lame, but I let Wes leave anyway, pressing my back to the wall behind me so I don't fall over. When I focus my attention back at the kitchen, the girl and Cade are gone, and I'm trying to pretend like I don't care where they've disappeared to. I still hope it's not one of the bedrooms upstairs.

And then my eyes meet Kevin's. He stands in the kitchen, right in the middle of a group of girls, and even though he seems to be pouring drinks for them, his attention is on me. I'm not sure how long he's been watching me, but I can tell he *has* been watching, and from the way he smiles at me while he's setting a cup of beer in front of some loud blond girl, I think maybe he wants me to come over.

I think about Cade, off with some girl he just met, and I move toward Kevin. The girls seem to scatter when I get there, but Kevin keeps his eyes on me. I wonder if he'll flirt with anyone, if I'm just one in a long list of girls that he's looked at this way at a party, like he's ready to devour them. Does it even matter?

"Want to dance?" I'm not much of a dancer, more of swayer, but I know from years of watching girls make their move on Luke that dancing is a good way to get a guy's attention.

Kevin puts down the bottle of tequila in his hand and sends me a warm, confident smile before sliding a shot in my direction. I swallow it, and as soon as it makes its way down my throat, burning a path that I almost immediately regret, I start to feel a little woozy.

And then Kevin is beside me, pulling me into the swarm by the tips of his fingers hooked through mine. The music is loud and pumping, the Nova song having faded away long ago, and Kevin pulls me against him until I can smell the sweat on his neck.

If I have any doubt about Kevin's intentions, they go out the window when his hand moves down to settle low on my back, his fingers resting on the curve of my ass.

"What's your name?" he asks with his mouth pressed against my ear, and I giggle because it seems hilarious that he's practically groping me but doesn't even know my name.

"Ellie."

He reaches down and takes one of my hands in his, bringing it up to loop around his neck. The action makes me a little dizzy, and I clutch at the collar of his shirt to stay steady.

I grab his hand and am immediately taken by how warm it is, how wonderful it feels in mine, how long it's been since I let someone touch me without flinching away, really touch me, not the shaken hands at Luke's funeral or the pats on the back from my mother. Or the seemingly oblivious way Cade pulled me along, our hands entwined, or put his hand on my arm to comfort me. This isn't a comforting hand on mine. This is something else entirely.

Out of nowhere, the room tilts a little, and I stumble away from Kevin, tripping backward, but warm hands keep me from crashing to the ground.

"You are so plastered," a voice says in my ear from behind, but doesn't make sense because Kevin is standing in front of me, watching me with wary eyes, his empty hands stretched out toward me. I push away from whoever has me and spin around too fast. Cade is standing in front of me now. He reaches out to steady me, and his hands are startling. They're hot and burning my skin.

Behind me, I hear Kevin say, "Oh, hey, man. Can you pass me my date?"

Is that what Kevin thinks I am? His date? But I get more caught on the fact that he asked Cade to pass me to him like I'm a salt shaker over the dinner table or something. And I realize that Cade is still holding me, his hands wrapped around my upper arms, and I look up at him, and he looks down at me, and I could melt right through the dance floor.

"Do you want to go?" Cade asks, and I keep myself from asking *go where* because the only place to go is a hotel room.

"Don't go, Ellie. You just got here," Kevin says. I've almost forgotten that he's there, but he's immediately in my personal space again, and I have two sets of hands on me now, instead of just one. I am suddenly very aware of how tingly my fingers are, how numb my lips feel.

"I'm just going to find Wes." I don't know why, but this suddenly seems imperative. In my mind, Wes becomes a solid, like home base, the place I always come back to. It was always the three of us, him and me and Luke. Ever since I was little, home was where they were. I turn away from both of them, searching, and I hear Kevin walk away, muttering under his breath. When I turn around he's gone, and somehow, I'm alone with Cade. Well, alone in a room full of dozens of people. It's enough to make my cheeks heat up. Or maybe that's the tequila.

"If you don't want to leave, at least go somewhere and lie down for a second," Cade is saying from behind me. "We'll find you a safe place. You're about to fall over."

"That's not true." I still feel relatively stable on my feet, despite my previous inability to keep them under me. Cade sighs, and I realize too late that the reason I can hear him sighing so quietly is because he's standing so close to me. He's holding me up again. Damn it.

Tired of listening to his disappointed grumbling, I say, "What are you even doing with me? Don't you have a date? Where is she?"

He squints at me. "What are you talking about?"

I wave in the general direction of the kitchen, as if the girl might still be standing there in the doorway. "That girl. She was pretty. Why aren't you with her?" I want to put a hand over my own mouth to get myself to stop asking stupid questions and making it very obvious how much I actually care about Cade's romantic life, but I'm too busy trying to get information from him that I care very much about.

He glances at where I'm pointing and then back at me. "I bumped into her outside the bathroom. Turns out we had a mutual friend. It wasn't, like, a *thing.*" There's amusement in his voice.

"Are you making fun of me?"

He rolls his eyes. "God, Ellie, no. I'm not making fun of you. You're just drunk."

I glance over my shoulder and realize I'm a few inches from a wall. I lean back against it, and it's cold and solid. I close my eyes.

"Do you ever think about that night at the drive-in?" Of all the stupid things that could have dribbled out of my mouth just then, this is probably the worst. I have definitely lost complete control over my vocal cords. I've spent a year trying to forget that night, but it's hard to forget with him so close, reminding me what it felt like to mean something to him.

When I open my eyes, he's watching me, his face blank. Cade is definitely much better looking than Kevin, and my body is starting to take notice, going tingly under the weight of his gaze. I feel a little like I've been going around on a carousel, spinning and dizzy but bursting with excitement nevertheless.

I look up at Cade and want him. I want how close we were a year ago, I want the way he used to look at me like I was the most important thing to him. I grab onto the fabric of his shirt and lean against him.

"I think you're right," I say, tilting my face up toward his, the way that girl did earlier. "I think I want to lie down. Walk me upstairs?"

He looks skeptical but then he nods. "Okay. Slowly." He puts an arm around my shoulders and tucks one of my arms around his waist. I feel the hardness of his side under my fingertips and shiver. He anchors me to him as we move into the hallway and upstairs.

Most of the bedroom doors are closed, but there's one at the end of the hall that's open, and we move straight for it. Cade pushes the door open all the way and flips on the light, showcasing a mostly bare room with white walls and minimal decoration. The only indication of who might live here is a picture on the nightstand, a framed photo of a polo-clad boy with his arm around a pretty girl.

"Lie down," he says, depositing me on the navy blue bedspread. It has little white anchors on it. They're dancing in my vision. "I'm going to get you some water. I'll be right back." He moves toward the door and then turns back to me. "Don't move, okay? Please."

He doesn't wait for me to make the promise, but the room is spinning, and there's no way I'm going anywhere.

It seems like only half a second before Cade is back, carrying a red Solo cup. Cold, wonderful water slips down my throat, cooling my skin and clearing my head a little. I feel like I can breathe again.

When the cup is full of nothing but melting ice, I set it aside and stand up, feeling more stable than I did downstairs but not by much. Cade watches me with a wary eye, his arms half stretched toward me just in case I lose my footing. He's close enough to the bed that it only takes two very unsteady steps to get to him, and when I do, I fist my hands into his shirt.

"Ellie," he begins, but I cut him off with a kiss, just barely managing to line our lips up in my shakiness, in my urgency.

A part of me is prepared for Cade to push me away, but those ideas go up in smoke when he kisses me back, sliding his fingers up the back of my neck and moving his mouth on mine so superbly that it feels like downing another shot of tequila. The alcohol hasn't made my lips and tongue nearly as numb as I thought, and for just a second, I forget everything. I forget where we are, why we're here, what happened to my brother two weeks ago. I let myself revel in the fact that Cade actually wants me. Still wants me.

My hands move from his shirt to his hair, grabbing and tugging, and then they move to his buttons. His fingers collide with mine, and he grips me for a second more before taking a step back. He sighs. "That's not what this is about."

"You wanted to kiss me that night at the drive-in," I say, shocking myself. "I know you did." It's something I've thought about over and over for the past year, but I never thought I would say it to him. I try to get back to where I was, pressed against him, letting him make me feel more alive than I have in a year, but he keeps his distance.

"Ellie, don't. You're drunk."

His words are pinpricks in my skin. I know I rejected Cade, I know that the distance between us is completely my fault, but knowing that doesn't quell the hurt. "You want me, don't you? I mean you—"

"Of course I do. But not like this. Not when you're ..." He trails off, and I can think of a thousand ways he could finish that sentence. *Drunk. Sad. Confused. Lost. Messed up.* They all work right now.

I can't be here with him like this, when it feels like he can see everything. I try to go around him, but he steps in my way. "Ellie, come on, let's talk about this. Let's talk about *anything*."

I don't want to talk. I just want to get out of this room. Cade is my ever-constant reminder. In the halls at Eaton High, at the garage right outside the shop's window, in the aisles at J-Mart, always, always reminding me of how my life *should* have been. But instead, it fell apart, and I just need him out of the way right now, need to put some space between us.

I try to shove him out of the way, but it has the opposite effect, causing me to ricochet off him and stumble backward. He steps forward to catch me, and his kindness is even more infuriating. Why couldn't he have just been an asshole?

"I want to go." I can't even look at him anymore, as we stand here, his hands still holding onto me, my eyes on the door. I want this night to be over. I want it all to be over. What did I really think was going to happen? That Cade was going take my virginity, right here in this stranger's room, and that I would somehow feel better afterward?

Finally, he says, "Let me help you."

"Leave me alone, Cade. Why can't you just leave me alone?" I don't mean to sound defeated. I mean to sound angry, but all the fight is going out of me, leaving that numbness behind. And I want it. I want it to eat up everything I'm feeling, swallow it whole until there's nothing left. Because being numb is so much easier than the alternative.

"Because I care about you," he says, his voice so soft, so full of comfort and sincerity that it makes something inside me ache, something that feels like it'll swell until it won't fit inside me anymore. "You can talk to me, Ellie."

I stare at him for a minute, something creeping up inside me, something that threatens to come pouring out.

I hear someone calling my name in the hallway. And then there's banging on the door before it opens. The door hits Cade in the shoulder, and Wes's face appears in the crack. His eyes connect with mine, and he shoves the door until Cade moves away from it. I can see Gwen in the hallway behind him.

"What's going on?" Wes moves into the room and his eyes fall on Cade. His eyes flash to me. "Are you okay? What happened? I went outside for one second, and you were just gone." I can see real fear in his eyes.

Cade grimaces. "I brought her upstairs so she could sleep it off."

Wes latches onto my arm. "Sure, you did." There's acid in his voice, and I can't even figure out why he would be talking to Cade like that.

Gwen comes up behind me and herds me forward. Wes helps me down the stairs, his fingertips digging into my arm and my side. But when we finally emerge outside, the night air the cleanest thing I've ever breathed in, Wes turns to me, his face angry. "What is the matter with you? You can't just disappear like that."

I sigh and run my hands over my face. I really need to sit down. "God, can you just leave me alone?"

"I'm not going to leave you alone!" he shouts, making my head vibrate, making the world seem twice as quiet when the echo finally dies. "You're at a fucking college party in a town you've never been in. You can't just disappear like that!"

"Stop treating me like a child!" I scream, louder than I mean to. My entire body quakes with anger.

"Stop acting like one! You're drunk and going up into bedrooms at strangers' houses with strange guys." I'm about to argue that Cade is not a strange guy, but Wes isn't done talking. "What do you think Luke would think if he saw what you just did in there?" As soon as the words are out of his mouth, I can tell that he's sorry he said them. His eyes go wide, and his arms fall by his sides.

I feel like I've been hit by a truck. But I won't let Wes see it. I step up close to him, until it feels like we're breathing the same air. "Luke didn't care what I did or who I hung out with. Luke left. He didn't give a shit about me anymore, just like he didn't give a shit about you."

Wes and I stare at each other, and I see the same hurt in his eyes that I feel in my gut, a kind of hurt that can never be made better, a kind of hurt that didn't start with us.

I turn, not sure where I'm going, but I see figures silhouetted in the doorway of the house. Cade watches with shock on his face while Gwen steps all the way out of the house, coming toward me. I hear Wes move behind me, and when I turn to look, he's walking away from me, down the street, probably to the car.

"Come on," Gwen says when she reaches me, rubbing my arms gently. There are tears streaming down her face. But I can't move.

I double over and vomit beside her shoes.

The boys booked a room at a hotel downtown while Gwen and I were at the party, and we go straight there. Gwen helps me up to the room, but Wes goes the opposite way down the hallway, disappearing around a corner, while Cade mutters something about finding an ice machine before ditching, too.

Inside the room, the air conditioner is on full blast, and I shiver immediately. I lie down and try to take a deep breath as the room spins around and tilts to the side.

"Are you okay?" Gwen whispers, and I try to make out her face in the darkness of the room, the only light coming from the window, where the glow of Shreveport floods in. Every time she asks the question, it gets harder to lie.

I shake my head. I can't believe any of that just happened. I close my eyes and then feel the mattress dip beneath me, and when I open them again, Gwen's face is inches from mine. She blinks at me, still wearing her glasses.

"Are you going to puke again?" she asks, and I'm surprised by the lack of urgency in her question.

"I don't know why I did that," I say instead of answering her.

A crease appears between her eyebrows. "Ellie, cut yourself some slack."

I turn away from her, facing a wall. Halfway up, there's a painting of a cowboy on a horse, and it makes me feel like I haven't left Texas at all.

I feel her fingertips on my scalp, moving the hair away from my face gently. "So, what's going on between you and Cade?" On any other day, a question like this might upset me. But today, it's easier than talking about anything else that's going on.

"Nothing, really."

I roll back over, and she lies down beside me. She pulls her arms up between us, wrapping them around herself. "I remember him," she says, her voice quiet. But even though she's whispering, her voice seems to fill the whole room. "From when I used to come over to your house. You guys were pretty flirty back then." Her mouth makes a weird shape, and she doesn't say anything else.

I shrug, my clothes rustling as they move against the clean sheets. "We went out once. Nothing happened after that. I guess we're just friends." It's a weird way to describe him now. Cade and I were friends before. But things are different now.

After a minute of quiet, I start to think about what happened back at the party. I squeeze my eyes shut, like I can block it all out, erase it, go back to before and just say no to the party in first place. "I said shitty things. I shouldn't have been so mean."

She sighs. "He wasn't exactly an angel to you. Wes will get over it. He knows you. He knows you didn't mean those things."

How can Wes know me when I don't even know myself?

The door opens at our feet, and I hear the rattle of ice in a bucket before the door slams shut again. I close my eyes and listen to Cade move around the room. The water in the sink runs, and then he comes to the side of the bed, and I can feel him standing beside me, even though he doesn't touch me.

"Is she asleep?" he whispers.

Gwen doesn't say anything, but I hear her shift. Maybe she nods her head or shrugs, but I pretend to be asleep either way. I can't look Cade in the eye right now.

"Okay, well, I'm going to put this water on the nightstand." I hear him set something beside my head, and then I listen as he goes into the bathroom, and then I really do fall asleep.

———————

Cade looks over at me with his lips clamped together. "Peanut butter?"

"It's a perfectly normal milkshake choice, Cade Matthews, or it wouldn't be on the menu."

Cade scoffs and takes his vanilla milkshake from the counter before handing my peanut butter one to me. He pays for both of them, and we walk back to the car. It's a double feature, but the first movie, a movie about a woman trapped in a haunted hospital, was so bad that I don't have much faith in whatever's next.

"They also have fried pickles on the menu."

"Don't you dare blaspheme fried pickles."

"They're gross."

I shake my head at him. "What a boring life you must lead, only liking vanilla ice cream and regular, unfried pickles."

"I don't even really like normal pickles."

"You know what your problem is?"

Our feet crunch over the gravel of the parking lot, and we get back in his grandmother's car. It smells a little floral and antiseptic, but I try to ignore it.

"What?"

"You're not a real Texan."

He throws his head back and laughs. "Is that necessary in order to like peanut butter and fried food?"

I shrug. "It can't hurt." We're quiet as the screen lights up, immediately jumping into two teenagers being killed during a camping trip. They can't be much older than Cade and me, and I can't imagine a world where my mom would let me go off camping with him. I ignore the movie and pick up the con-

versation again.

"Where did you come from?" He sends me a confused look, and I laugh. "I mean, before you moved to Eaton."

Cade moved to Eaton when we were in the fourth grade, but no one seems to know that much about where he came from, including me.

When I ask him now, his eyes seem to dim a little. "Indianapolis."

"That explains it. There's no way you're being brought up on fried pickles and funnel cake in Indiana."

He smiles, but the shadows are still there, so I shut up. When he speaks, his voice is easy, amused. "They have fried pickles in Indiana. It's Indiana, not Antarctica."

I smile down at my feet. "Try a sip," I say, holding my cup out to him.

He grimaces. "Absolutely not."

I yank the cup back quick. "You're not allergic to peanuts, are you?"

"No. Peanut butter is just gross."

I shove the straw in his face again. "Just one sip."

He shakes his head.

"Come on, what are you, man or mouse?"

He chuckles then, his eyes bright, and I watch, awed, as he wraps his lips around the straw and sucks. I have to look away because the act feels too intimate, but I look back when he makes a choking sound. He looks away from me and shudders, and I have to laugh. He coughs dramatically and then lunges for his vanilla milkshake.

I shake my head and drink from my shake again, trying not to focus on the fact that my mouth is exactly where his was a second ago.

He sets his head back and sighs. "And here I thought you liked me. You don't try to kill people you like."

I scoff. "I never said I liked you."
I sip from my milkshake, and he grins over at me.

———————

The air is wet. Wet and thick. And then it's not the air. There is no air. I've slipped below the surface of the water. It closes around my head, and I fight, clawing and thrashing, trying to get back to the sunlight, but I can't. I sink to the bottom like a rock and stare up at the surface. My lungs are closing up, filling up. I feel dirt under my hands.

And then I'm in a pit, a closed pit of rock and dirt. As I'm screaming, pounding for someone to let me out, it begins to fill with water. I panic, tearing at the earth around me, but nothing happens. I scratch and rip and pry, but the pit stays the same, closed over my head. I scream, and I feel hot tears on my cheeks, but it does no good. The pit fills, and I'm submerged, gasping and clawing.

I wake up in a sweat. Outside, it's storming. Fat, heavy raindrops slam against the window. Lightning flashes. My heart rate spikes, and I clutch handfuls of the hotel comforter. Beside me, Gwen is fast asleep, snoring just slightly, and I can see the shape of the boys on the bed next to us in the moonlight coming in through the window.

I sit up, clutching my stomach, certain I'm going to be sick again. I find the glass of water that Cade left on my nightstand, gulping down half of it. But then thunder crashes again outside the window, and I drop the glass on the carpet.

"Damn." I reach for the glass, but the carpet is wet.

"Are you okay?"

I gasp and spin around. Cade looks over at me from his side of the room, his skin pale in the moonlight. He's not wearing a shirt, and even in the darkness, I can make out the planes of his skin.

"I'm fine," I tell him.

The party comes back to me in a flash. His lips on mine, the anger on his face, the way he watched from the open door as Wes and I fought. Last night, I had Cade's hands on me. And maybe they were drunk hands or maybe they were pitying hands, but I can't possibly look at the boy in front of me now and not remember the way he pressed his fingers into my skin.

"You should go back to sleep." I turn away and pull the covers up to my shoulders, staring at the wall and pretending to sleep.

In the morning, we pack the car in silence, and even though I send Gwen desperate eyes, she sits up front with Wes, leaving me in the back with Cade.

I can't stop thinking about last night. Not just the kissing. But the other stuff. Getting mad at Cade, yelling at Wes, puking in front of that house. I have to have better control over myself. College parties are not why I'm doing this. Without thinking, I reach into the bag at my feet, my fingers finding the paper edge of the map. I run my fingers down, feeling the places where the tip of a pen made an indentation. This is why I'm here. I just have to make it to Dexter.

We're almost an hour down the road when I glance at Gwen and Wes and decide that even though I don't have a whole lot of privacy here, I need to say what I need to say before we have any more road behind us.

"I'm sorry about what happened at the party," I tell Cade, as quietly as I can. "I acted like an idiot."

His expression changes, from casual to concerned so fast he doesn't even look like the same person. "Don't say that."

"It's true though. You didn't deserve any of that. I—" I look at Gwen and Wes again. They're probably not listening, right? I swallow, but I still feel a little bit like I did when I woke up in the middle of the night, like the whole world is closing in on me. I tell him the truth anyway. "This is just harder than I thought it would be. I'm sorry." I'm not good at apologies, not sincere ones at least. But Cade deserves an apology, if only for getting mixed up in my screwed-up life. Once we're back in Eaton again, I'll cut him free like I did before. I ache at the thought.

Cade bites his bottom lip in a way that is both appealing and childish and leans in close to me, his voice quiet under the noise of the air conditioner. "It wasn't all bad."

It takes me a second to understand what he means, but when I do, I blush. For the last hour, I've been trying not to think about what it was like to kiss Cade. But right here, with Cade looking at me with his clear green eyes, I start to think about what it would be like. Something real. Maybe in another life, Cade and I could have been something. Maybe I would be sitting here, his doting girlfriend, driving across the country with him with hearts in my eyes. Maybe I wouldn't have damaged the whole thing last year. He's so close, but I can feel that it's ruined, the way rotten fruit is soft to the touch.

I lean away and watch Louisiana fly by outside the window.

Chapter Seven

We pull over when we cross into New Orleans.

"What are we doing first?" Wes asks, turning around in his seat to look at me. This is the first time we've spoken in the six hours since we left Shreveport, and I'm so shocked to see his attention on me that at first, I don't even really know what he's asking me.

"What?"

Wes raises his eyebrows at me. "Where are we going in New Orleans?"

I think about the map in the bag at my feet. I can feel it there, like a small sun that I'm trying to cover up with a backpack stuffed with clothes and toiletries.

"Oh, um. Mississippi River?" I almost choke on the words as they come out, thinking about the day we put it on the map, about the way Luke got so excited and immediately drew a long line along the path of the Mississippi as it moved through America, a big smile on his face.

Wes doesn't say anything. He just plugs something into his phone and then we're off.

The sun is high in the sky when we get to the river. People mill around

Jackson Square, sitting on the benches and chasing their kids at the edge of the water. We walk until we've reached the river, finding a concrete staircase that leads right down into the water without stopping. We sit on the steps, scattered, like we can pretend that we're not all here together, our feelings still bruised about everything that happened last night.

I've been to beaches, to the Brazos, to the Gulf, but there's something about being here. Maybe it's because it's the first time I've been to the water without Luke. I think about the time we went to Padre Island, and I got so caught up in the fun that I forgot to put on sunscreen and got a second-degree burn. Luke drove me to the store and bought me aloe gel, rubbing it on my back in the hotel room while my mother scolded me for not being more careful. If I close my eyes, I can almost pretend I'm there again, under the sun with Luke, the waves roaring loud around us. For a second, the smell of the river in my lungs extinguishes everything else inside me. I'm sitting closest to the water, so close that the gentle lapping starts to wet the tips of my shoes.

I open my eyes when Wes's shoes scrape on the concrete step behind me. He shifts and nods in Cade's direction. "Hey, you know history stuff, right? Got any facts about the Mississippi?" He asks the question like he's talking to a search engine, but I can see what he's doing, trying to reach out to Cade, offering him a lifeline after the way he acted last night. It comes out stilted and awkward, and when I look over at Gwen, she sends me a close-lipped smile, like she can see what Wes is doing, too. I should be grateful that he's even trying.

Cade smiles, but he doesn't take his eyes away from the water. "Well, I know it's the second longest river in the United States. Fourth longest in the world. And that the first riverboat to sail it was called the *New Orleans*."

We all wait, but Cade doesn't offer any more information.

"That's it?" Wes asks. "I thought you were like an encyclopedia." I kind of hate the way he says it. Cade's encyclopedic knowledge of things that no one else in Eaton tends to care very much about is one of the reasons that people like Luke and Wes said he was odd. As if intelligence and passion about an academic subject are the thing that could make a person the weirdest.

Cade shrugs. "I don't study bodies of water very often. Sorry to disappoint."

I hear someone shift behind me, and I know without looking that it's Cade. I know that he's coming to sit beside me.

"What else is there to do around here?" I ask when he's settled, his hip almost entirely pressed against mine. I focus on a weed floating down the river so I won't be so distracted by the heat of him.

Cade looks sideways at me. "What makes you think I know?"

I smile down at the murky water. "Maybe you don't know much about the Mississippi, but I find it hard to believe you don't know anything about the French Quarter. Especially since we read about the Louisiana Purchase in world history last year."

Cade looks at me, obviously torn, and then he rolls his eyes. "Yes, okay. I did a little bit of research on Jackson Square over Thanksgiving break. I finished the textbook so I was looking for something else to pass the time." He says this part quietly, and I can't blame him. Even *I* think reading a whole textbook over break is a little much. I can't imagine what Wes would have to say about it. "Jackson Square is actually the very spot where Louisiana was declared part of the U.S. in 1803, and it's actually modeled after a square in Paris. And that statue behind us"—he doesn't look back, but I do, at the large, black, horse-bound statue in the center of the square—"is Andrew Jackson, hero of the Battle of New Orleans, and the seventh president of the United States. There's a shit-ton of history in this square, and honestly, it would take all day for me to recount it all to you. But I could, you know, if you wanted me to."

He smiles at me, and I just watch him, watch the way his mouth moves and the way his eyes light up. He's looking at me, and I'm looking at him.

"You're kind of a fucking nerd," Wes says, and we both whip around to look at him, to see the humor in his eyes, but the movement makes me lose my balance on the edge of the step, and even though Cade reaches out quick to grab me, I plummet into the Mississippi.

The murky water closes over my head, and I fight not to immediately suck in a breath. I can feel the concrete ledge beside me, but the current is already moving me away. I scrabble for something to hold onto, my hands finding the ledge I just fell off of, my chest constricting in utter panic, my nails scraping along the concrete.

Something splashes into the water beside me. Arms encircle my waist, and I'm being yanked up, my lungs finding fresh air in seconds.

Someone pulls me up onto the concrete step from above while a pair arms are still wrapped around me. I gasp and wipe the grimy water off my face. I grab at the hand that's clutching at my stomach and look over my shoulder. It's Cade that has a hold of me, just as wet as I am and refusing to let go even though we're on solid ground again. Wes has a hold of him, wet up to his elbows and still clutching the soaking fabric of Cade's shirt. Gwen clutches my other arm, her hand wrapped around my wrist in a death grip.

"Shit, Ellie," Wes says, his words quiet, but he's not really being quiet. The commotion around us is just so loud. People have gathered around us, most of them pointing phones or offering to help, and I turn my face away from them, holding on harder to Cade.

"So, we've seen the river," Wes says behind us, and I set my head against the concrete and shut my eyes.

———————

I struggle in the back seat of Wes's car, trying to shimmy out of my dripping jeans without getting the seats wet. Cade, Wes, and Gwen each cover one of the windows with their backs so that no one can see in, and I move as fast I can out of my wet clothes and into dry ones. I smell like the dirty water, and I consider asking them if we can get a hotel room now, so that I can shower, but I've already been enough trouble as it is.

When I'm dressed, I switch places with Cade, standing with my back pressed to the passenger-side window while he changes. Beside me, Wes grabs my wrist, quick and insistent, before dropping it.

"What?" I ask. I'll never be able to get the picture out of my head of him breathing heavy, his hands holding tight to Cade. His arms have a sheen of mud on them.

His eyebrows are furrowed, and there's something desperate in his eyes. "Hey, look, I think we should tell Gwen about the map." He says it so quietly, leaning in close so that only I can hear him.

I glance over at Gwen, the width of the car between us. She notices and smiles at me. I look away, immediately feeling so guilty it makes my stomach hurt. She held me when I came out of that water, and all I've done is lie to her. "I thought you said it was a bad idea."

He glances back again, obviously nervous, but this time, Gwen doesn't notice. "I mean, it might be. I don't know if she ever got over it, you know, what he did to her." Wes says. He bites his lip, like he's holding something back. "She's hurting too, and I thought was a reason not to tell her, but maybe it's the one reason we should."

I try to imagine the situation from her point of view. I try to imagine being with someone, anyone, for over a year, just to have them vanish one day. I wonder if she's hiding something, too, pressed down deep, just like me. I wonder if something slides around under the surface for her, a constant threat. I swallow down the need to ask her.

Gwen and Luke met in Spanish class, when he was a junior and she was a sophomore. She used to tell me it was one of those love-at-first-sight, fairy-tale moments. Luke would say he didn't believe in things like that, but Gwen didn't care. She would tell the story like she was reading it straight out of a book. Back then, Gwen painted my nails, baked cupcakes, talked Luke into a rom-com when he wanted to watch *Fight Club* for the eight-hundredth time.

I watch Gwen now, see the way her eyes rove around the square, watching people walk by. Is she going to be upset when she finds out that we've been following Luke? That we're going to Michigan to find out more about where he was before he died? She smiles big at Cade when he gently pushes the door open behind her. She moves out of the way. I don't want her to be angry. I don't want her to stop being happy. I definitely don't want her to hate me.

"We'll tell her later," I say. I don't want to do it now. I don't want to take away whatever she's found on this trip that's made the sadness I saw in her eyes the day of the funeral disappear. If she's the only one who can feel something like joy then she deserves to feel it.

Wes hesitates, his eyes going to Gwen and then coming back to me. Gwen and Cade are talking softly, and for a split second, I admire the slope of Cade's shoulders in his fresh T-shirt, one that's just tight enough for me to see the muscles along his back as he talks to Gwen. His hair is slicked back and damp. I don't even care that he probably smells like river water.

"This was your idea," I remind Wes.

He nods, rubbing at the back of his neck. "Yeah, I know. You're right. We should wait."

"Come on, guys!" Gwen calls to us, and even though there's a smile on her face, there's still something about her, and I can't help but wonder if she's just as wounded as the rest of us.

The shot goes off, and I flinch. I don't know what it is about that sound, but it always puts me on edge.

My mother sighs as soon as Luke takes off from the starting line. "He always starts with too much energy. It tires him out before he's made it to the last hurdle."

This is what she says at every meet, and then after, when she's with Luke. He always pretends not to hear her, and then starts the exact same way at the next meet. His coach doesn't seem to have a problem with it.

111

I just roll my eyes and leave my parents to discuss Luke's technique among themselves. I walk down the metal bleachers and stand against the fence that separates the bleachers from the track. The metal is cold, and I pull the hood of my jacket up over my head and follow Luke with my eyes around the far side of the track.

"Your mom talking about Luke's energy levels again?" Wes asks, coming to stand beside me.

I groan. "Of course." I shiver, and Wes steps closer to me. He's like a walking space heater, and I resist the urge to burrow into him. I don't want to give anyone the wrong impression. Someone steps up on my other side, blocking the cold wind, and I turn to see a frilly, colorful unicorn hat in my face.

"Nice hat," Wes says, sarcastic, and Gwen grins at both of us, plucking at one of the unicorn's ears.

"What, you don't think I'm cute?"

Wes sputters. "Of course not. I mean, I don't mean you're not—it's just that I don't—I don't know if cute is—" He makes a weird gesture around his head and then drops his hands. "I'm going for candy. If Luke asks, I saw the whole thing."

And then he's gone.

"Weird," Gwen says and then tugs me closer, looping her arm through mine. "Cold," she says. She sets her head on my shoulder. "You coming to the party?"

I shrug. "I don't know. I'm kind of tired."

Luke crosses the finish line second, and the stands erupt in cheers. Golden boy strikes again. He does an intricate handshake with one of the guys on the team, and then spotting us, he rushes over. He boosts himself up against the fence, his shoulders and head poking above the metal bar, his hands gripping the rail tight, and next thing I know, he and Gwen are making out mere inches from me.

"Well, that's pleasant," I say, looking away.

"Oh, hey, Ellie," Luke says, winking at me.

"Oh, hey, Ellie," I mimic, and he grins. I feel a tiny burst of pride. I like being able to make Luke laugh. It's like the highest of compliments, especially because I don't consider myself to be that funny.

"You're both coming to the party, right?" He looks pointedly at us both, and Gwen nods her head enthusiastically.

"I don't know if I feel up to it," I say, pulling my coat tight around me. I don't know how Luke can wear that uniform, shorts and a tank, in this weather. I guess he doesn't have much of a choice. A sheen of sweat covers his arms and shoulders, and goose bumps travel up over his arms.

He looks at me, his eyebrows tilted in, and the corners of his mouth pulled down. "What are you talking about? You always come to the parties. Who's going to duet Nova songs with me during karaoke?"

I gesture at Gwen. "Maybe your girlfriend?"

Luke looks at Gwen and then drops down to the track before pulling himself up again, this time directly in front of me. His arms tremble with the difficulty of holding himself up, his only anchor the chain-link fence that separates us.

"Ellie, I need my sister with me. You're my best friend. Everyone expects you to be there." He gives me a pleading look, his lower lip stuck out pitifully.

I roll my eyes, pretending to be annoyed, but I get that warm feeling deep down that I always do when Luke says stuff like this to me. I'm fairly used to being invisible in this town, but if Luke needs me, that's all that matters. "Fine. I'll go. But I don't want to stay late."

Luke leans forward and kisses me on the cheek. "Knew I could count on you. Milkshakes for everyone!" Luke smiles big up at the stands behind me, and several people cheer.

New Orleans is the complete opposite of Eaton in every way. The streets in New Orleans are narrow and crowded. We pass bars and shops and tourist traps aplenty, and then, like she's twelve, Gwen latches onto my arm and says, "Look! A fortune-teller! Let's go in there!"

We're stopped outside a very small door in a row of businesses, and I look at the sign that reads FORTUNES, red lettering against a yellow sign.

"You're kidding, right?"

Gwen rolls her eyes. "Ellie, come on. It's New Orleans! You have to go to a fortune-teller!"

I look over at Wes, who's looking down at his shoes with a smile on his face. I look back at the door. I would almost believe there's nobody inside. The doorway is completely dark, with a bead curtain slung across the entrance. I look at Gwen again, her eyes shining. "I'm only going in there if you promise that you don't actually believe in fortune-tellers."

Gwen grins at me, and then she's gone, the bead curtain swaying gently behind her. Wes goes in after her, and then Cade and I are walking through the doorway, shoulder to shoulder, and I'm completely weirded out.

Inside, there's a little desk, like maybe there's supposed to be someone sitting behind it, telling us what to do, and the place is so dark, lit only by strong-scented candles, that I almost run right into Wes and Gwen, who have stopped by a display of strangely-attired animal statues, separated by bottles of oil and incense holders.

"Hello?" Cade calls, and I hear footsteps coming from the other side of another beaded curtain before a woman parts it and steps into the room with us.

"Hello!" she says, her smile wide. I have to admit, she doesn't look like I imagined she would. I guess I expected robes and jewels and rings, the kind of thing you see in the movies. Instead, our fortune-teller looks a little like a soccer mom. She has chin-length blond hair, pale skin, and high-waisted jeans. "Is anyone looking for answers?" she asks, and we all immediately look at Gwen, who clasps her hands in front of her.

"I don't know about answers," she says, smiling shyly. "But I've always wanted to sit for a reading."

The woman smiles brightly at Gwen. I'm sure Gwen is pretty much her ideal customer, so I'm not surprised when she comes forward and puts an arm around her. "Oh, I'd love to do a reading for you, darling. What's your name?" And then the woman is leading Gwen back into the room that she just came from, behind the beaded curtain, but just before they disappear on the other side, the fortune-teller shoots us all a look over her shoulder.

"Absolutely no eavesdropping," she says sternly, "or your readings won't be so favorable."

The beads sway behind them, and Wes looks over at me. "I'm a little terrified," he says, backing away from the curtain, apparently so he won't accidentally hear something he's not supposed to and get a curse put on his head or something. There's a sitting area on the other side of the small room we're in, past the little front desk that apparently nobody actually mans.

I sit in a chair, covered in a moon-and-star-patterned fabric and pull my feet up with me. There are four chairs surrounding a small table, and there's an honest-to-God crystal ball in the center. The boys each take a seat, and I hold in an agonized groan.

"This is so stupid," I say, putting my chin on my knee. I don't know why I'm so anxious. It's definitely not just the fortune-teller. I'm ready to move on, ready to get out of here, ready to be done sightseeing so that we can get to Michigan already. But it doesn't matter that I'm in a hurry because we're here for the night and no matter what I do, we still have two days before we reach Michigan. My leg jiggles up and down, and Cade sends me a strange look.

Wes levels me with a harsh expression. "Give her a break. She wants to have fun. Why don't you just lighten up?"

"Lighten up," I say, more to myself than to him and tip my head back so that I'm looking up at the black ceiling. There are little stars painted on it, too. The person here who knows the truth is Wes, so he should be the last person telling me to lighten up.

"Do you believe in telling the future and all that?" Cade asks, and I can tell by the cadence of his voice that he's asking Wes, not me. I think I've made it pretty clear how I feel about all this garbage.

Wes shrugs. "I don't know what I believe. I guess I believe in, like, making your own destiny, but I guess I also believe in a higher power, so mostly, I just do whatever the hell I want and hope that I've been a good enough person to merit the favor of whatever being is calling the shots."

Cade smiles, big and sincere. And then he leans forward and pulls something off a shelf, and I realize it's a services menu in a Plexiglas display case. Cade examines it, like we've just sat down at a restaurant and he's planning on ordering an appetizer.

"Tarot, palm reading, crystal ball. Who knew there were so many options to choose from?"

Wes snorts.

The beads twinkle again, and Gwen comes out of the back room.

"That was quick," I hear Cade say under his breath, and then we all shut up when we realize—even in the dark room it's obvious—that Gwen has been crying. Her features are swollen, her eyes bloodshot. Great. Wonderful. Fantastic.

Gwen drops down into the empty seat beside Cade, but I'm already halfway out of my chair, ready to be out of this place.

But the lady, whose name I still don't know, mistakes my immediate desire to leave with an eagerness to get my palm read or whatever, and next thing I know, she has a hand on my back, and she's steering me toward the beaded curtain.

"Oh," I say, looking over my shoulder at the three of them, all of whom are watching me with wide eyes. "No, I don't want to have my future told. I just wanted to—"

"I think you could really benefit from a card reading," the lady says, and maybe it's my imagination, but I think she leads me toward the doorway a little more forcefully. I try to turn to the others for help again, but the beaded curtain is between us, and I decide that it's probably my best bet just to do this and get it over with. It's probably more painful if you fight.

"Have you had a reading before?" the woman asks me as I sit across the table from her. It's covered in a red crushed velvet tablecloth, and I'm relieved to see that there's no crystal ball to be found.

"No," I tell her, watching as she shuffles a deck of tarot cards. For a very short period of time when I was in middle school, I was obsessed with astrology, obsessed with reading my horoscope every day and then bursting into Luke's room so that I could read his as well, usually as loudly and quickly as I could as he ushered me back out into the hallway. He didn't believe in horoscopes or anything else.

When she's finished, she sets the deck of cards between us. "Cut the deck for me, sweetheart," she says.

I resist the urge to roll my eyes and reach out to pick up half the deck, which I set beside the half I left behind. She does something with the cards, and then she looks me right in the eye.

"Is there something you want to know? Something particular that you want to see?"

I shrug. "I guess not."

She makes a humming noise in the back of her throat. "Okay. How about some guidance? Your friend told me the four of you are on a journey. That's a good place to start. How about some words of wisdom as you continue on your way?"

I open my mouth to tell her that this isn't a *journey*, but before I have a chance to say anything, she flips over the first card, and I'm looking right at a skull, wearing an elaborate gold crown. In bold letters beneath it, DEATH.

I push my chair back away from the table. "Is this a joke?"

She looks at me, her eyes wide. She doesn't seem worried or scared, just observant, like she's waiting to see what I'm going to do. "I don't joke during readings, hon. Is there something here that scares you?"

I snort. "Don't give me that bullshit. What else did Gwen tell you?"

She shakes her head. "She didn't tell me about the boy who died. Not directly at least. But this..." She presses the tip of her finger into the card. "This isn't about him. This is about you, dear. Death reversed, a fear of change, an inability to move on. That's in your heart, no one else's."

My hands are trembling, out of anger or fear or something else entirely, I'm not even sure. "It's not true," I say, my chair still pushed away from the table, my legs ready to lift me and take me away from here.

"Honey," she says, one of her hands resting on top of the deck, ready to flip over another card. "I could have told you all that without even turning a card over. It's written all over your face."

I should walk out. I should stand up right now and leave, but I feel all the blood drain from my face. It's not real, this sort of thing. I know that.

She flips another card. A hand holds out a golden cup, and just like last time, it's upside down, with the words under the image facing her instead of me.

"Hmm," she says, placing her hand over the card. "The Ace of Cups tells me that you have some repressed emotions."

I think about the monster that crawls around in my chest. I'm not repressing the monster. The monster is repressing itself. If anything, I have no emotions to repress. There's nothing there inside me. Just emptiness, like knocking on a drum, the sound of it echoing.

She doesn't give me a chance to argue this time. She just keeps going. "Ace of Swords, reversed," she says, turning over a card, a hand holding a sword, light sparkling from its tip. "Confusion. And a lot of it. I'll take a stab in the dark and say that your confusion is the reason you're here."

I ball my hands into fists. I'm not confused. I know exactly what I want. I want to find out who sent me that map and how they knew Luke, how they know me. "The reason I'm here is Gwen having some sort of lifelong dream to have her future foretold."

But she's already shaking her head. "I mean, the reason you're here in New Orleans, the reason you're running from home. You're confused about what you want, which isn't surprising. How old are you, sweetie?"

I hesitate. "Seventeen."

She hums quietly, her hands preparing the next card. "I've never met a seventeen-year-old who wasn't at least a little confused about what they want in life."

She flips another card, and I think it's the last one, based on the way she sets it beside the others, three cards perfectly centered under the first one that she drew. "Five of Wands. Conflict. Animosity."

"I don't understand," I tell her before she can go on about how full of animosity I am. "I thought this was supposed to give me wisdom. I thought it was supposed to give me guidance or something."

She smiles at me, and I hate the way she does it, like I'm a child, like I've just told her the world isn't fair, and she's about to say, *you're right, it isn't.* "This *is* guidance. You have to let go of what you're holding onto, stop concealing your emotions, and put away the conflict that's keeping you from moving forward."

I don't know what to say to that. I'm afraid if I argue with her, she'll just accuse me of being full of animosity again. So I grit my teeth, even as she leans forward across the table, pressing her hand flat to the table-cloth. "You're like a thunderstorm," she says and then takes her hand away and presses it to her chest. "Inside here, you've got so much con-flict: love and hate and sorrow and anger, and you can't hold it in forever."

My hands grip the edge of the table, and when I stand, I bump the table, tipping it just enough to jar the tarot cards and send them into disarray. "I don't believe in fortune-telling." I turn and whisk aside the beaded curtain. I put some cash on the counter because I know that's what I'm supposed to pay even though it wasn't my idea to come in here in the first place.

The three of them haven't moved from where they were when I went in, and they all watch me as I approach. I grip the back of the chair that I vacated and look at Wes. "Palm reading?" I say simply, and he shakes his head, his eyes wide.

I hear the displacement of beads behind me and the woman doing something around the front desk, and as I watch, prepared to bolt from the building at any moment, Cade pushes up from his chair and walks around me, heading right for the fortune-teller. I watch them over my shoulder, him approaching her, her nodding at something he's saying, and then the two of them disappearing behind the beaded curtain.

"He's kidding, right?" I say, watching the curtain sway and bump and then go still.

"Guess not," Wes says behind me.

I stand exactly where I am for as long as it takes Cade to get whatever he's getting out of that woman. I can't even imagine him in there, having tarot cards turned over in front of him like I did, or having his palm read, or gazing into a crystal ball. It's all just so preposterous.

As soon as his figure reappears on the other side of the beads, I'm walking toward the door. I have one foot out the door before Cade is back on this side of the curtain.

———

We walk Bourbon Street until we find a bar that's loud and crowded, the sun finally falling below the horizon behind us. There's a live jazz band playing at the front of the room, people's faces turned toward it like flowers to the sun, and we slip in, seemingly undetected. We snatch a small cocktail table, with just enough room for the four of us to stand around it.

"Anyone want something to drink?" Wes asks, leaning into the center of the table and looking around at everyone. My skin is already sticky from the moisture in the air and the close proximity of this particular bar, so I ask Wes to get me a soda, imagining how good it'll feel to drink something ice cold. I'm still a little irritated about what happened back at the fortune-teller's, but I try to listen to the music and unclench. I feel like any control I had over this trip is starting to slip out of my hands.

Some people are dancing in the aisle that cuts the room in half, separating the bar from the booths and cocktail tables. Couples wrap around each other, swaying to the music, even though it's moving faster than they are. Others sway by themselves. Maybe they're drunk, or maybe they just really like jazz, but either way, they look happy.

We listen to the music, none of us saying anything, and I'm glad for the contented silence between us. I'm tired from spending almost all day on the road and ready to crash even though it's barely evening. Despite the cold soda, my skin gets hotter, and I lean against the table in an attempt to stay upright. The exhaustion is winning out.

But then it's not the table that's holding me up, it's Cade's arms, and he's pulling me into the center aisle, where we're bracketed by strangers.

We sway back and forth, and I feel myself going numb again. I feel everything slipping out of my body, until I can just be, no thoughts, no emotions, nothing. Cade is warm, and I press my cheek to his shoulder.

When we turn, I see Gwen and Wes at the table, where we left them. They're standing close to each other, much closer than they were before, having what looks like a serious conversation. I feel like this is something I should process. But I'm so warm and tired, and I can feel Cade's chin against my hair.

I pull back and tilt my head to look up at him. I slide my hand up to his neck, and I'm intoxicated by how hot his skin is. He presses his forehead to mine, and then his mouth slides closer to mine, and I want him to kiss me more than I've ever wanted anything.

"Ellie, we have a problem."

I pull away from Cade. When I turn, it's not Wes I see but the bright screen of his phone. I flinch away from it and take the phone front his hand, putting it at a more reasonable distance for me to see what's on the screen.

"A friend of mine from Tate just sent that to me."

I almost drop the phone when I realize what I'm looking at. It's a missing persons ad, and it has Cade's face on it. And mine.

"Let's think about this logically."

Gwen, Wes, and Cade look up at me from the hotel bed where they're all seated.

"Who knows where we are?"

The three of them all look at each other and then back up at me, not saying anything.

"Wes, did you tell anyone where we were going?"

Wes shakes his head. "Nah. My parents think I went on a road trip with the guy I roomed with last semester. They think I went with him to look at graduate-school programs."

"Okay. Gwen?"

Gwen's eyes go wide. "No. My parents are in California all month to see my sister's new baby. There's no way they even know I'm not home. I've been talking to them like I am so they wouldn't get weird."

I sigh. "Okay. Cade. Your face is on this thing. I can almost guarantee that this is my mother's doing, but your grandmother would have had to play a part in it, or you wouldn't be on it." I tamp down my anger. I shouldn't even be surprised. I knew she would do something like this, but it's barely been two days. Why can't she just leave me alone, even for a few days? She knows I'm not missing. She knows I didn't get kidnapped or anything awful like that. She has to know, so why all the drama?

Cade plants his hands on his knees. "Well, I didn't tell them I was leaving." He shrugs and looks up at me like I might judge him, as if I didn't do the same thing.

Wes groans. "You probably gave her a heart attack."

Cade grimaces, then shakes his head. "No. There's no way she would jump to this. It's not like her. It's only been a day. She's not a worrier. If I tell her I'm staying out for the night, she doesn't ask where I'm going to be. She never asks me where I'm going or who I'm with. I mean, I didn't exactly think she wasn't going to notice, but I definitely didn't think she was going to do something like this."

Gwen puts her hands up. "If it's not typical for her to freak out, then why the missing person report? Why wouldn't she try to call Cade first?"

Cade and I look at each other, and we don't have to say anything. Gwen's shoulders slouch. "You turned off your phone, just like Ellie, didn't you?"

He bites his lip and then meets my eye again. "I was afraid that if I told her where I was going, it would mess things up for Ellie." He speaks to me directly then. "You never said, but I figured you were running away."

Gwen sends me a strange look. "Is that what you're doing? Running away?"

It sounds like an accusation. "You didn't tell your parents, either."

"That's different. They're on the other side of the country. I knew it wouldn't make a difference. But running away? Just like—"

She stops, but she doesn't have to keep going. *Just like Luke.*

Her words are a punch in the gut. Yes. Just like Luke. My mother didn't expect him to run, and she certainly didn't expect me to, and that's enough to make me want to walk away. I don't want to be her predictable kid anymore. I want her to be just as shocked as Gwen is right now that I had the guts to run, even if neither of them understand what this is really about.

"Things with my mother could get ugly," I say, crossing my arms and letting Gwen's comment slip by. I don't want to argue right now. "I won't blame anyone if they want to go home. But I'm not. I don't care about some report my mother filed. She does stupid shit like that. She'll get over it. I'm going to keep going."

I'm going to keep going because there's something I don't know at the finish line, and I have to make it there.

"I have to do this. For me." Something inside me shifts, making room for this revelation. This trip isn't about Luke, not really. Luke got what he wanted. He took his trip. This is about me. *I* want to know what's in Michigan. *I* wanted to get out of Eaton and away from my mother. I'm doing this for me.

"Does anyone still want to come with me?"

They glance at each other again, and my chest clenches. Fear. Even though I was pretty sure I wanted to go on this trip by myself when Wes first decided he was coming with me, I don't think I can go the rest alone. I want them with me. And I'm terrified they're going to turn back now.

"I'm coming with you," Cade says, and I almost sigh in relief.

Wes leans across Gwen, sitting between them, to look at Cade. "Won't your family just call your grandmother as soon as we get to Indianapolis?"

Cade's eyes drop to the carpet. "I doubt it. They don't really talk anymore." I watch him, feeling something nudge at me. Cade never made it seem like there was anything wrong, but I can see it when he looks up at me, that there's more to this trip for him than he's telling us.

"I'm still in," Wes says, changing the subject, shifting my attention.

Gwen is the only one who hesitates, and I guess that makes sense. She still doesn't know why we're really doing this, and probably, to her, it seems like a big risk to take for a road trip, but she has to know by now that it's not just a road trip. My need to get to Michigan is like a siren, sending off signals that everyone within a mile can hear. Can't she tell?

She stays silent for a long time and then says, "Yeah. Okay. Let's keep going."

Chapter Eight

I swing my putter at the ball for the fifth time and groan when it rolls close to the hole before careening in the other direction.

"Dammit."

Cade laughs, and I glance nervously at the line of other players that's forming behind us. Without looking at Cade, I rush for the ball and drop it into the hole.

"Cheater!" Cade calls, pointing at me. "You can't do that."

I pick up my putter from where I dropped it. "You're the one who cheated. You totally downplayed your mini-golf skills. That's deception."

Cade smiles and comes to stand beside me. He holds out his hand, and I put the ball in it, rolling my eyes. He sets the ball where it was before I tried to cheat, and then he comes behind me.

"I'll teach you my trick," he says into my ear as he positions himself behind me, reaching around to grasp the putter, his hands wrapped around my own.

"You are such a cliché," I say, laughing.

He doesn't move for a second, and then I feel a fingertip along my shoulder, right beside the spaghetti strap of my dress. "You have a sunburn."

I turn my head, aware and excited by how close he is, his nose almost brushing mine. "I went to a Nova concert last night."

His eyes are already on my mouth, all the humor gone, and I wait, certain he'll kiss me.

"Hey, Johnston!" One of the guys in the line behind us calls out. "If you want to get lucky, that's what the back seat is for!"

I blush hard and pull away from Cade, swinging the putter gently and finally sinking the ball.

———

Halfway to St. Louis, we have to pull over for gas. I offer to fill up the tank, and Wes agrees without asking questions. Maybe he wouldn't have if he weren't so groggy, but his eyes are half-lidded, with dark circles beneath them.

While Gwen and Wes walk to the convenience store, Cade comes to stand beside me. I try not to be overly aware of him as I pick the kind of gas I want. Everything feels different now, like we're criminals, a whole new kind of weight settling on us all. I don't know how much more I can withstand before I crumble.

"Are you hungry?" he asks, leaning against the side of the car, his legs crossed and his hands in his pockets, and for a split second, I can't help but thinks he looks a little like James Dean. I have to look away.

"Sure, I guess. I don't know. Mostly tired." It hasn't been that long since we stopped for lunch. "Maybe some Oreos."

Cade smiles, and he crosses his arms. "You do realize that the kind of Oreos you pick will lead to all sorts of judgment, right? This is basically a compatibility test, happening live right before your eyes."

My stomach flutters when he says compatibility test. Does he want us to be compatible? Even though I shouldn't want it, I do. I want us to be a perfect fit. "Well, I mean, it's a gas station. Not many options."

Cade shrugs, and he looks so relaxed for someone who just found out last night that our faces are probably all over Eaton, reported missing, and I can't tell if he's just talking to me like this to make me feel better. "Enough options to really figure out what kind of person you are."

I snicker because I missed this. I've missed Cade for the last year. "Fine. I want the thin ones."

Cade's mouth falls open. "Ellie Johnston, you've got to be kidding me. I don't know how you could have possibly made a worse choice. Those aren't even real Oreos. Those are Oreos for people who don't like Oreos."

"No," I argue, "they're Oreos for people who like the cookie part of the Oreo more than the cream part."

He throws up his hands. "The cream is the best part! Next thing, you're going to tell me that you like Golden Oreos."

I don't say anything, but I hold his gaze long enough to get my point across.

Cade pretends to choke. "You know what? I can't talk to you anymore. I'm going to go inside and buy your blasphemous cookies now."

I watch him go, my cheeks aching from smiling so big. I wish it could be like this all the time. I wish I could just erase everything between us and everything that's happened and go back to my normal life, but I don't even know what normal is anymore.

My smile falls. I pull my phone out of my back pocket and turn it on. I know it was probably stupid to turn it off in the first place, but I knew she would do this. I knew she would overreact.

My phone starts to vibrate as soon as it boots up. Text messages. So many of them. And they're all from my mom.

Why is your phone turned off?
Ellie please answer. I'm worried.
If you don't answer your phone I'm calling the police.
ELOISE

I've never considered myself a vindictive person. Luke used to hold grudges. Sometimes I think Luke was holding a grudge against my mom, but I could never decide if it was one big grudge or a million little ones. Like, he would get over one just to be handed new ammunition the next day. Or if maybe she did something when he was a kid, and he just never got over it. He was the king of grudges, and I don't think I would be even a little surprised to find out that his entire life was one long grudge against the woman who bore him.

But sometimes I wonder. Sometimes I think back to that argument they had in the living room, the one neither of them ever knew I heard, and I wonder if it was the grudge to end all other grudges, if it was worse than I could have imagined, whatever he felt toward her after that. Sometimes I felt bad for not hating her right alongside him. But it was never bad enough, not really. She never crossed that line where I couldn't forgive her anymore. Looking down at my texts right now, I wonder if she's finally crossed the line. I wonder if I even understand her or Luke or anyone else. I always thought I did, always thought all of our secrets were right on the surface, but that can't be true because there's always that thing, whatever they fought about, that no one ever told me the truth about.

I put my phone in my pocket and stare down at the concrete, feeling empty. A part of me wants to be home again, but only home like it used to be, with Luke on the other side of the wall, listening to his music too loud and Mom downstairs grading papers at the dining room table, and Dad making chicken legs on the grill. I'll never have that again.

When Gwen comes back out to the car and stops beside me, I turn to her. "Do you remember two years ago, when I had a crush on Jake Douglas and Ava Jennings kissed him even though we were friends and she knew I liked him? Luke said he would never speak to her again, even after I got over it?"

Gwen puts her hand against the passenger-side window, and it's the first time I notice that her fingernails are hot pink and that she has a slim silver band around her middle finger. "Yeah, I remember. He was always talking about how much he hated her after that. Said she was a bad influence on you."

I think about our mother. I think about the things Luke said about Cade. I think about all the people Luke held grudges against over the years. I think about the night I came home, and he was gone.

"All gassed up?" Wes asks, walking right past us and tossing a handful of junk-food packages through the open driver's side window just before the gas pump pops. I replace the nozzle where it belongs as Cade steps around the car and holds something out to me: a package of Oreo Thins.

"I feel like I just betrayed everything I believe in," he says, and I watch as he rips open his own package of Oreos. Double Stuf. I know he's still joking with me, but whatever humor found me before has vanished, falling flat inside me. I have to look away from his expectant expression.

"Want me to drive?" I know Wes is just going to decline. He hasn't let anyone else drive in two days, even though I know he's just as exhausted as the rest of us.

"No," Wes says, ripping open a bag of Cheetos and shoving a few in his mouth. "My parents got me this car because they felt guilty for making me go to Tate, and there's no way I'm going to let anyone else drive her."

I get into the back seat with Cade. I shrug, and Cade smiles. He leans forward between the seats. "You didn't want to go to Tate?"

Wes is quiet for a minute and then he shrugs. "I don't know. It wasn't Tate exactly. Just seemed like an opportunity, you know?" He glances over at Gwen, and she reaches across the console to hold his hand. "I guess things worked out."

His words are like a knife. Things might have worked out for Wes and Gwen. But they didn't work out for Luke. And I don't think they're working out for me.

"So, how long have the three of you lived in Eaton?" Cade asks, out of nowhere.

"All my life," Gwen says, and Wes nods.

Cade's eyebrows are raised high as he sits back in his seat. We pull out of the gas station and onto the highway. "Ellie?"

"Yeah, all my life. I mean, technically I was born in Austin, but we moved when I was a baby. When, uh, when Luke was almost three. Been there ever since."

Wes looks into the rearview mirror, narrows his eyes at Cade. "You're not a lifer?"

Cade shakes his head. "Indianapolis until I was nine. But I like Eaton."

Wes snorts. "You like Eaton? What's there to like?"

Gwen reaches across the space between their seats to smack him on the arm. "What's wrong with Eaton? It's not that bad."

Wes looks over at her, and even in the back seat, I can see the conflict in his eyes. "Why would you want to live in the same place your whole life? Don't you want to see the world?" He gestures out the front windshield, like he needs to remind her that that's exactly what we're doing.

"Well, sure," Gwen says. "I want to see the world." She shrugs. "But Eaton is home."

"I don't know," Cade says. "I remember how crowded Indianapolis was. Like, how many kids were in my class and how long we always had to stand in line at the grocery store, and Eaton is just so different. It's like going underwater."

I hear Gwen sigh. "I like the quiet. I've been to Dallas a few times. All that city noise, it makes me feel like I can't think."

"Eaton is a fucking cage," I remember Luke saying. I hear him in my head, his voice so clear he could be in the car with us. He used to say stuff like that all the time, always itching to get out. "It's where people go to live out their boring lives, to die like boring people. It'll suck you in, and you'll be stuck, and you wouldn't be able to leave, even if you wanted to."

Gwen looks over her shoulder at me. "What about you, Ellie?"

I shrug. I don't know what to think anymore.

The party isn't boring, since the baseball team and the softball team showed up and are having a contest to see whose biceps are bigger. So far, the girls are winning, but I'm enjoying the boys' heroic efforts nonetheless.

"It's time for karaoke," someone announces, rolling out a karaoke machine. I'm not sure why, but the track team parties always end in karaoke. The boys' relay team sings "We Are the Champions" even though they didn't place at

the meet tonight, and then the girls sing "Bohemian Rhapsody" which turns into a party-wide sing-along.

And then Luke takes the stage. Luke and I don't always do a duet. I'm not even really a fan of karaoke, but when Luke asks, it's always impossible to say no.

After he takes his place atop the makeshift stage, which is actually just an elaborate fireplace ledge, I wait for him to call me up, wait for him to say we'll be singing "Lose Yourself" by Eminem or "How Can I" by Nova or "Sgt. Pepper's Lonely Hearts Club Band" by The Beatles, our three favorite songs to do together.

Luke smiles into the microphone and says, "I'd like to invite my duet partner up to the stage." He smiles out at the crowd, and I think he's looking for me, but his eyes graze right over me, and I think that he probably wants to sing with Gwen after all. She's is his girlfriend, and they've done karaoke duets more than once. But when I spot her in the crowd, over by the kitchen with some of the girls on the track team, I realize Luke isn't looking for her, either.

His eyes lock on someone, and he points into the crowded room. "Miss Emily Crowley, please come to the stage."

Emily Crowley is a sprinter for Eaton High and has known Luke for years, but I've never seen her and Luke in the same room before. She's a freshman, in my grade. Emily rushes over to Luke and crowds in close to the microphone with him, a blush spreading across her face, making it shine pink.

I glance over at Gwen. Her eyes are glued to Emily and Luke, unblinking as Luke speaks again. "Emily and I just realized a few minutes ago that we're both obsessed with Kanye, so here's 'Gold Digger.'"

They launch into the song, and Gwen steps away from the group she's with.

She reaches for her coat and her unicorn hat, both of them hanging over a chair, and pushes her way out the front door.

Up on the fireplace stage, Luke has seen the whole thing. The music is going, but he's not singing. His shoulders slump, but he whispers something to Emily before handing her his microphone and rushing through the room to get to the front door.

I maneuver to the kitchen and watch out the window as Luke intercepts Gwen at the end of the walkway. Their mouths move as they argue.

She angrily throws her hands in the air, and he gestures over in my direction, the direction of the party. I'm afraid that they'll see me watching them, and I consider hiding, but their eyes never leave each other. Gwen's mouth snaps shut, and for a long moment, neither of them says anything. Then finally, Luke says one thing, calmly, and Gwen nods. Then Luke steps forward and wraps his arms around Gwen. I watch for a second and then turn away from the window.

I'm alone in the kitchen for a long time. No one says anything to me or comes looking for me, and the next time I check out the window, Luke and Gwen are gone.

Sometime after midnight, when I realize that Luke isn't coming back for me, I ask Wes to give me a ride home.

It's chilly and dark and rainy in St. Louis, the Mississippi River tumultuous in the wind, and it almost feels like a punishment, like maybe we shouldn't even be here. I can't stop thinking about that missing persons ad, my mother actually calling the police like she said she would. And now everyone has to deal with my baggage.

From far away, the arch didn't look that big, but now, standing below it and looking up, I feel tiny. We all shield our eyes as we look up at it. There's a break in the clouds, and the glare from the sun shimmers off its surface as it curves up over us and down on the other side. It's like looking at a twisted skyscraper, and after a few minutes, staring up at it starts to make me dizzy, and I have to look away.

"Do we want to go up?" Gwen asks, and I can see in her eyes that she wants to, but that she'll pretend like she doesn't if we all agree to stay on the ground.

"We have to go up," Wes says, smiling over at her, obviously seeing in her the same excitement that I do.

The four of us get in line to go up in the special elevator instead of a normal one. They're like little lounge pods, and I hurry to take the seat next to Gwen because I don't know if I can stand every inch of me being pressed against every inch of Cade, but that just means he has to sit across from me, and our knees brush through the whole ride. I'm lightheaded by the time we reach the top.

And then I'm light-headed for an entirely different reason. I've never been a big fan of heights, a quirk that my family, Luke included, often tormented me about. I was always the one waiting at the bottom of the roller coaster for them, the one who closed her eyes as we went over the extra high bridges, the one who stood back from the windows of any high-rise building we were in while everyone else gawked down at the ground, so far below.

The hallway at the top is narrow, and I'm pretty firmly buffered by people on either side of me, most of which are standing with their toes against the outer wall, bent over the curve of it to see down below.

If I don't think about it, if I just let myself believe that I'm somewhere I've been a hundred times, like standing beside my locker at school or behind the register at Books and Things, I can almost pretend everything is okay.

I press myself stomach-first against one of the walls, more for stability than because I actually want to look out, but when I do look out the window, down at where we were standing just minutes before, and realize that there's nothing between me and the ground below but the metal under my feet, I feel a little queasy. I try to focus on something solid, the material around the window, the cement ground below, the buildings of St. Louis in the distance.

Cade comes to stand beside me, his leg brushing mine. "Ellie, you okay?"

I press my face into my hands, and then I take a deep breath and look out the window again. "Yeah, I'm fine."

"You're solid on your feet," Luke used to say when I had my hands over my ears and my eyes clamped shut. "You're not going to fall."

"But what if it's not me that falls?" I would ask, when we were standing too close to the edge of a bridge or looking out a high window. The first time I said it, we were on a carnival Ferris wheel. I was sitting as still as possible, trying not to rock the seat Luke, Wes, and I were sharing. My mother was so convinced that once I got in, once I got to the top, I would love it. That the view from the apex would be so breathtaking, looking out over Eaton, that I would forget my own fear.

There isn't enough distraction in the world to make me forget. I didn't forget on that Ferris wheel, and I squeezed my eyes closed, as tight as I could, telling myself that I was somewhere else. Anywhere else.

This time, I stare out the window and let the Mississippi take my mind off of it. We followed it all the way here, and something about the gentle lapping of the water in the wind makes my stomach settle a little bit. People sit by the edge of it, walk along beside it, stop to look out at it like I am.

"Do you want to go back down?" Cade asks, but I can't focus on what he's saying. Down by the river, I see a figure. He's far away, but everything about him is familiar, his dark hair, his broad shoulders, his baggy jeans. From up here, I watch him turn and look up at the arch, and I swear, just for a second, that it's him. My pulse jumps, and I grip the edge of the window, everything else fading as I try to focus, try to make out the features of the person's face so far away.

"I'm not going to let you fall," I can almost hear his voice in my ear saying, and even with my eyes closed on that Ferris wheel, I could feel him beside me. Solid. Luke was always solid, always present, always a rock.

"You can't keep this thing from falling," I said to him then.

"You think the nuts and bolts holding this Ferris wheel together would dare defy the will of Luke Johnston?" He laughed about that one, and so did I, and by the time we were done discussing whether the Ferris wheel shaking apart around us was a possibility, the ride was over.

"Luke," I say, pressing my hands to either side of the window, leaning over as far as I can to watch the figure. Everything in me stops. I stop breathing; I stop moving; I swear my heart stops beating. I want it to be him. I want to pretend like I live in a world where he could still be alive, walking right to the arch, just to see me, like he never left, like we're just on this vacation together, and he's going to be waiting for me down at the bottom of this tower so that we can listen to Nova in the car and go for milkshakes.

"Ellie, what's going on?" Cade stands closer to me so that he can see out the window, too, and I want to point down at the guy, still walking toward the arch, up the stairs that lead down to the river, his hands in his pockets. But my arms don't move. I'm clutching the window so hard, a slight pain forming at the ends of my fingers. *Be Luke*, I think to myself, something pressing up into my throat, against the wall of my chest, maybe a scream, maybe a sob, maybe just *something*.

I want it to be him because I want to tell him that I came here, all the way to Missouri, and that I'm just as brave as he is, and that things can go back to the way they were if he'll just take me with him.

"Ellie," Cade says, and I hear the sadness in his voice, feel it settle over my skin. "That's not Luke, Ellie."

"Here," Luke said, grabbing hold of my hand, even though we were firmly on the concrete. He helped me out of the seat and back onto solid ground. "Better?"

I watch the guy move across the expanse of concrete below. Of course it's not Luke. He doesn't look anything like him. His hair isn't as dark as Luke's, his shoulders sloped down at a sharp angle, his back too hunched and his walk too uneasy. I feel sick.

I feel Cade's hand on my arm, his voice in my ear, and it startles me. I back away quick, moving away from him too fast, and I swear, I feel the arch sway beneath my weight. Or maybe it's just me. I feel like there's no solid ground anywhere on the planet.

"Ellie?" Gwen appears at my side and puts an arm around me, and I ignore the eyes of the other people in the building as she helps me to the floor under the window, across the arch from where Cade stands, watching us. "You okay?" she asks, and I nod even though it's a lie. "We should go back down." She glances over at Cade, who looks between the two of us, and I can't read the expression on his face, but it's anything but comforting. My stomach lurches at the way he looks at me. He can see that I'm breaking.

We get back into the elevator, Gwen pressing me between her and Cade, where I can feel their warmth. Gwen is watching me closely, so I try not to look at her, and as we move back down the tower, her hand crosses the small distance between us and takes mine.

There's a mist in the air by the time we make it back down to the ground, and I shiver. Gwen puts a hand to either side of my face and makes me look her in the eye. "Are you okay?" she asks. "I'm so sorry. I can't believe I forgot that you don't like heights."

I look past her, at Cade, and he watches me carefully. He knows it wasn't the height that got to me, not really. It wasn't looking down from that high up, seeing all the empty space between me and the ground.

It was that guy. Even now, I fight not to look around for him. Maybe he's still here, and maybe he's not, but I keep my eyes focused on Cade and Gwen. It's not Luke, I remind myself. Luke is gone.

I gently pull Gwen's hands away from my face. "I'm okay. Thanks." My stomach is still a little queasy, but I don't feel like I'm going to fall over anymore, and that's something.

Wes, floating on the periphery, nods in the direction of the river. "Look, you can walk right down to the Mississippi." He attempts a smile, but his face is completely devoid of joy, and I can't blame him. There's something about this place. It's something ominous, like the sky is going to swallow us whole.

"Let's go down," Gwen says to Wes, and they both turn to me, but I just shake my head. The Mississippi and I clearly don't get along.

"Will you be okay?" Gwen asks. I assure her I will be and watch them go, descending down the long, wide concrete staircase until I can just barely see them against the gate that separates us from the water.

I stand directly under the arch, right in the center, and crane my head back to look up at it. I have to think about something else. I have to distract myself, just like Luke told me, so that I don't fall apart. I'm okay. I have to be okay. I can't shatter now. We still have a long way to go until we get to Michigan, still a long way after that, and I can't stop until I know what's waiting for us.

"It's six hundred thirty feet tall," I hear Cade say, and I look back down so fast that I get a little dizzy. "The Gateway Arch is over twice as tall as the Statue of Liberty," he says, but he doesn't sound very enthusiastic. He stands beside me, his eyes on one of the silver legs of the arch at our side. "It took them two years and thirteen million dollars to build it."

I'm a little surprised that he's still reciting facts, but then I think that maybe this is his way of comforting himself. It's always been a point of embarrassment for him, but maybe it's because it's his coping mechanism. But coping with what, I don't know. And I realize that maybe I scared him up in the arch. Maybe I'm the reason he has to recite facts to find comfort. I reach out and brush his hand with mine. I'm relieved when he laces his fingers through mine, even though I know I should be putting distance between us. If I'm causing him this much stress, I should back off. Only, didn't I already try that once?

"You okay?" he asks. "What happened up there?"

I start to say yes, even though I don't have an explanation to follow it, but the wind picks up again, blowing my hair into my face, and it starts to rain, big fat drops that land startlingly heavy on my skin. Lightning crashes over the river, and I jump, moving away from it and from Cade. The rain is coming down, and I can see Wes and Gwen down by the river, putting out their hands to catch raindrops.

I feel like the world is getting louder, ready to sweep me away, and there's nothing here for me to hold on to. Why do I feel like this?

"Ellie?" Cade's face is dripping from the sudden downpour, his concerned eyes on me. "What's wrong?"

The whole world feels like a monster, like some larger than life version of what's inside me, dead set on eating me alive. Lightning crashes again, and it's like I'm stuck in that world I dreamed about. I'm buried alive; I'm drowning; I'm going to die.

I turn and run. I have no idea where I'm going. I don't even really know where I am, but I'm not the only one running. People are scattering in all directions like pigeons on the sidewalk, and I run with them, until there's a building in front of me, and I throw the door open. I can still hear Cade calling my name, but it's absorbed by the sound of the rain, the wind, the thunder. By the door that slams shut behind me.

I'm in a church, an honest-to-God cathedral, and I'm trying to catch my breath. I bend at the waist, and notice that I'm dripping on the hardwood floor. With my luck, they're probably the original floors, put here by some settlers in the sixteenth century or something. I take a few steps farther in, still gasping for breath, but I'm afraid that has more to do with my panic than how far I just ran.

My shoes squeak on the floor, so I rush to a pew and take a seat. The last time I was in a church was at Luke's funeral, and this cathedral is nothing like the little Methodist church in Eaton. The ceiling is domed; there are huge, white columns lined through the pews, and at the front, where I assume the priest stands, there's a huge painting of Jesus hanging on the cross.

I run my hand along the pew in front of me, leaving water along the wood. It's just cool enough for goose bumps to sprout along my arms, just light enough for me to see the raindrops still puddling up along my fingers. I focus on these things to drown out the sound of the rain on the domed roof. To drown out my own thoughts.

I gasp when someone drops into the seat next to me, and for one unbelievable second, I think it's a priest, like someone who works here, works for the Lord, has seen my pain and come to intervene. But then I remember that this isn't *It's a Wonderful Life.*

It's Wes.

His eyes stay glued to the painting at the front of the building for a long while. He's just as wet as I am, his fingers laced together in his lap. And then his head falls forward, meeting his crossed thumbs.

"What are you doing?" I ask him, whispering so as not to disturb the few other people in the church. I don't know how I feel about him being here, sitting so close when seconds ago, I couldn't stand even Cade's hands on me. I don't think I want attention or comfort. I think I just want to disappear.

Wes cracks one eye and looks over at me. "I'm praying."

We stare at each other for a second.

"Why?"

Wes shrugs. "What else am I supposed to do right now?" He watches me for a beat and then he lowers his head again. I haven't said a prayer since I was a little girl, visiting church with a friend from school and doing what everyone else did. My parents have never believed in God or any other high power. They're members of the Church of Don't Kill Anyone.

My hands are still trembling, and I tuck them against my body, trying to push away whatever tried to destroy me outside. I'm okay. I'm okay. Maybe if I keep thinking it, it'll make it true.

I'm not sure what I'm supposed to do or what I'm supposed to say to him, but before I've decided, his head comes back up, his eyes opening and focusing on me. His voice is low when he speaks. "Do you remember when Luke went away to that church camp? He was gone for a month."

I squint over at him, thinking. We've switched gears so fast, I feel a little disoriented.

"It was the summer before our freshman year. The summer before you started middle school? My parents wouldn't let me go with him because they're atheists."

"Right." I remember now. I'm not sure how I ever could have forgotten. Luke spent the majority of his summer at the church, where there was always something to do. I remember Luke telling me about it with a laugh. "Idle hands are the devil's playthings," he would say, in a nasally voice that always cracked me up. "He said he went because the girls at the church were the hottest."

I expect Wes to laugh at this, but he doesn't. His jaw is firm, his fingers still laced together. Why are we talking about this right now, when my heart is still pounding, when the storm is still raging outside?

"Yeah," Wes says, "he joined to meet girls. He came back from church camp with Court Rodick as his girlfriend. I was so damn jealous." He flinches and looks around quick. "Jealous. I was just plain old jealous."

He reaches out and drums his finger on the pew in front of us, and I notice that his arms, at least up to the elbow, have dried in the cool air.

"I remember."

"Right before he left, he told me to watch over you. He told me I had to be your big brother for the summer because he wouldn't be there to do it himself."

I just stare at him. I've never heard any of this before. That was years ago. "Really?"

Wes nods. "He was worried about you. Scary things happen to kids in middle school, and you were hanging out with Ava Jennings, and she was always getting you in trouble, and I think he was just really freaked out about leaving. So the day he went, he came to my house, and he told me I had to be your big brother for the summer."

My skin goes hot when I hear all of this. I remember that summer. I remember Luke dating Court Rodick. I remember him dumping her at the end of the summer. I remember him dropping the youth group when he started high school. I remember walking to get ice cream with Ava and having my first kiss at a party with her cousin and getting grounded for being out past curfew. But now it all looks so different.

Wes glances sideways at me, but I ignore the look. "Why are you telling me this?"

"Because I didn't hold up my end of the bargain." He says it loudly, and a woman in the first row looks at us over her shoulder. Wes lowers his voice before speaking again. "Because when he left last year, I should have stayed with you, Ellie. I shouldn't have not called you and not checked in on you. It was a jackass thing to do, leaving you to handle it all yourself."

I feel a weird ache in my bones, a tightness that I can't identify. "You're not responsible for me."

He makes an incredulous sound in his throat. "I wanted to be. I loved being your big brother, Ellie. I loved having you as my little sister. I loved being defensive over you and making sure you got on the bus and talking you into eating your vegetables. You were *my* little sister, too. When Luke left, I did, too, and that was a fucked-up thing to do."

I'm shaking my head before he's even finished. It isn't his job to look out for me. It was never his job. It was . . . Luke's.

"Luke was supposed to look out for me. He was my big brother. He was supposed to be there for me, and he's the one that left." The words sound empty coming out of me. I'm like Cade, reciting facts from a textbook, and I feel sick again. I think of Luke in the living room, yelling at our mom. A week later he was gone. He left. *He left.* And he never came back. I hold my stomach. *Breathe. Breathe. Breathe.*

Wes squeezes his eyes shut. "I get that." He sighs and runs his hands over his face. "I'm telling you this because when I turned around at that party on Friday, and you were gone, I panicked. And then I found out you were upstairs with Cade, and I panicked harder. I was scared out of my mind because I'd fucked up all over again, and I knew that if you were hurt, I'd never be able to fix it. I'd never be able to take it back."

This is about the party. This is about him and me. There's so much messed up shit in my life that I can't even keep it all straight anymore. I forgot all about the party. I forgot that we yelled at each other outside the door. I forgot that, for a second, I let the beast inside me run free, let it scream and be mean and get angry.

Angry at Wes for something that isn't even his fault. And the beast wants to be free again. It claws at me. It tells me I have a right, but that can't be true. I can't be angry. I can only be numb. I can only miss Luke with every part of me.

Wes is rubbing at his index finger with his thumb. "You're the only family I have, Ellie. And I can't let anything happen to you." His voice goes raspy, so I look away from him. I can't see him cry. Wes has always been that guy who never cared too much about anything, and I don't think I can take seeing him this way. So I press my forehead into his shoulder and close my eyes.

"I'm sorry for what I said at the party," I say it to him, but only because he can't see my eyes, can't see my face, pressed against his shirt. "I didn't mean it."

"Didn't you?" he asks, the words vibrating through his body and through mine. "He left. What else are we supposed to believe but that he didn't give a shit about us?"

He's right, of course. I was right. But I don't want to believe that. I don't want to hear him questioning it. I start to argue, to take back what I said when the monster was in control. But before I can say anything, he opens his mouth, and I'm silenced.

"I have to tell you something."

I don't like the way he says it. It makes my skin prickle, like the hairs on your arm standing up when there's electricity in the air.

"Two days before Luke left, he told me he was going to leave."

I can't process his words. I feel like he just said them in another language, all sounds and consonants. "What?"

Wes sighs, his shoulders hunching. "He came storming into my room, saying that he was done. And that he had to leave Eaton. That it was time to go. And he told me to pack my stuff."

I understand the words now, but they don't make sense. "He wanted you to—"

Wes nods. "To go with him. But I told him no. I wanted to go to Tate. That was *my* plan. But he called me a coward and walked out. And two days later, you were calling me to tell me he was gone."

My hands are shaking, and I know Wes could see if he looks, so I ball my hands into fists. That feels better anyway. "He told you he was going to go?" My voice is quivering, too, and I can tell that Wes isn't expecting that from the way his eyes find mine. The way he looks worried.

"Ellie, don't be mad."

Don't be mad. *Don't be mad.* It takes me a second to realize that the wetness on my face isn't the rain from my hair. It's tears, and they're hot, and they're from me, and they're from anger. I've lost the ability to hold it in.

"He told you he was going to leave?" My voice is rising, and I can't seem to get it to stop.

Wes's eyebrows crease in. He's looking at me like I'm crazy, like I've just suggested we burn this whole church down. "Ellie, come on. Don't be upset. It was a year ago. What's done is done."

I'm shaking my head before he's finished talking. "You could have said something." I stand and back away from him. "Why didn't you tell me?" I don't even know who I'm angry at. The anger just flies around without a destination. "Why didn't he tell me? Why didn't he ask me to go? I don't understand."

"Ma'am." Someone is walking toward us, someone who looks official and like he is definitely going to throw us out of this church, but Wes reaches me before the other person can, and when he puts his hands on me, both of his hands on my shoulders, I let him. I don't know what to feel anymore, don't know what to do.

By the time the person, clearly a priest, has begun to herd us toward the door, I gladly march away from Wes to find Cade and Gwen standing at the door, watching us. I'm about to throw open the door, to get away from the stifling room that feels like it's getting smaller by the second, but Wes stops me, his hand curling around my arm. I can feel Cade's and Gwen's eyes on us.

"Ellie, I know it doesn't feel like it right now, but everything is going to be okay."

I pull my arm away, not because I'm angry at him. That's died away quickly, dissipating like fluid in the ocean. I just can't stand his hands on me. I don't want to be touched. I don't want to be told everything is going to be okay.

"I'm sorry, but I have to ask you leave." The priest has followed us, and he's standing beside a giant basin of holy water, looking like he might need to hide behind it.

Wes spins around, and I see anger flash in his eyes, like he's just as angry about all of this as I am. "Look, man. It's storming outside. Can't we just have a second?"

The man folds his hands together. "You're creating a disturbance. I'm sorry, but if you don't leave, I'll have to call the police."

I think about the image on Wes's phone, mine and Cade's faces. *Miss-*

ing. If this guy calls the cops, there's a chance we won't make it away from them.

"We're leaving," I say, tugging at Wes until he finally gives in and follows me. I turn and walk out into the rain. I can hear it hitting the arch, giant above us, and it doesn't seem scary anymore as we walk through it to where we parked the car. There are scarier things in my life right now than this beast of a storm.

And knowing that Luke asked Wes to go with him and not me is scarier than anything else.

———

We all stand shivering in the lobby of the hotel while Wes gets us a room. When I planned this trip on my own, I fully intended to sleep in my car, somewhere in a quiet parking lot, but now that there are four of us, that's not really an option, so thank God for Wes's brand-new credit card.

Gwen stands beside me, her long hair dripping fat drops onto the tile floor. The lady at the front desk looks at us, glancing first at Gwen and the floor in front of her, and then at me. Her eyes examine my face for a long time, and I feel paranoia in my blood. I know there's no way a missing persons ad from Eaton, Texas, made it all the way to a woman in Missouri, but I don't like the way she scans my face like she's trying to memorize it. I look away, down at the floor, letting my wet hair cover my face.

Wes hands me a room key, and I take it without looking back at the lady behind the desk. I wish I could explain what's happening to me. I wish I could explain this feeling I have, like I'm scattering into a million pieces, like I need something to grab hold of but everything is moving too quickly.

In the room, I don't bother to shower. I slip off my wet shoes and climb into bed. It's not even that late. We only agreed to get a hotel room because we're all tired and Indianapolis is still four hours away.

"Ellie?" Gwen asks, her voice small. "Are you hungry?"

I turn my face into the comforter and shake my head. I feel off-kilter, like my outburst at the church has thrown me into disarray, and now I need a second to balance myself again.

I hear the door open and close, and then the room is silent. I listen to the sound of the storm outside. It seems like it's following us, first in Shreveport and now here, and I honestly don't know how much more of it I can take.

"After I graduate, I want to be one of those superfans who follows a band all over the country," Luke says, typing away at something on his phone, the master of multitasking, or maybe multiconversing.

"I think they call that a groupie. You want to be a groupie?"

Luke rolls his eyes and finally looks up from his phone, his eyes focusing on the stage at the front of the room, where a tech crew is setting up and testing instruments and connections. "Not a groupie. I just mean, you know, I'll go to every show they do."

This is our fifth time seeing Nova together, and it never stops being exciting. We've already watched two opening acts, and any second now, Jack Olsen is going to step on the stage, and I'm vibrating with excitement.

"Isn't this their last show in North America? You'd have to, like, fly to

Japan. I don't know if you'd be able to get excused absences from your profes-sors."

Luke looks at me, and his casual smile has vanished. Maybe it's just be-cause the room is so dark, but I swear I see shadows in his eyes. He looks like he wants to say something, his eyes traveling over my face, but then the al-ready dim lights plummet into darkness and the room erupts into cheers.

On the way home from the show, Luke is quiet. Nova's second album, his favorite, plays from the speakers, muffled in my fuzzy-feeling concert-dam-aged ears. Luke finally looks over at me.

"You know I love you, right, El?" His words catch on the air, like he had to force them out, like he's still having to force himself to even look at me. He finally looks away, back at the dark and empty road, flying past empty land-scape. We had to drive all the way to Austin for the show.

"Are you okay?" I ask. He's acting weird, and I suspect it has to do with classes starting soon. Every day that he's gotten closer and closer to his first day at Tate, he's been acting more and more strange, like he's not even here, his eyes always a little dreamy and his body always a little restless.

But he doesn't say anything about that. He doesn't glance at me. He tight-ens his hands on the steering wheel and then reaches over and turns down the music. "I guess I've just been thinking a lot, you know, about happiness."

I sigh and turn in my seat to face him. "Luke, you're going to be happy at Tate. You will. I mean, what about Gwen? She'll be there with you next year. And Wes. And as soon as it's over, you can, like, kayak to Africa or whatever. Just give it a chance."

He's quiet for a long minute, his eyes barely there in the darkness of the car. "Yeah. I know. You're so smart, El. You've still got time, you know. You could apply somewhere else before Tate eats you alive."

I laugh. "Not everyone is terrified of Tate. It's just a school." I close my eyes and lean my chair back just a little. "It's okay, Luke. It's just four years."

This time, when I'm in the pit, it's open at the top, and then I realize it's not a pit at all. It's a grave. I lie in my own grave, the soft dirt under my back, watching as someone shovels dirt, first onto my stomach and then onto my chest, getting heavier and heavier. Someone is doing this to me. I open my mouth to scream, to ask for help, to say something, but dirt is shoveled onto my face, and I can't speak without choking on it.

I push the dirt from my eyes, and then someone leans over, looking down into the grave, and I realize it's Luke.

The rattle of thunder wakes me up, and I gasp impulsively, like I might still be choking on dirt.

I sit up and look around. The hotel room looks exactly like it did when I fell asleep: dark, the only light coming from one of the bedside lamps, and cold. I can hear the hum of the window unit. I see Cade sitting by the window, reading a book. He shuts it and stuffs it in his bag.

"You came back," I say. I don't know where they went, but I know they left. I remember hearing the door shut behind them.

"I didn't leave," he says, coming to stand at the foot of the bed. I try to remember him still being here, but all I remember is the room being really quiet. "I hope that's okay."

I don't say yes or no because I don't know.

"What happened up in the arch, Ellie? What happened in the church?"

I turn over, burying my face in the blanket. I want to sleep for a few days. I'm so tired that my body aches, and I feel a little sick to my stomach with the need to just close my eyes. "I don't know," I tell him honestly. I can't tell him that I lost it. I can't tell him that everything I've been holding in is clawing its way to the surface.

My face heats, and I stare into the darkness out the window, the glass shimmering under the rain drops and the city lights. They blur, and tears leak out of my eyes, roll down my face, and I turn as far away from Cade as I can so that he can't see. I can't just go around crying in front of everyone. I cried back in the cathedral, and I'm crying here, and I'm so weak. I'm supposed to be stronger than this. I'm not supposed to feel anything. I have to be tough enough to get through this trip, to get all the way to Michigan, to face whoever sent me the map and whatever they have to tell me about Luke.

What if it's worse than what Wes told me?

What if it's nothing at all?

"What did Wes tell you?" Cade asks gently, and I know if I answer, my words will be thick with tears.

I clear my throat, take a deep breath. "That Luke told him he was going to leave and that he asked Wes to go with him."

There's a stretch of silence, and I finally look over at him. He sits on the edge of the bed and laces his fingers in his lap. "I don't really know what to say to that."

I choke on a laugh. "Yeah, well that makes two of us. I mean, why would he ask Wes to go and not me? I'm his sister. This trip, it was something the three of us planned."

Cade's eyes move over to me slowly. "What's the deal with the trip?

The map?"

I'm too exhausted to try and keep anything from Cade. If Gwen were here right now, I would tell her everything, too. Keeping secrets is exhausting, and I don't have any energy left in me. "It was something we did with Luke years ago. And then Luke kept the map, and me and Wes forgot about the whole thing. But someone sent it to me, someone in Michigan."

Cade taps his fingers on his leg. "So that's why we're on this trip? To go to Michigan and find out who sent you the map?"

I nod, my hair sliding along the comforter, and Cade just watches me. I can't tell what he's thinking, his eyes straight forward, his hands restless. So I just keep talking.

"All this time I thought he didn't tell anyone," I say, my voice just a whisper over the sound of the air conditioner. "But he just didn't tell me." I have to suck in breath after I say this to keep from crying again. Now that Cade is looking right at me, I fight harder against the tears, even though it's like waging war.

Cade watches me, but he still doesn't say anything.

"I've spent a year trying not to think about what he did. But he left. He didn't say one word to me. He just disappeared, and I was supposed to go on with my life like everything was normal." My voice cracks; my breath trembles; my stomach twists.

He looks down at his hands. "You were like a ghost. You were completely different. After. You were a totally different person."

I don't know how to explain it. How do you explain that you're full of something toxic? How do you explain that there's a monster that's threatening to break out of you, that the only person who might have been able to speak the same language as you is gone, and now what's the point in ever trying to speak to anyone again?

How do I explain that when Luke left, I spent all of my time trying to pretend I was okay when I knew for certain that I would never be okay again?

I try to imagine the impression that Cade must have of Luke by now. He didn't know Luke, only knew *of* him, only has an idea of him based on stories and rumors and gossip, the bite-size moments when they encountered each other in our living room or the library or the hallway, just like Luke had of him. I wish I could sit him down and tell him everything about Luke, the real Luke. Luke, who loved being the center of attention but hated it when people would swarm him after a track meet, when all he wanted to do was take a hot shower. Luke, who snuck out at night, but only because our mother was like Big Brother, surveilling him from every possible angle at all times. Luke, who took me to my first concert and taught me how to ride a bike and never left me behind, even when he was the most popular guy in school, even though I was two years younger than him.

The hotel door opens, and Gwen and Wes come in. They're talking in whispers, and when they see Cade sitting on the end of the bed, they stop talking altogether, and I wish there was some way I could hide. If I thought I could pull this blanket over my head and they would just let me be, I would do it.

Wes is holding a brown paper sack, and he comes over to me, holding out a paper-wrapped hamburger. It has spots of grease all over it, and my stomach growls. "Please don't be mad at me."

I take the burger and sit up, wiping at my face quick and hoping that the room is dark enough to keep them from seeing my swollen and wet face. "I'm not mad at you." The monster inside argues a little, but I think I mean it. I don't think I'm mad at Wes.

"So what's next?" he asks, sitting in the chair that Cade vacated earlier.

I look over at Cade. "Indianapolis?"

He purses his lips and nods. "Yeah. Indianapolis."

I unwrap my burger while Gwen and Wes try to find something to watch on TV. Cade digs through the bag Wes left on the comforter and pulls out another burger. I expect him to stay where he is, at the end of the bed, far from me. But he kicks off his shoes and scoots all the way back, until his back is against the headboard, right beside me.

I take a bite of my burger, trying not to focus on the way he smells like fabric softener and slight traces of cologne. I stare at the TV, but I can feel Cade looking in my direction, and then his hand comes up, and he presses his thumb to my cheek, wiping away what's left of a tear trail on my skin.

I look up at him, just barely taller than me, and his hand drops back down to his lap. He looks away and makes quick work of the wrapping on his burger, but even with my eyes trained on the TV again, I can see Gwen out of the corner of my eye, watching us.

———

Cade and I lie back on the hood of his grandmother's car and look up at the stars. His fingers brush mine, and I shiver, even though it's hot enough outside that I'm sweating. The drive-in is empty; we're the only ones left besides the crew cleaning up, and the huge screen at our feet is dark.

"Do you remember field day, sixth grade?"

I'm already laughing before he's done speaking.

"You were so pissed at me," I say through my laughter.

"You broke my nose!"

I gulp in a breath. "Cade Matthews, I did not break your nose! It was just a nosebleed!"

"Yeah, because you threw a kickball directly at my face!"

"I thought you called me Ellie Belly!"

He snorts and smiles up at the sky. "I would never call you Ellie Belly. I had way too big a crush on you."

I blush and focus on the sky, the stars spread across it. I think I'm ready for this, for feeling, for him to start saying sweet things, for us to move from friends to more, but I still can't quite meet his eye, can't quite take the way he looks at me when he says things like this.

I watch a plane, with its little blinking red light, traveling through the clouds, disappearing somewhere around the moon.

"How much do you know about astronomy?"

He smiles up at the sky. "Astronomy is my favorite. It's the kind of thing you can study your whole life and never know everything about. I mean, can you believe we're just a speck in the grand scheme of things? There are countless galaxies, and here we are, acting like we matter, like we know everything."

I laugh and, in a bold move that I can only pull off because I'm tired and the stars are shining down on us, I scoot closer to him. He turns his head, his eyes drifting from my eyes to my mouth and back again.

"With you around, I can almost pretend the stars don't exist."

He looks serious, but I laugh hard, holding my stomach. "Oh man, Cade. That was cheesy."

He laughs, his white teeth sparkling in the dark. "Sure, but did it work?"

I bite my lip. "Maybe a little."

He leans close to me, and I close my eyes, waiting for the brush of his lips against mine, something I feel like I've been waiting for my whole life.

And then the lights at the drive-in all turn off, plunging the world into utter darkness.

An inch from me, Cade's breath puffs against my mouth. "I should probably get you home." He glances at his watch. "It's almost one."

"Wow." I look at my phone, surprised not to see a million texts from my mom. She said she would lay off the helicopter parenting for one night, but not a single message from her is pretty impressive.

We hop off the hood, and my stomach sinks when I realize I'd give anything to stay here with Cade instead of going home to Eaton.

Chapter Nine

Cade watches me all the way to Indianapolis. I can feel his eyes on me, but I don't look at him. I can't. I can't get distracted anymore. This trip isn't about him and me. This trip is about getting to Michigan. This trip is about getting some kind of answers, even though I don't even know the questions. All I can think about is what Wes told me. I can't decide if it changes everything or changes absolutely nothing. We're all quiet. It's a four-hour drive, and the only time we speak is when Wes pulls into a gas station and asks Gwen to buy him an iced tea from inside.

It's not until we're down there, in the shadows of Indianapolis, that Cade finally speaks. "Why in the world are there catacombs in Indianapolis, and why are we *in* them?"

"Because of the article," I say, like that'll clear everything up. When we first planned the trip, and even when I was consulting the map before we set out from Eaton, the catacombs always seemed like a good idea. But now that we're down here, I'm starting to wonder what the point of coming down here *is*. What the point in *all* of these stops is. What's the point in chasing a ghost when we already know where he ended up?

"What article?" Cade asks.

The four of us walk through the empty catacombs, the walls made of brick and covered with about a hundred layers of dust. I reach out a hand to touch the wall, my fingertips coming away dirty, and I get a chill up my spine. Maybe there's more than one reason why this was a bad idea.

"*Rolling Stone*," I answer. "Like three years ago. They did an interview with Jack Olsen, and he said that he and the other guys from Nova met down here. Apparently Jack used to come down here to play, and the Harper brothers heard him one day. The start of a beautiful friendship."

I remember how excited I was to hear the story then, but now it isn't quite so cool. Luke thought it was amazing, three guys forming a band underground. "Hardcore," he said that day when he brought me the article to read, his face the picture of exhilaration.

"Is that true?" Gwen appears at my side, her eyes still roving. She can't seem to make them stop. "Nova met down here?"

I shrug. "That's what the article said, so I guess it's true."

Gwen and Wes walk together, away from Cade and me, and next thing I know, Cade has taken my hand and turned us in the opposite direction. I expect him to let go, but instead, he threads our fingers together, and everything in me goes warm in that way that it always seems to when Cade's skin is against mine. I've lost track of whether I want to pull away, so I don't.

"This is so creepy," I say as we walk down one of the dark hallways. The only lights in the catacombs come from lamps hanging intermittently from the ceiling. Arches line the walls, leading us in a mazelike formation, going on as far as the eye can see. "I feel like I just walked into a horror movie."

Cade smiles down at me, and some of the tension in me starts to ease. There's nothing I can say, other than perhaps the complete and utter truth, that will get us to Michigan faster, so I should try to take in this trip the way I'm supposed to, like the grand adventure Luke always wanted it to be.

"I don't know. I think it's pretty cool." Cade's eyes lose a little bit of their focus then. "I can't believe I forgot about that day in chem. Feels like a million years ago."

I look over at him, confused, and then remember. The day Luke found the *Rolling Stone* article, he was so excited about it that he interrupted our chemistry class. Cade and I were partners, and our chemistry teacher wasn't exactly thrilled about letting Luke into the room just to give his little sister a magazine, but Luke charmed him, just like he charmed everyone.

"I liked you then," I say because he still hasn't said anything, and I'm so consumed by the heat of him against me that I'm ready to spill every secret I've ever had. What is it about Cade that makes me spit things out like this? I wiggle my hand out of his, mostly out of embarrassment.

He lifts his head, his eyes finding mine, shadowed in the meager light. "When?"

"That day in chemistry, and really pretty much ever since freshman year."

He tucks his hands in his pockets and nods in a weird way. "You should have told me that," he says with a shy kind of smile. "I wouldn't have been so self-conscious, and I would have asked you out a lot sooner." His eyes meet mine again, soft and so full of him, even in the dark.

"It wouldn't have done any good," I say. "It's not like anything ever happened."

He stops walking, and I do, too, looking back at him. I know he wants to say something. I know he wants to talk about that night. I've been completely silent on the subject since then and now that we're here, now that I've been unable to stay quiet around him, maybe he thinks this is his chance. But I can't talk about it. I can't even begin to explain why things happened the way they did. I don't even understand it myself. It was like a bomb went off, and when the smoke cleared, I was the only one still standing.

"What did the fortune-teller say to you?"

He looks at me like just asked him to recite The Book of Mormon. "What?"

"The fortune-teller. On Bourbon Street."

His brow smooths. "Oh. Right. Um. It's kind of stupid."

I shrug. "Well, sure. The whole thing is stupid. But tell me anyway." I think about my own reading, the woman trying to decipher what kind of person I am based on a stack of cards, and it makes my face burn. It can't work like that. I can't work this hard to bury everything inside me just to have a complete stranger come along and expose it like it's no big deal.

"I, um, I asked her if she could communicate with the dead."

My eyes shoot to him. He's rubbing the back of his neck, his head down, like he's embarrassed, but what I feel toward him is less shame and just more shock.

Cade shrugs. "She told me she doesn't do that kind of thing. Which is fine. I don't really believe in, like, spirits walking the earth anyway, so it's probably for the best." He says it with a reasonable amount of conviction, but I can see that he's looking for hope somewhere. I never could have imagined this kind of desire in Cade, someone so easygoing, so unexcitable.

"Who would you want to—" My attention is diverted by a sound, something far away, coming from the other end of the catacombs.

"Is that music?" Cade asks, but I'm walking away from him, back the way we came, passing the point where we split, the music getting louder as we go, until we finally come upon Gwen and Wes. They stand close together, Wes's arm wrapped around Gwen's shoulder, her face pressed into his chest, tears falling across her skin and darkening the fabric of Wes's shirt.

Between them, Gwen holds her phone in the palm of her hand, a Nova song spilling out of it. A song I know so well, a song whose words are tattooed on my brain. They're never going to fade, no matter how much I wish they would.

I know I should feel something. Every time I've heard Nova since Luke left, it's felt like being ripped open, like someone pricking at my skin until I'm bleeding. But now, I hear the words, and I just stare at the phone. I don't have anything left. I feel like I've been scraped raw.

My eyes meet Wes's, and he holds my gaze. I can't fathom why they decided to do this, to listen to this song in the middle of these catacombs. I thought we were trying to keep Gwen away from Luke. I thought we were trying to act as if this trip had nothing to do with him. These catacombs aren't even really about him. They're about Nova.

But I guess it doesn't matter. Nova was Luke, always. They were his favorite band, and just bringing her down here, just mentioning that Jack Olsen met the Harper brothers down here was enough to turn her into this, and I have to look away because if I don't, she might break me.

"I'm sorry," she whispers against the fabric of Wes's shirt, and I feel guilty that she even feels like she has to apologize, as if she's not allowed to grieve. As if she's not allowed to be sad, just because she's moved on, if that's what she's done.

How can I blame her for feeling what I don't want to?

––––––––––

We're walking down Monument Circle, trying to pretend that things haven't gotten really awkward. Gwen and Wes don't hold hands, and I try to keep my distance from Cade, and I feel like we're a bunch of balloons that someone just let go of, floating off in different, completely undetermined, directions.

"Are you hungry?" Cade asks, and I shake my head, even though I'm not positive it's true. I can't interpret the signals my body is sending me anymore, and so I can't even really decide if I want to eat.

"I'm going to run in here and get some water," Wes says, stopping us and motioning toward a convenience store.

"Yeah, me too," Cade says, sending me a sad smile as he follows Wes in.

"Are you okay?" I ask Gwen, and it's so strange to be asking someone else the question that always gets under my skin. I know she's not okay, but I guess I mean a new kind of not okay, something piled on top of the already very much *not okay* we all are.

Gwen shrugs, and we cross the street to sit on the concrete steps at the base of a large monument that towers above the square. She curls up, resting her forehead on her knees, like she's trying to make herself disappear. There are so many people moving around us that I don't think anyone has even noticed us.

Then, after I'm certain that we're just going to sit here in silence, listening to the cars drive by and the noise of conversation, Gwen turns to me and says, "It's like he died twice."

I just blink at her. "What?"

She sits up, pressing her hands into her knees. "Luke was gone so long, it's like he was already dead. To me, anyway." She shrugs. "I could almost forget he even existed. I grieved for him, you know? And now . . ." she trails off, presses her face into her hands.

I've never thought about it this way, but now that she's said it, the truth of it cuts deep. Luke has been dead to us for the last year. When he left, he might as well have been dead already. He vanished into the night, and for all any of us knew, he had driven right off the face of the planet.

It hurt then. It felt like death. It felt like being stabbed in the chest. I spent hours crying, days, weeks, until there was nothing left inside me, until I had cried all of my insides out. And then I got over it. I went back to my life, even though it didn't make sense without him in it anymore. But I got used to a life without Luke, without the other half of me. And now that he's dead . . . what's changed?

I have to look away from her to catch my breath, and I focus on the cars driving past, watching them until I'm dizzy so that I don't feel anything else.

"I've been so mad at him."

Her words scratch at the surface of what's moving around in my chest. She was mad at him. She was mad when he left. She says it so simply, so calmly. I have to look back at her, and when I do, I feel a stab of jealousy for the way she feels everything out in the open, and not just today. I remember her crying so openly during the funeral when I couldn't. She's never tried to hide, never tried to stifle it.

I nod. I can see that, of anyone, she has a right to be mad for what happened between her and Luke. Even now, after he's gone, she has a right to feel anger over grief. No one will blame her for that. "Because he left without a word."

She shrugs. "That, yeah. But the whole thing with Margo, too." I look at her, confused, but she doesn't see me. She scrubs at her face with the palms of her hands. "All that shit that went down, it messed me up. I couldn't get over it, and when he left, that made it that much harder. It's like never getting closure, never really getting to say everything I wanted to. I guess I thought I'd get a chance someday."

"Margo?"

Gwen sniffles and nods. "Yeah. You know, Margo Smith. She's the one Luke cheated with."

My whole face goes hot, like someone just turned the temperature of the whole city up twenty degrees. "Cheated?"

Gwen looks at me for a minute, blank, and then her eyes go wide, and her back straightens. "Oh God. Ellie, I thought you knew."

My stomach churns. "Luke cheated on you? When?"

She bites her lip, but it's not like she can take it back now. It's already in the air, and she has to tell me the truth. "A few weeks before he left."

"But you . . . I mean, you guys were together. When he left, you were together."

She shakes her head. "We weren't. We broke up."

I just stare at her, and she stares back, and I think maybe she's waiting for me to react, waiting for me to say something, but I'm too confused. I feel like we're talking about someone else now, not Luke, not my brother, some stranger that I didn't know.

Out of the corner of my eye, I see Cade and Wes cross the street, heading in our direction. "Then why did you come to the house that day?" I hear the words come out of my mouth, as if somehow this is the most important thing I need her to explain to me. The morning after Luke left, Gwen showed up on our doorstep, and I had to tell her what happened. I had to tell her that her boyfriend—at least, I thought he was her boyfriend—had picked up in the middle of the night and vanished without telling anyone where he was going. And she cried, right there in our dining room.

Gwen glances at Wes, and I see his face change from calm to concerned as he moves to her side. "I wanted to talk to him. I wanted to try and figure out if there was still something between us before I let him go." She says it so gently. She's trying to comfort me, even though it happened to her.

I look out over the square, at all of the people going about their normal routine. I want to know what normal looks like. I keep waiting for my life to feel normal, and it never does. Maybe my new normal is not really knowing my brother. Maybe my new normal is having the people I thought I knew constantly tell me things I can't even understand, rewriting my history until not even the past looks like the normal I remember.

I can hear Gwen and Wes talking, and I know she's telling him what she just told me, but I can also tell, by the rhythm of her voice, that he already knew. Maybe he knew when it happened; maybe he knew later, when they broke up; maybe he didn't know until he and Gwen became more than friends. Either way, he knew before I did, and I know that it's not about me. I know that on the list of ways that Luke hurt me, this isn't really one of them. This is how he hurt Gwen.

But I still feel it, the residual pain, bouncing off of everyone else until it lands on me, and I'm just the culmination of all of it. This is my new normal.

"Ellie?" Cade sounds confused, and when he comes to stand in front of me, a bottle of water dangling from his fingertips, I feel sorry for him. He's an outsider, a spectator to our lives as we live them around him.

"Ellie," I hear Wes say, "this doesn't change anything."

"I don't get it," I say, pushing onto my feet, perching at the end of one of the concrete steps. My voice is low, free of inflection. I don't feel the need to accuse or get upset. I just want to know. That's all. I just want to know my brother. "How could he have so many secrets I didn't know about?"

"Luke didn't tell you everything, Ellie."

I look up at Wes, standing on the step beside Gwen, still so much space between them, and something burrows inside me. "He was my best friend. He told me *everything*."

"No, he didn't." Wes looks defeated. "He always felt like he had to pick and choose with you. I know he didn't tell you about losing his virginity or about the time he got the shit kicked out of him when we were freshmen. Or the time he ran away for three days and hitchhiked down the highway. Luke had secrets, Ellie. Even from you."

I think about that fight in the living room, the envelope Luke waved around, like it was a grenade he was about to launch into the room.

Something heavy forms in my throat, and I can't bring myself to look at any of them. I can't admit to them that Wes is probably right. He kept that stupid map, cheated on Gwen, broke up with her, asked Wes to leave with him and got mad when he wouldn't, and then took off. I try not to think about what else he was hiding from me. What else did he think I wasn't strong enough to handle?

I turn and walk away from them, heading for the other side of the street.

"Ellie!" Wes shouts to me, but I turn to face them and throw up my hands.

"I'm just going to find a bathroom," I say, not even a lie. I wait for the traffic to open and plunge across the street, ducking into the first place I see, a bar. It's mostly empty, which I'm grateful for, and I keep my head low as I make for the back of the small building, right into the ladies' room.

I clutch the edge of one of the porcelain sinks and try to breathe, but every time I think I have a grasp on something, every time I think I'm getting closer to understanding what the hell happened to Luke and to me and to all of us, I just get further away. I'm not getting answers; I'm just getting more questions.

I wash my hands and splash water on my face. I lean back, my face turned toward the ceiling, and let the cold air from the vent blow on my face, cooling the blush that took over back at the monument. Once my face is a little less splotchy, I feel confident enough to open the bathroom door and step back out into the dark bar. I can't stop, not even for a moment. I have to keep moving, until we're in Michigan, even if knowing I might find more secrets there is almost enough to make me falter.

I stand in the hallway where the bathrooms are, and I wait. I wait to see if someone is going to come after me, any of them, but they don't. I stare at the door, at the outline of sunshine that makes it through around the edges. Maybe I can just stay here. Maybe they'll never come looking for me. Maybe I can just disappear.

I hear the crack of billiard balls and look over to where one of the only patrons of the bar is playing pool.

In the light of the red wall sconces, I almost don't recognize him. He's wearing sunglasses, and I wonder how he managed to hit any of the balls if he can't see them. He doesn't seem to be playing with anyone, but he has a drink balanced on the edge of the table, something honey-colored with melting ice.

There's something so familiar about him, something that tugs at something deep in my brain. It's the way he carries himself as he moves from one side of the table to the other, the way he gently grasps the pool cue, the way he leans against the table with the weight of one slender hip and takes a drink from his glass. The more I watch him, the more I know it's him, and I can't seem to take my eyes off of him.

Jack Olsen.

I have to be hallucinating. There's no way that Jack Olsen is here, in this bar. There's no way that the one place I walked into in Indianapolis is the one place where Jack Olsen, lead singer of Nova, just happens to be at seven o'clock on a Monday. It's probably just my eyes—or my brain—playing tricks on me the way it did back at the arch. I'm just seeing Jack Olsen here because it's what I want to see.

"Are you in line?"

I drag my attention to a girl who's a foot taller than me, motioning at the bathroom door behind my back.

"Oh. Sorry. No." I move out of the way to let her pass, and when I look back, Jack has abandoned his game of solo pool and is leaning against the bar, talking to the bartender. He laughs, and it's the laugh that does it, the familiar smile, the way he grips his drink in one hand and gestures wildly with the other. It's definitely Jack Olsen. I've seen the way he moves on stage, in music videos, in interviews, enough to be sure, even if it's dark and his sunglasses are obscuring so much of his face.

I try to seem natural as I sidle up to the bar, praying that now, of all times, Wes or Cade or Gwen doesn't decide to come into this bar to check on me.

Feeling bold for some reason I can't even begin to fathom, I take the stool one over from Jack's, a red vinyl stool still between us. Jack glances over at me, but he doesn't miss a beat in his conversation with the bartender.

"I'm not saying the Colts are going to the fuckin' Super Bowl or anything, I'm just saying that if they keep up the way they are, they could sweep the AFC South, okay?"

The bartender makes an incredulous sound and then glances over at me. "You want something to drink?"

I tap the bar, like I know what the hell I'm doing, and say, "Jack and Coke." I've never actually had a Jack and Coke, but Luke used to drink them in Wes's basement when they could talk the guy at Liquor House into selling them Jack Daniel's for twice the sale price.

The bartender glances at Jack and then the two of them start to laugh. The bartender comes to stand in front of me. "You look like you're about twelve, so why don't I just bring you a Coke without the Jack?"

He turns away, and I watch him, terrified to look at Jack. I focus on a group of girls by the front door who seem like they might already be on their way to drunk. But then again, I'm fairly certain Jack has already had one too many.

"Did you think that was going to work?"

I turn and look at him, struck by how different he looks now than he did the last time we saw him in concert. His hair is longer, his face covered in days-old stubble. One side of his mouth is perked up in amusement, and I decide to take advantage of that.

"I figured it was worth a shot."

He snickers and throws back the rest of his drink. "You're better off flirting with a cashier at a gas station or something. Bill's not the kind to serve anyone who's underage."

With that, Bill sets a glass of Coke in front of me with a grunt. "Damn right. I'm not losing my liquor license because some teenager wants to get drunk." He sets another drink in front of Jack and turns to help someone else.

I glance at the door, certain that any second now, someone is going to come after me. But when I turn back around, Jack is off his stool, taking his drink back to the pool table.

"I just came from the catacombs," I say loudly and then mentally curse myself for acting like an idiot. There were definitely smoother ways to strike up a conversation with someone like Jack Olsen.

Nevertheless, this makes him pause. He presses his hip against his vacated stool and looks at me. "Oh yeah? Teenagers love that place. Used to be a lot less of a tourist spot." He cocks his head and takes a gulp of his drink, his eyes never leaving mine. He smacks his lips and sets his glass on the edge of the pool table. "Used to spend a lot of time down there when I was your age."

"Yeah. I know."

He raises an eyebrow at me. "Yeah? And how would you know that?"

I shrug. *"Rolling Stone."*

He pauses, looking at me, and then a smile spreads across his face. He nods at Bill, behind the bar, and Bill nods back. I guess that means he's getting another drink.

"Should have seen that one coming. You know—" He points one long finger at me "—they made it seem like that article in *Rolling Stone* was going to put us on the map. But that didn't happen at all."

I shrug again. I'm really making a good impression here. "I think you guys do okay." Nova isn't exactly selling out stadium shows, but they're not playing to drunk crowds in dive bars, either.

He smiles at me. "You don't see my paychecks." He picks up a pool cue and chalks the end, and I just watch because I'm not nearly as good at pool as I am at foosball, so there's no way I'm going to suggest I join him. Not that I should anyway. I'm supposed to be on my way to Cade's family's house right now. "Where are you from?"

I perch one hip on the side of the pool table and watch as he lifts his sunglasses, takes a good look at the table, and then sinks a ball, all in less than thirty seconds. "Texas."

He whistles. "Long way to come just to see the catacombs."

I pull at one of my cuticles, unsure whether I should drop this on him. He's a stranger. I'm a stranger. But I grip the pool table and do it anyway because I'm never going to get a chance like this again.

"Actually, we came here because of you. Because of what you said in the article, about meeting the rest of Nova down there."

Jack grins at me and adjusts his sunglasses. "A fan, huh?"

My stomach drops. Nova was always Luke's band. He took me to all the concerts, uploaded all of their albums onto my iPod, played them in his car when he drove me to school or to football games or anywhere really. Nova is Luke's band, not mine.

"My brother was the real fan." This is not an answer to his question, not really, and I know how it sounds as soon as it leaves my mouth. I know it's the kind of thing you say when you want someone to ask questions.

His grin persists, and he pushes his sunglasses up to look at me. "Let me guess, he loved the *Rolling Stone* article and the one they played on the radio, but he lost interest when we fell off the radar."

"Actually, um, no. He always loved you guys." The words catch in my throat, and there's a creeping up my back, an uncomfortable awareness that I'm talking about Luke to a complete stranger, even if it feels like I've known Jack Olsen for a long time.

Jack blinks at me like he already knows what I'm going to say.

"He died. Two weeks ago."

"Fuck." His smile is gone, and he sets his pool cue against the table. "Hey, Bill!" I watch as he makes eye contact with the bartender and nods at him. "Get us that Jack and Coke."

Bill makes a strange face but reaches for a bottle anyway.

Jack sits on the edge of the pool table. "I'm fucking sorry. That's . . . Christ, that's awful."

I decide immediately that even if he's being kind, I won't go into the details. The last thing I want to do is ruin Jack Olsen's night with mine and Luke's story, with the way things seem to be unraveling with every step, with the fact that the three people I came here with across the street, waiting for me.

Bill slides the Jack and Coke across the bar to us, and I watch as Jack goes to get it, looks down into it, and then hands it to me. Bill doesn't say anything, just raises his eyebrows and walks away.

"Thanks."

"Is there anything I can, uh, do or . . . ?" He looks so uncomfortable that I'm almost sorry for saying anything about Luke. He fiddles with his sunglasses.

"In that *Rolling Stone* article, you said that being sad over people who'd died didn't do anybody any good." I remember the night I sat in my bed, reading the article again for the fifth time while Luke snored on the other side of our shared wall. I remember reading that line over and over again and thinking how cynical it sounded. Cold. Emotionless. It felt like something only someone who was heartless could think.

I forgot about those words he said, that article a piece of my past from two year ago, but standing in front of him now, the man who said them, makes them come roaring back like a tidal wave.

Jack groans and rubs a hand over his face. "Shit, kid. I gave that interview right after my dad died. I was bitter. It wasn't supposed to mean anything. I was just . . . talking."

I just look down at the floor. I don't even know why I brought it up. There are no answers anymore, no magical ways to cope, no seminar on how to deal with a scenario in which your brother dies a year after he completely abandoned you. I'm certainly not going to find what I need here.

I set my still-full glass on the bar and tuck my hands into my back pockets. "I should probably go. I have people waiting on me."

He nods, and I can't tell if he's looking at me because he's pulled his sunglasses back down over his eyes.

But when I turn to leave, he says, "Hey!"

I turn back around, and he's got one hand extended toward me, like he can physically stop me, even though there's so much distance between us.

"When I said what I did, what I meant was, how you feel about someone who dies, it doesn't change what they did when they were alive, and it's certainly not going to change anything after. You can't take anything back. You know?"

He sounds so hesitant, like he's not sure he's saying the right thing, and I don't know how to tell him that there is no right thing.

"Yeah. Thanks."

Outside, the sun is setting, and it's like I just stepped out of an alternate dimension. What happened in the bar behind me doesn't feel real, and I don't know how I could possibly explain to anyone that it was.

"Ellie!"

I look up and see Gwen, Wes, and Cade, all of them waving their arms wildly in my direction from across the street, and I stand there for just a second, letting the cars pass by between us, before I take a step toward them.

———

"I still can't believe you met Jack Olsen. And that you wouldn't let us go in after you," Wes says, and Gwen groans.

"I think you have to let it go," she says, glancing out the window as houses fly by outside.

"I couldn't let you ambush him," I tell Wes for the tenth time. "It was bad enough that I approached him while he was trying to be low-key."

"It's this one," Cade says as Wes slows in front of a house. The car falls silent, and I can feel Cade's eyes on me as I look at the little white house we're parked in front of, quite a ways from the house next door, on land that stretches back and disappears into a thicket of trees. The house looks new, at least with a fresh coat of paint on the wooden slats.

When I glance up at Gwen, she's watching me. Sad, that's the expression she's wearing, and I know we've ruined whatever easiness she might have been feeling before. Now, her mind is on Luke and what he did to her.

Wes raps on the steering wheel and looks at Cade over his shoulder. "So what makes you so confident that your grandma didn't just call them the second she realized you were missing?"

Cade's eyes are on the house. I see a figure move in one of the front windows, and it startles me.

"Well, that's the thing," Cade says, and I hear the hesitation in his voice. "I haven't actually seen my aunt and uncle since I was a kid. There's always been sort of a, um, rift between them and my grandmother, so there's no way my grandmother would have called them. She'd never think I would come here."

I look over at him slowly. "But they know we're coming, right?"

He sends me a look, and that's my answer.

We're halfway out of the car when the door of the house springs open and a woman steps out onto the porch, her hand up to block her eyes from what's left of the sun's rays. She frowns and then takes another step in our direction.

"Cade? Is that you?"

Cade freezes, his hand clutching the open car door. "Um. Hi, Aunt Sam."

Sam's eyes go wide, and she's still making her way slowly down the porch steps toward us when the door flies open again, and a small figure shoots out of the house and onto the porch. Sam catches the person before they barrel off the porch steps, and I realize it's a little girl wriggling in her arms. Together, they finally get to us at the car.

Sam's a young Asian woman, with dark eyes that seem to inspect us all, even while her daughter, who looks just like her, bounces around in her arms. Sam bites her lip and smiles at all of us as Gwen and Wes get out of the car.

"Are you really here?" she asks Cade, her voice full of wonder, and I can't believe that this is the first time Cade is seeing his aunt since he moved to Texas when he was nine. What kind of rift would make people not want to see their family?

"Who are you?" the little girl asks, and Sam rolls her eyes.

"Everyone, this is Laney. And I'm Sam. Laney, this is your cousin, Cade. We've told you about him."

Laney nods. "You live in Texas, with the horses. Where's your cowboy hat?"

Cade grins at her. "Not many horses where we come from."

"You're Cade's aunt?" Gwen asks, walking around the car to shake the woman's hand, and I can't tell if she's trying to diffuse the tension or if she's just unable to let the politeness of introducing herself pass her by.

Sam blinks at her before extending her hand. "I am. Well, you sure are pretty."

Cade clears his throat. "Sam, this is Gwen and Wes, and um . . ." He gestures toward me. The car still sits between me and everyone else, and they all turn to look at me. "This is Ellie."

Cade's aunt's eyes find me, and she smiles bigger. "It's so nice to meet all of you." Her smile falters, and she looks over at Cade. "But what are you doing here? I mean, of course, I'm glad you're here, and James will be so—"

"Is he here?" Cade's eyes travel past Sam, toward the house, but if James—who I assume is Cade's uncle—is here, he doesn't seem to be in a rush to see who's come to visit.

Sam shakes her head. "No. He's at work."

Laney rolls her eyes dramatically. "Daddy's *always* at work. Can I try on your sunglasses?" She's switched gears so fast that we all just stare at one another for a second before we realize that she's talking to Wes, who's got on a dark pair of sunglasses.

"Laney, stop," Sam says, swatting at her daughter's hand, but Wes rushes to take them off and hand them to her.

"I have a few pairs in the glove box. Sensitive eyes."

Laney nods like what he's saying is very serious and then puts the glasses on. She's only about five, and Wes's sunglasses are comically big on her, sliding off one ear so that they sit crooked on her face.

"It's so dark," she says, and I look at Sam, who's looking at Cade, and I feel so awkward standing here, showing up on the doorstep of someone who didn't even know we were coming. Why didn't we just stay in a hotel, instead of coming to these people?

"We should talk," Sam says. "I just made dinner. Sandwiches. I hope everyone is okay with tomato basil soup."

"Sounds great," Cade says and follows her up the path to the house.

The house is the kind you might expect on a prime-time sitcom: picture frames of the family of three smiling, hung on sunflower yellow walls; a spotless hardwood floor, decorated by colorful rugs; a recliner from which I'm sure Cade's uncle watches the Super Bowl or the World Series or March Madness; the scent of lavender in the air, probably coming from the candles lit in every room we walk through.

The tomato basil soup is still warm and delicious when we're served, which doesn't surprise me because I can't imagine that fresh food would ever dare go cold in Sam's kitchen. She's the kind of person who has a KitchenAid mixer on the counter, but the bowl isn't sitting in its spot, ready to be used, because it's already been used recently. The clock above the stove is a wooden knife and fork.

"Cade, I'm glad you're here," Sam begins, lacing her fingers in front of her. She's already had her bowl of soup and a chicken salad sandwich. I'm savoring mine. "But I'm confused. What's going on?"

When Cade looks at his aunt, I see something in his eyes that I've never seen before. It's almost like he's embarrassed, like he's not sure what to say. Cade always knows what to say. "I've wanted to visit for a long time. But James and Grandma—"

"I know." I see the way Sam deflates a little, and I suddenly feel like I'm intruding on a private moment, some secret family drama that I shouldn't be witnessing. "James, he—" She cuts herself off, her eyes traveling over the three of us, the intruders, and then back to Cade. "Maybe we shouldn't be talking about this right now."

I blush. I don't know if it's just that we're not family or that she doesn't trust us with whatever happened in their past that kept Cade from ever seeing them, but it doesn't matter because Cade agrees and falls silent.

At the head of the table, little Laney dances in her seat excitedly, her small hand wrapped around a big spoon as she tries to eat soup without coating her shirt with it. "Are you going to live with us?"

I expect Sam's cheery demeanor to endure, but her face twists in a strange way. "No, sweetie. Cade isn't staying."

Wes and Gwen glance at each other across the table but stay quiet. I watch Cade. His neck goes red and then his ears. "Actually, that's kind of why we're here. We're on this trip, sort of a big blowout before senior year, and it would be great if we could crash here tonight." The tiny lie comes out so naturally I wonder if that's what he believed about this trip before I told him the truth.

Gwen's wide eyes shoot to me, and I feel a little bit of the panic that's written all over her face. After our awkward greeting and this silent, tense dinner, it doesn't feel right to stay here. It doesn't feel like we're welcome. This isn't what we expected at all.

"We don't have to stay," I say, putting my hand out on the table, like I can put a halt to this whole thing with one gesture. "We've been staying in hotels, so it's not like one more is going to be a problem." When Cade said we could stay here, I thought he'd arrange it. Or at the very least, I thought he knew the people we were going to be staying with. But they haven't seen each other in eight years?

Sam is already shaking her head. "Oh, no. We have plenty of room for all of you. Please, stay."

When Cade looks at me, I feel like he reads my mind. He knows exactly what I'm thinking because he sends me a look, his eyebrows puckered in and his mouth pressed tight. And I know that even though I'm uncomfortable, even though I can see the stress in the way Wes's eyebrows crinkle and Gwen's mouth make a little O, Cade needs to be here. We need to stay, even if it doesn't make sense.

"Okay," I say despite Wes's foot finding mine beneath the table and giving it a nudge. "Yes. We'll stay."

Sam smiles, and she looks tired. "We've got a guest room we can set up for the girls, and Laney's room and the couch are open for the boys."

Cade shakes his head. "No way. Let Laney keep the room. I'll sleep on the floor."

Sam scoffs and waves him off. "Absolutely not. She sleeps with us half the time anyway. I'll just throw some blankets on the couch and get clean linens for Laney's bed." She sighs, but not in an unpleasant way, and looks at Laney. "Laney, sweetie. Bedtime."

"No," Laney whines. "I want to stay up for the party."

"There's no party, baby." Sam strokes her daughter's hair, and I don't miss the way Cade looks away, almost like the affection makes him uncomfortable. "It's past your bedtime, and I won't be dealing with a cranky kiddo in the morning. We need to get you to bed." She looks at each of us with a smile. "I'll just get her settled."

She's not gone a second before Wes lets out a whistle. "I feel like I just walked into *Mr. Roger's Neighborhood*."

Cade shrugs, but I can see the tension in his shoulders, in the way he sits with his hands folded in his lap. "I think it's nice. I didn't even know I had a cousin."

Gwen purses her lips. "Want some of mine? I have, like, twenty-seven."

Cade smiles at her and then yawns. "God, I'm tired. Sorry if, uh, you guys feel weird staying. I'm just sick of hotel beds. I'm not used to sleeping in strange places."

We're all quiet for a long time, and I can feel the exhaustion starting to eat away at me, starting with the back of my eyeballs and moving all the way to my stomach. I'm queasy with it.

"Come on," Cade says, and I open my eyes. I don't remember shutting them. He's leaning down over me, his hands on my arms, and I let him help me out of my chair and down the hallway. We pass by a closed bedroom door that must be Sam's. I hear her and Laney inside, having a conversation, and then we walk right by and into another bedroom, with a queen-size bed in it that I want to let swallow me.

"This is really nice," Gwen says, walking in and pressing her hand down into the mattress, covered by miles of comforters and sheets and pillows.

I turn to say something to Cade, but he's already stepping back into the hallway and shutting the door, so I join Gwen over by the bed.

"I could just sleep in my clothes," she says, yawning. "God, why does spending all day doing nothing make you so tired?"

I laugh. "We drove over two hundred miles today."

Her eyes go wide. "No way. I've never been able to measure distance in miles. Isn't that weird?" She's rambling now, taking off her shirt and her jeans and fumbling around inside her bag that Sam must have deposited in here when we were helping ourselves to dinner. "I can only measure distance by how long it'll take me to get there. So if someone tells me that a town is four hours away, that would be far, but if they said it was seventy miles, I have absolutely no clue." She giggles, and I can't help but watch her as she slides off her glasses and then climbs between the sheets. She looks like a little girl on a sugar crash.

I change and get in beside her, and I'm pretty sure she's asleep by the time I turn off the lamp on the nightstand beside me. I'm starting to sink, starting to let sleep take me, when Gwen speaks, low and quiet, startling me awake.

"Are you mad at me?" I can't see her face in the dark, only the outline of her as my eyes adjust to the darkness.

I blink over at her, confused. "Why would I be mad at you?" If anyone should be angry, it's Gwen, not just at Luke for all the things he did, but at Wes and at me. But she doesn't even know how angry she *should be* at us. She doesn't know she has reason to be. Guilt churns inside me. I hate that she's so worried she might have upset me when I've been lying to her this whole time.

She burrows down into the thick blanket, pulling it up to her chin. "Because I didn't tell you about what Luke did. Or because, I don't know, because of Wes?"

"Because of Wes?" I feel a little jolt of surprise at hearing her mention him. Why would I be mad at her and Wes? Is there more I don't know about, or does she know something about this trip that I don't know she knows? All these secrets are making me dizzy.

She nods. "Because we're together?"

"Oh." That isn't what I expected at all. Does she expect me to tell her that she did something wrong? At what point after someone has vanished from your life do you assume they're not coming back? How long did Gwen wait after Luke was gone before moving on? Does it even matter? He dumped her. "Definitely not mad." Confused, maybe. But not mad.

She chews on her lip, shifts onto her back to stare up at the ceiling. "He knew I wasn't over Luke. He was so patient with me. And now . . ." she trails off.

I'm motionless. I can't figure out why she's telling me this, what reason she has to dredge this all up now, when the waters are already so muddy. But I hear the desperation in her voice, like she's been waiting to say this for a long time. "And now what?"

Her voice is even quieter when she speaks again. "And I think I might love him. Is that messed up? He was Luke's best friend."

I'm not surprised when she says it. It's been there in the way they look at each other, always orbiting each other so subtly. I stare at her silhouette, trying to see this through her eyes. Luke left her just like he left me. What would I do if I had been with a guy for almost a year and he'd left without a word? If one day he was there and the next he was gone and I had no idea where he was? Even as I try to keep the thought from forming, I imagine if it was Cade. I imagine a reality where we became a couple after that night at the drive-in. If we had, and a year later, he cheated on me and then disappeared, well, I can't even imagine it.

"Gwen, you can love whoever you want. No one's judging you." I say it, even though I'm not sure it's entirely true. Maybe people *will* judge her for being with Wes, but I'm not one of them. "You can't beat yourself up," I say, keeping my voice low just in case the walls here are thin. "Luke is—" I feel the words rise in my throat like bile. "Luke is gone. You can't help who you have feelings for."

I thought my words would comfort her, but they seem to make it worse. She presses her face into her pillow and sobs. I panic. I've never been good at comforting people when they cry. I'm always just awkward. I immediately start blurting things.

"I mean, what else are you supposed to do?" I ask her. "Luke just picked up and left without a word to you. And after . . . after what he did, you can't honestly think that you were supposed to sit around and—"

"I think it was because I was satisfied with Eaton," she says, her voice thick, making absolutely no sense. "I knew he was going to leave, and I knew he was done with me."

My stomach twists. "He told you he was leaving?"

I can't see her do it, but I feel and hear Gwen shake her head, and for some reason, I'm relieved. It was hard enough knowing that Luke told Wes, and even though I know it's petty to be jealous of something like this, I don't think I could stand knowing that he told Gwen, too, without telling me. "No. But I knew something was wrong. I knew he was going to do something. That's just the way he is. *Was.*" Her breath stutters and so does my heart. "When I came to the house the day he left, I guess I wasn't all that surprised to find out that he took off. Mostly, I was just sad. He was acting weird a long time, and then he slept with Margo, and it just felt like he was freaking out. Maybe I saw it coming."

Saw it coming.

I think about that day in the living room, Luke yelling so loud at our mother, his whole body shaking with anger. Maybe I should have seen it coming, too. Maybe if I had paid more attention.

"Toward the end, I don't think he loved me anymore. I think he knew I didn't want to leave Eaton. And it was like, I was a waste of his time if I didn't want something more. He wanted somebody who wanted adventure, someone with wanderlust, just like him. And I didn't have that."

She falls quiet, and I try to process everything. Something about knowing this, it turns anxiety into a weight on my chest. Maybe it's knowing that Luke *did* cut all of his ties. Maybe he didn't just walk away from all of it like I thought he did. He wasn't friends with Wes when he walked out that door, and he wasn't Gwen's boyfriend.

But he was still my brother. He still walked away from me.

Gwen's quiet for a long time, and then I hear the soft cadence of her breathing, and I realize she's fallen asleep.

All the lights are on in the house when we get there.

"That's weird," I say to Cade as we walk up to the front door. I imagine my mother waiting angrily at the dining room table.

"Think you're in trouble?" Cade asks with a grimace.

I shrug. "No clue." I'm used to my mother's anger, to her disappointment and her fits, but not even she can ruin this perfect night.

On my doorstep, Cade stands with his hands in his pockets. He looks nervous, and it's so adorable, it makes my skin tingle.

"Thank you for taking me to the drive-in. It was awesome."

He smiles down at me. "I've thought about taking you there for a long time."

I take a step closer and tilt my face up to his. "You can ask me out anytime."

His eyes drop to my mouth, scan my face, but he doesn't move. Is he waiting for me to make a move? I'm not feeling quite as brave as I was back at the drive-in, and I wait for him to close the distance between us, but he doesn't. He takes a step away from me, one foot resting on the step below us.

"I'll see you later?" he asks, and for just a second, I imagine waiting for him at the garage, holding his hand at school, going on dates every Friday night.

But he obviously isn't going to kiss me tonight. He takes another step, now completely on the step below me. I try to hide my disappointment.

"Good night, Cade."

He smiles and takes the rest of the steps down to the sidewalk. "Good night, Ellie."

I watch him get back in his grandmother's car and drive away.

———————

I get out of bed and tiptoe out into the hallway. I know where Sam and Laney are sleeping, so I go the other way, opening a door beside ours that has Princess Laney written in pink glittered letters on the door. The room is completely dark, but this side of the house is right under the shine of the moon, and I see in its light that Cade isn't asleep in the bed. Wes is.

I back out, shut the door, and keep moving until I'm in the living room, right where we first came in. The moon is shining down through the windows in here, too, and I see Cade, his eyes open, looking up at it, spread across the sofa.

"I thought I heard someone moving around," he says, and then his eyes find mine. He doesn't move, just keeps his head propped in his hand as he watches me, waiting to see what I'll do.

I lean against the doorway. I don't even know why I'm here, other than that I can't seem to stay away from him. "Tell me why you came on this trip."

"Ellie—"

"Tell me the real reason. Is it because you wanted to come here and see your family again? What happened to make your grandmother keep you away from them?" I'm feeling bold. It feels like Cade knows everything about me after the past few days. Well, almost everything. I still can't bring myself to tell him why I put an end to what was so obviously starting between us that night on my doorstep, haven't even told him *why* we're on this trip, why I've been so eager to get to Michigan. So maybe I don't have the right to ask him this, when I'm still holding on to so much, but I want to know something about him, and seeing as how I've just walked right into the center of his family drama, now seems like a good time.

The smile falls from his face. He pushes himself into a seated position, the blanket falling to his waist to completely reveal his *Star Wars* T-shirt.

I can practically hear the wheels turning in his head, can practically feel his hesitation in the air. He takes a deep breath, and it's so quiet in the house that I can hear it as loud as I can hear the ticking of a grandfather clock somewhere.

He swings his legs over the side of the couch. "Come on, I want to show you something."

———

"This might be a little crazy," I say as Cade leads me out into the woods behind his aunt's house. It's so dark, even with the moon shining high above us, and I've read my fair share of news stories about people getting lost in the woods and never being found.

Cade laughs. "Don't worry. There's a path."

I feel a little ridiculous, walking through the woods in my pajamas, but he's wearing his, too, so I guess that makes it a little less ridiculous. But I still feel exposed, naked, in my thin clothes in the open air.

"I want to go to school out here, in Indiana."

I stop walking, feeling like he just dropped something right in the path that I can't get around. "Really?"

He nods and motions with his chin for me to keep following him. We go in so deep that the house disappears and all I can see is trees and shadows. The only thing keeping me from freaking out is the shape of Cade in front of me.

"My parents met at the University of Indiana," he says. "My grandmother used to tell me the story."

"Really?" I've heard stories of people meeting in college, falling in love during orientation or a dorm hall party or whatever. But I've never known someone directly who had that kind of story, someone who was the product of it. My parents met at a mutual friend's wedding.

Cade stops walking, and I almost run into him. When he turns, I can just make out the lines of his face, the way his mouth is turned down just slightly, a frown. "They died. That's why I moved in with my grandmother. That's why my grandmother doesn't really talk to my uncle anymore. She took me, moved to Texas, and tried to forget about Indiana."

I feel like my heart has completely stopped beating. "Cade, I'm so sorry. How did I not know this? How have I known you for so long and not known that?"

Cade shrugs. "My grandmother didn't want people gossiping about me, so she's tried to keep it quiet. You know how it is in Eaton."

The muscles in my stomach go rigid. All this time I thought we were the only ones who lost someone, and here Cade was the whole time, hurting. "You could have told me." I've known Cade since we were kids, we've been friends for so long, and I could have been there for him better. I could have helped him somehow.

The thought almost makes me laugh. How can I help Cade, if I can't even help myself?

"Anyway, that's why I'm here."

I look over at him, confused. "Because of your parents?"

He starts walking again, and I follow him, even though I feel like my whole body has gone numb. "I've always felt like I was missing out on a part of them by never coming back. But it was so hard for my grandmother when it happened that she never let me." He stops again, and I stop beside him. He finally looks down at me, finally sees me.

"I know you came on this trip because of your brother. I don't understand it, and it's okay if you don't want to tell me, but when I saw that map in your car, I knew it had to do with him, and I was so jealous of how brave you were, taking the leap, leaving Eaton just like that, and I wanted to be brave, too. I wanted to come here. I wanted to . . ." He stops, presses his hand into his stomach, exhales. "I wanted to bring you here."

I take his hand, overlap our fingers. "I'm here," I say, and even though it's meant to comfort him, it comforts me, too. I've been so lost on this whole trip, so confused about what we're doing and why we're doing it, what I'm going to find in Michigan and what I left behind in Eaton. But with his skin against mine, I feel grounded. "I'm sorry about your parents."

He leans close to me. "I'm sorry about Luke."

We're quiet for a long time, and I set my head against his chest, listen to his heart beating. It's the loudest thing in the world right now, drowning out the sounds of the wildlife and the occasional car on the road.

I look up at him, at the way his eyes are focused on me. "Why didn't you kiss me that night? At the drive-in?"

His mouth opens a little, and I think I caught him off guard, saying the thing he least expected. Maybe it was the thing I least expected, too. His hands wrap around my arms, his fingers digging into my skin just a little, like he's keeping me from floating away. "I guess I thought I had time."

I have to look away from him. I thought we would have time, too. I imagined a nice future for us, complete with candy hearts and prom dresses. "I'm sorry," I say. I probably should have said it a year ago, when I stopped answering his calls and stopped looking at him in the hall and stopped being his friend. "I never meant to hurt you."

"What happened?"

It's too hard to explain. It's too hard to try and put a name to the rift between my life before and my life now. There's no simple definition. "I guess I just don't even know who that girl is anymore. I don't make sense without Luke."

He doesn't reassure me. He just looks down at me for a long time, and then he takes my hand, steps backs, and pulls me farther down the path. I follow him in silence, and stop when he does.

"Want to go up?" he asks, and I realize that I've been so busy looking at him that I didn't notice the treehouse directly beside us.

I look up at it and laugh. "Do people really build treehouses in the woods?"

Cade smiles at me and starts to climb the wooden ladder. I watch him go, smiling at the way his bare toes curl around the wooden planks. Who knew that feet could be cute?

When he's at the top, he sits at the edge of the little porch that hangs past the doorway, dangling his feet over the edge and looking down at me. He pats the wood beside him, and I crane my neck.

"Um. That's kind of high."

His smile falls. "Oh. Shit. Sorry. I'll come back down."

"No," I say quickly. "No. I want to come up." I'm still feeling brave. I've come all this way, followed Cade into the woods, said things I never thought I'd say. I can certainly climb a damn wood ladder.

He stops, his hand still wrapped around one of the wooden slats. "Okay."

When I was a kid, my parents took Luke and me zip-lining. The tree was taller than the one Cade is in right now, the line extending through the forest, to a tree so far away that you couldn't even see it.

"Don't forget to throw down the rope so we can stop you," the instructors told me. The idea that whether or not I was going to crash into a tree on the other side was dependent on my own competence was too much for me. I made it halfway up the tree before I stopped, unable to go any farther.

Down on the ground, my parents called to me that I was okay, that I could do it, but I couldn't. Luke had already started climbing up behind me, so they told me to slide as far as I could to the left of the ladder to let him up beside me. I held on with a death grip, and then I felt Luke's body slide past mine. He was moving so fast, completely unfazed. I watched him climb over the lip of the wooden platform and then heard his far-off celebratory noises when he reached the other side while I climbed slowly back down to the ground.

I look up at Cade, focus on his legs dangling over the edge as I force my way up, my limbs trembling as I go. When I get close enough to the top, Cade's hand wraps around my arm, and I know that if I slip, he won't be able to keep me from falling, but it's nice to know he would try.

I pull myself up onto the platform and swing my leg up, grabbing onto the wooden slats and finally landing all of my weight onto it, flat on my back. Just past the edge of the treehouse's roof, through a break in the trees, I can see the stars. I hold my fingers up to the sky, looking at the way the stars are the same color as my pale skin. I let my hand drop.

"It's not so bad once you're up here."

He smiles and lies down beside me, our faces side-by-side, our bodies pointed in opposite directions.

"I thought you'd like it. My dad and my uncle built it when I was a kid. We didn't have as much land as my aunt and uncle do, so they let us do stuff like this here. As you can tell, Laney has sort of adopted the place." He points at something on the wall inside the treehouse, and I realize it's a crayon drawing of a unicorn, galloping atop a rainbow. It's actually pretty good.

Cade turns his head, so I turn mine, and I feel like I should memorize every crevice of his face. The freckle he has on his right cheekbone, the way his top lip has a little Cupid's bow dip in it, the way his eyes shine with moonlight.

He takes a deep breath, and I wait for what I know he's going to say, what I can already feel seeping in through my pores. "I know it feels like you're not you without him. But you are, Ellie. You're still that girl from the drive-in."

I shake my head, feeling like I can't pull air into my lungs. "That girl was someone else."

He nods, turns to look up at the stars. "Maybe. But when I look at you, I still see her in there. Maybe a little different, but still the same person, just without all the pieces she adopted from her brother."

I scowl at him, his words driving away the unease in me. "What do you mean?"

He shrugs, his shirt making a rustling noise as it slides against the floor. "You liked all the things he liked; you did what he wanted to do. This is the first time you've ever had you all to yourself."

I feel like someone just cut me open. I've never thought about it like that before, like the reason I've felt half complete since Luke left is because so much of me was just made up of *him*. Nova, the parties, the map, even Gwen and Wes. Everything is him. So what part of it is me?

"You'll figure out the rest," he says, so casually, so gently, like he didn't just gut me. "You want to know something?" he asks in a way that I expect him to say something about the stars or about the history of Indianapolis, but instead, he says, "This might sound totally twisted, but when I heard about Luke, I guess I just felt maybe you would understand."

"Understand?"

"How I felt when I lost my parents."

I'm still searching for something to say, but he keeps talking. "I know things have been weird between us, and I'm not saying I thought we'd get back together or anything like that. It's not about that. I just want to be your friend again. I just wanted you to know that I'm here, and I know what you're going through."

"So, what? You thought you could save me?" I don't mean for it to sound so harsh, but it does anyway. I'm falling apart, right here outside of this treehouse.

His eyes go wide. "God, no. If anything, I thought maybe I would be able to save myself."

I don't know what to say after that. I don't know the right things to say to comfort him. I can't even reconcile what I know about Cade with what I didn't know until tonight. He didn't just lose someone, he lost two someones. And he still feels it. Maybe I'll still feel it, too, a decade from now.

When I open my mouth, I'm not sure what I'm going to say, but somehow, I end up saying, "I can't believe I met Jack Olsen in that bar today."

Cade turns to me with his whole body now, flipping onto one side so that he can see me entirely. "Yeah, how did that really happen?"

For some reason, the ridiculous look on his face makes me laugh. I cover my face, laughing hard, trying to speak but unable to find the air. "Oh my God," I say, pressing my hand to my stomach. "I have no clue. I went to the bathroom and when I came out, there he was." I gasp for air, laugh more. "He was playing pool, drunk, wearing these awful sunglasses."

He snorts then, looks at me, smiling. He reaches out and thumbs away the tear that's tracked down the side of my face. The laughter dies down inside of me, and I have to look away from him. He's so close, I can smell a hint of toothpaste on his breath.

I look up at the sky, see the way the stars swirl above us in the dark. "Hey, are you still interested in astronomy?" I ask.

"Yeah," he says, his voice dreamy. His eyes start to close, but then he opens them quick and shifts onto his back again. "See, there's Ursa Major right there and Corona Borealis." His hand moves in circles, his finger making me dizzy. "And there's Polaris, also known as the North Star."

He keeps talking, and I close my eyes, listen to the soft cadence of his voice as he talks about the night sky.

When I open my eyes again, the sky is just barely starting to lighten with sunrise.

"Shit," I say, pushing up on the hard wooden slats, feeling how sore my back is. Beside me, Cade is still fast asleep, rolled onto his side, his arms tucked close around him like maybe he got cold during the night.

"Cade," I say, shaking him. "Cade, we have to get up."

He groans and shifts onto his back. It takes him a second, but his eyes eventually open slowly, staring up at the sky for a long time before finally shifting to me. "Ellie?"

I can't help but smile. "Treehouse, remember?" I point at the treehouse over my shoulder, and his eyes go there and then shift back to me.

"Right. That would explain all the pain."

Without waiting for him, I stand up and move to the ladder. Hopefully no one else is awake, and we can just sneak back into the house without any fuss. Going back down the ladder is way easier than going up, as my destination is solid ground, and I wait for Cade at the bottom.

We slip back into the house as quietly as we can, but it's no use. There's someone sitting at the kitchen table, and it's not Sam.

"Didn't mean to scare you," the man says. The sleeves of his dress shirt are rolled up to his elbows, and there's a suit jacket slung across the empty chair beside him. He has a mug in front of him, the single light over the kitchen table shining down on him. He looks up at me, and I'm surprised by how much of Cade I see in his face: the same eyes, the same cheekbones, the same mouth. "I'm James. You must be Ellie." He looks behind me, at Cade. "Cade." He takes a sip from his mug. "Want some coffee?"

Cade and I don't say anything, just watch James take another sip. There's something ominous about the situation. Not about him, necessarily, but about the way he watches us over the lip of his cup.

He uses his foot to push the chair beside him away from the table, inviting us to join him. We both take a seat, and I feel like I shouldn't make any sudden movements as I settle into my chair.

"I'm sorry I missed dinner." When we say nothing, he says, "I work with businesses overseas, so I do a lot of middle of the night conference calls. I miss dinner a lot." He takes another sip. "Of course, I didn't know that we were going to have guests. I'm going to assume you spent the night in the treehouse and that nothing inappropriate happened." With that, he sends us both a stern look.

We both nod, like children being chastised.

"I guess I understand why you thought your grandmother wouldn't contact me. I certainly didn't think there was any way you were going to show up on my doorstep, either, and that's what I told her when she called me yesterday."

My heart plummets into my stomach, and I hear Cade start to say something, but James isn't listening. He leans forward on his elbows, leveling Cade with a heavy gaze. "What were you thinking, ditching your grandmother like that? Whatever it is, you better rethink it because you're getting your ass straight back to Texas."

"Uncle James—"

"I don't want to hear it. God, and have you seen the missing persons ad? I couldn't even show Sam. It would have terrified her. Why did you even—"

I hear a board creak, and we all look up to see Gwen and Wes hovering in the hallway, watching us.

James throw his hands up. "How many of you are there? How many runaway kids do I have in my house?"

I shake my head, ready to tell them that Gwen and Wes are adults, but Cade is already talking over me, standing away from the table. I watch the two of them, my entire body frozen still.

"I just wanted to come back here," he says, and that seems to get James's attention. His eyes travel up to Cade. "It's stupid that they won't let me come see you. It's stupid that there's this thing between all of you."

James exhales and balls his fist on the table. "Cade, you don't need worry about all that stuff."

"How am I not supposed to worry about it?" Cade says, a little too loud. "My parents died." At this, my eyes shoot to Gwen and Wes, who look as shocked as I felt when he told me last night. "I know it was grandma's son and your brother, but they were my parents, and the fact that you can't look at each other affects me. But none of you have ever even thought about that."

I can see James grinding his teeth, but then he sighs. "You're right. But that's not something I can fix right now. Cade, when you're eighteen and you're in charge of your own life, you can come back here. You can stay as long as you want. But this was not the way to do this."

"You can't tell her we're here," Cade pleads. I'm surprised by the desperation in his eyes. I've never seen him like this, pleading, scared. "Ellie has to keep going."

Everything in me pulls tight, and I'm certain that right here, right now, Cade is going to let everything out. He's going to tell Gwen and everyone else that we're trying to get to Michigan, that we're following a map that I made with Luke and Wes three years ago, about whoever is in Michigan that knew Luke.

But then I remember that Cade doesn't know about all of that. Or least, he doesn't know most of it. The only one who knows we're going to Ann Arbor is Wes.

"Her brother . . ." Cade starts to say, but then he looks down at me, still sitting at the table. I hold my breath, waiting to see what he'll say next, how much he'll tell. When he looks back at James, he says, "This trip is important to her. If you want to make me go back, that's fine, but don't make her go back, too."

I shoot up from the table then. "What? No. I'm not going on without you. Either we all go, or none of us do."

James's eyes are wide as he looks back and forth between us.

"What's going on? Why is everyone up so early?" Sam comes into the kitchen, squeezing by Gwen and Wes to get to us. She looks from James to us and back again, and we wait for James, to see what he'll say, to see if he'll condemn us back to Eaton.

His jaw works, his fingers tap on the tabletop, his eyes shift between the five of us. And then he says, "No reason. Cade and Ellie heard me come in, that's all. It's still very early, so maybe everyone should head back to bed." He sends Cade and me a look, and we take the hint, going our separate ways, me back to the guest room and Cade back to the couch.

"What's going on?" Gwen asks after she closes the door behind us. "Is everything okay?"

I get in the bed, the sheets cold from the air conditioner, and pull the blanket up over me. "I have no idea."

Chapter Ten

It's warm in the guest room when I wake up, feeling dried out and groggy. Gwen is sitting up in the bed, looking down at something on her phone.

"What time is it?" I ask, wishing I could just roll over and go right back to sleep. Who knew that road trips could be so draining? Not to mention spending most of the night in a treehouse. Everything comes back to me, and I'm not sure whether to smile or groan or just pack my stuff as fast I can and get the hell out of here.

"Already after noon," Gwen says, and I groan, rolling back over, but when I do that, the bright afternoon sun shines directly in my eyes, and I hate everything so much. I cover my face with my hands, but then realize something smells good.

Gwen laughs when she realizes I'm sniffing at the air. "I think Cade's aunt is cooking something." Her amusement seems to die a little, descending back into the worry that I saw on her face when I first woke up.

"You okay?" I ask her. So much happened last night and this morning that I can't even begin to understand how I feel about it all, can't even begin to understand where we go from here.

She wraps her arms around her legs, pulling them up to her chest. "I've just been feeling weird," she says. She runs a hand through her hair and turns to face me. "I think it's because we're going to Michigan.

Just . . . because of everything."

She doesn't have to say it. Because that's where Luke died. The thought is a million needles in my skin. I can't think about that. I can't, or I won't go. And I have to go.

And I have to tell her about the map, about the person we're going to see in Dexter, about everything.

"Gwen, look, there's something—"

Her phone chimes, and she smiles when she looks down at it. "It's Wes. He wants us to go eat with them."

I watch her rush to get out of bed and change into real clothes, and I know I should say something, but she looks so happy, smiling down at her phone again before tossing it onto the bed and struggling into her jeans. So I leave it. For now.

In the kitchen, Cade and James are huddled together, discussing something in low tones, while Wes and Laney discuss the merits of *Sesame Street* over *The Muppets*.

"They're in two completely different categories," Wes says to Laney, who just shakes her head.

"Elmo," is all she says, and Wes sighs like he's been defeated.

"I know. Everyone likes Elmo. But what about Kermit? He's badass."

Sam sends him a sharp look, and he cringes. "Oops. Sorry. Kermit is really cool." He points a finger at her. "Don't say *badass.*"

At the stove, Sam sighs, and then she sees us. "Oh, girls, good. I didn't want to wake you up. I know you're tired. But I wanted everyone to get something to eat before you have to leave."

I don't mention that we're definitely already supposed to be gone. Some of the urgency has cooled in my veins now that we're so close.

We'll be Ann Arbor by the end of the day, and now that it's staring me right in the face, I'm in far less of a hurry.

I accept a plate of grilled chicken and vegetables gladly and take a seat next to Cade. As soon as I sit down, Cade and James separate, both of them smiling at me like they're hiding a secret.

"What is it?" I ask them both suspiciously.

Cade shrugs, but he's still smiling. "Just making plans for the future."

I smile because Cade's clear excitement is contagious, even if the word *future* coming from his lips sends a little thrill through me. "The future, huh?"

He nudges my leg with his. "University of Indianapolis? They have this Earth-Space Science program." He smiles down at the table. "I don't know. I thought it would be cool."

I reach out and squeeze his arm. "That sounds really nice."

Across the table, Wes pipes up. "You're not going to Tate?"

Cade's smile dims a little. "I don't think so, no. I think Indiana is where I want to be for a while."

Wes whistles. "Indiana's pretty far from Texas."

When he says this, my stomach twists. I didn't even think about that. About Cade being so far away, about him not going to Tate, not being in Texas, not being *around* anymore. I have to look away so no one sees the panic in my eyes. It's a strange emotion after being without him for so long already. How have I become so attached to him again in just a few days?

Cade seems to understand why I've gone silent. He reaches out and wraps his pinky finger around mine under the table.

I have too many things to think about to add this to the list. I pull my hand away from Cade's and go back to my food.

Getting in the car, we all move like robots. We pack our things in the back, get in the same seats we've been traveling in for days, turn on the radio to something I don't even have the energy to process.

As soon as we've stopped for gas and are back in the car, Cade slouches down in his seat and closes his eyes. I don't know how he can sleep. Between sleeping until noon and the coffee I got when we stopped for gas, I feel like maybe I'm not going to sleep until I turn thirty. But I watch Cade sleep because there's not much to do, and he's nice to look at.

"His family was nice," Gwen says, and when I look up, she's looking at Cade, too, her hand curled over the back of her seat.

"Yeah."

Wes catches my eye in the rearview mirror, and I look away quick. It's not like Cade and I are trying to hide anything, but since I have no clue what's going on between us, I'm not sure I'm ready to let Wes and Gwen in on it yet. I want something to be just mine, something I don't have to immediately dissect and try to explain to someone. *Just mine.*

I look out the window and watch the last miles of Indiana fly away behind us. It's hard to imagine Cade growing up here, living somewhere other than Eaton. So many people I know have lived in Eaton their whole lives, and I try to envision what it's like to grow up in Indiana. There are people who are born and raised here, just like the three of us were born and raised in Texas. And I wonder if Luke would have been unhappy anywhere, or if it was just Eaton he hated so much.

"Can you turn up the music?" I call into the front seat, hoping to drown out my thoughts.

———————

Somehow, even though I could swear I'm not even tired, I fall asleep in the back of the car, and when I wake up, we're pulling up against a curb and my head is on Cade's shoulder.

I push away from him before he wakes up and look out the window. There's a beach. Right there, as if it's no big deal, there's a beach, completely empty, the sun shining down on it. Cade stirs awake beside me, and we all just sit in the car and stare at it, until Wes finally gets out.

"It's not going to come to us," he says.

"Where are we?" I ask, getting out, too. Since Wes programmed all the stops so that we wouldn't have to consult the map, it's easy for me to lose track. There are countless stops between us and our return to Eaton, but I've stopped paying attention. The only one that matters to me is Ann Arbor.

"Lake Erie," Wes replies, closing his door and coming around the car to stand beside Gwen.

I roll my eyes. "Yeah, I get that, genius, I mean where? Lake Erie meets land in a lot of places."

"Oh." He pulls out his phone and scrolls around before saying, "Newport, Michigan."

I remember now. Wes is the one who picked this place. We all decided we were going to visit all five Great Lakes, but we didn't want to see them from the same places everyone else did. So we put our fingers to the map at each lake, and Wes's finger pointed here. Newport, Michigan. This would have been Luke's last stop before he went on to Ann Arbor. I shiver at the thought.

Lake Erie is sloshing quietly in the wind in steady intervals, and it's not until we're standing there, looking out over it from the edge of the beach, that I realize just how exhausted I am, a deep kind of exhaustion that seeps all the way down to my bones, and I can't tell if it's from the trip or from knowing where we're going after this. Perhaps the entire last year is finally catching up with me.

"We should swim," Gwen says, and we're all silent, probably in shock. At least, I'm in shock. I don't have a bathing suit, and stripping down to my underwear in front of these boys to go swimming in Lake Eerie is not on the itinerary.

"What?" Wes finally asks, but it's too late. Gwen is already pulling her shirt off over her head and tossing into the sand at our feet. I glance around quick to make sure no one is watching, but all I see is empty beach, golden sand.

"Let's go," she says as she walks toward the edge, wiggling out of her tight jeans. The three of watch as she goes, and then she's splashing into the water in her underwear, completely unconcerned about whether we're going to join her.

Wes moves next, lunging toward the water and stripping his shirt off as he goes. He never even takes his eyes off Gwen, already shoulder deep in the lake. I look away when he gets down to his boxers. I don't really want to see that much of him.

But when I look away from Wes, it's to find Cade in a similar state of undress, and my cheeks go hot as Cade reaches down to the button of his jeans.

Before he can drop his pants, I start to scramble out of my clothes. I will not let him fluster me, not when I can fluster him right back. And it's pretty clear I've flustered him because by the time I've stripped down to my bra and underwear, he still hasn't undone the button on his jeans, and it's obvious that he's trying not to look, but he's blushing anyway and also staring down at the sand instead of undressing.

I take off for the water, already regretting the decision to take off my clothes. I dive in and let the water be my shield, let it cover me so that nobody can see all of my bare skin. Gwen and Wes are swimming around each other, their hair wet, not even paying attention to me.

But then Gwen grins at me and swims over, and I'm a little shocked when she puts her arms around my waist, the water making our skin slip across each other. She presses her chin to my shoulder, and I let her hold me for a long time, thinking of the way she cried in the catacombs, the way she was afraid I would judge her for being with Wes.

I look at her, Gwen, the prettiest girl I've ever known, my favorite of all Luke's girlfriends, the only one who ever seemed to care that I was even alive. Luke dated tons of girls. They moved into our lives and stayed for dinner and then they disappeared into the hallways at school when he moved on, becoming just another face.

Sometimes, when I'm busy dissecting every memory I have of Luke, every time he sat beside me at the dinner table or took me to Wes's house or made me feel like the most important person in the world, it's easy to forget that Gwen is there in the memories, too. She helped me with my chemistry homework; she talked to me at dinner, asking me how school was going; she said hi to me when we passed in the halls, sometimes stopping on her way to class, leaning against a locker to talk to me; she took me to the movies when I wanted to see something the guys didn't. How have I forgotten all that?

I put my arms around her in the warm water, pressing my face into her neck and breathing in the wet, murky smell of the lake water. Guilt curdles in my stomach, but I don't know what to do anymore. It's too late to hope she won't be mad when we tell her we're going to Ann Arbor, to Dexter, to wherever the hell we're going, but not telling her was so clearly a mistake. Why did I think she couldn't handle it? Why did I underestimate her so much?

"Thanks for letting us come," she says against my ear, and I catch Wes's eye over her shoulder. I can see in his eyes that he's feeling just as guilty as I am, and I have to pull away from her, from her soft skin and her soothing voice and her kindness because I don't think I deserve any of it.

I pull away from her just in time to see Cade wade into the water and swim right toward me. I need to pull away from him, too. Because if I don't deserve Gwen's kindness then I certainly don't deserve Cade's. I haven't told either of them the whole truth, and all they've done is show me gentleness.

I turn and swim away from Cade, but he thinks it's a game and swims after me. He follows me far into the lake, until my feet can't find the ground anymore, and then he's got his arms around me, and I know he means it as a joke, but when I turn, kicking my feet against his, and find his bare chest, I just burrow into it. I press my head against the muscle there, and we float together, and maybe I don't deserve Cade, but I think I want him anyway.

I get tired of swimming long before everyone else. I've never been much one for the water, and it's getting kind of late anyway. My limbs are tired and sore from being folded up in the car for days. I put my dry clothes back on and stretch out on the sand. I listen to the sounds of them splashing in the water and close my eyes, but something is building just below my rib cage, no matter how much I try to fight it off, a constant reminder of how fast we're moving toward the person I've been waiting to meet.

"Ellie."

My eyes fly open, and I realize that Cade is bending over me, and that I must have fallen asleep, right here by the lake. As I'm still processing this, Cade drops down onto the sand beside me. He's still shirtless, but at least he put his pants back on, and I don't look at him as he settles in beside me.

"They look happy."

I tilt my head at an uncomfortable angle to see Gwen and Wes in the water. They're wrapped around each other, floating as a single entity, and I can hear that they're talking, but I can't tell what they're saying. But yes, they look happy.

I turn on my side and press my hand under my head so that I can just look at Cade. "Can I ask you a question?"

He smiles up at the sun, shining down on him, shining on the layer of water coating his skin. "Sure."

"How did they die? Your parents?"

I see him run his tongue over his teeth, not looking at me, and I regret even asking.

"I'm sorry. That was rude. I just wanted—"

"A house fire," he says over me, quickly.

My stomach clenches. "Were you there?"

He shakes his head. "I was on a camping trip with my grandmother in Yellowstone. I think that's one of the reasons she took me away and never let me come back. She's protective of me because I was with her that day. I think she feels guilty a lot, about everything, even though she couldn't have changed anything. If anything, she saved me, you know?" At this, he turns his head to look at me. "If I'd been home, I might not have made it out."

"That's awful. I'm sorry." But he's here. He *did* make it out, and I can't imagine living with that. I wrap my arms around myself, curl up like I can protect myself from Cade's sadness.

"I'm sorry I didn't really know Luke."

At the mention of Luke's name, my eyes shoot back to Cade's. "What do you mean? You knew him."

Cade shrugs, causing sand to bunch up under his shoulders. "I knew him the way people in Eaton know each other, but I didn't *know* him. It's like, all I have are these snippets, flashes of memory. We had speech together before he graduated, and he was always so confident at the podium when I was always so nervous; he was always hanging out with Wes when I came over to your house or had his arm wrapped around a girl at school. I remember these little pieces of him, like how they were always asking him to be on the morning announcements and he was always winning medals in track, but I never really *knew* him."

"Maybe if you know me, you know him." He's the one who said part of me is made up of Luke, that I took on so much of him. I never had his confidence or that thing about him that made it impossible not to be drawn to him like he produced his own gravitational pull. But there are still pieces of him here.

Cade shakes his head. "I think maybe you knew parts of him that other people didn't. What everyone else saw and what you saw aren't the same thing."

I think of all the nights Luke stayed in my room until he couldn't keep his eyes open anymore, just talking, all the times we took a detour on the way home from school just so we could finish listening to the song on the radio, every time he introduced me to a new band or a movie he knew I'd love or a corner of Eaton he found bearable that no one seemed to know about. I think of the way his eyes always went soft when he told me how proud he was of me or how much he loved me or how excited he was about the future.

I feel the hardness in my throat and look away from Cade so he can't see that my eyes have filled with tears.

I hear Gwen and Wes making their way out of the lake. A moment later, Gwen collapses on the sand beside me. She looks perfectly content to lie here in her dripping bra, black with little pink roses.

"What are you guys talking about?" she asks.

I'm hesitant to tell her. I don't even know where Gwen stands on anything anymore. I don't know if bringing up Luke will make her sad or angry or completely unresponsive. So I don't answer her.

Cade does, though. "Luke."

Gwen just nods, like this is exactly the answer she expected, but Wes sits down by our feet, wrapping his arms around his knees. "Remember that place on Fifth that shut down a few years ago? What was it called?" He looks to Gwen and me for confirmation, but it's Cade who answers.

"The Gorge," Cade says. "Best ice cream floats."

Wes grins at me. "We used to go there all the time. Their roast beef sandwiches were the shit. Luke used to order his root beer float first," he says with a chuckle. "Remember that time he ordered a float and when the waiter showed up to get his food order, he just ordered another float?"

I throw back my head and laugh. "And then he puked both of them up on the side of 377 on the way home."

"Gross," Gwen says, laughing. "That is *so* Luke."

"It's this place," Wes says quietly when we've stopped laughing. "Michigan. It . . . it feels like him." His voice is so soft I almost don't hear him over the sounds of the birds flying by, the traffic on the road, the sound of my own heartbeat in my eardrums.

Wes is looking at me in this way that's telling me he wants me to agree with him. He wants me to tell him that I can feel Luke here, like he's haunting us. I look away from him and push up off my back.

"We need to get back on the road," I say, even though it's not going to make much of a difference. Ann Arbor is our next stop, and we're not that far away. I wait for them to dress, and then we all traipse back to the car.

I don't feel Luke like some spirit with unfinished business. I don't think he's watching us from Heaven or anything like that, sending us signs and signals to let us know that he loved us. I think he's dead. And I don't think any amount of driving across the country is going to bring back the dead.

In the car, Wes glances at his phone, clipped into a holder beside the steering wheel, and goes north on 75.

"Why are you going north?" Gwen asks, absently, using the visor mirror to get something out of her eye. "It's south to Chicago."

But Wes keeps driving. Beside me, Cade leans forward, his eyebrows pulled together, but Gwen just fidgets, putting the visor up and looking over at Wes.

"Wes?" she asks, and I see Wes glance at me in the rearview mirror. I can't look at him or at her or at anyone, really. We never should have waited so long to tell her. She glances over her shoulder at me, and even though I don't look at her, I can practically feel her looking at me. I can *feel* the moment she realizes what's happening.

"No," she says, snatching Wes's phone out of the holder and looking down at the screen. "We're not going to Ann Arbor."

"Gwen," Wes starts, but she cuts him off.

I can see panic in her eyes, wide and so white around her pupils. "Shut up. You guys don't just get to hijack this fucking trip without telling me. We're not going to Ann Arbor. We're not going to where he—"

Wes slams on his brakes, pulling to the side of the highway and turning on the hazard lights even as cars zoom around us, honking as they go.

"Did you guys think you could just decide without me?" she asks, looking around at all of us, and I feel bad for Cade because technically, he had nothing to do with this decision.

"You don't get to just make a decision like that," she growls at us. "It's where he died!" Gwen says, louder than I've ever heard her speak. Her eyes are glistening with tears, and I have to look away from her as she wipes them away. "I mean, this trip isn't about that. This trip is about getting out of Eaton. It's about experiencing the world. It's not about going where Luke did." She looks at Wes then at me. "Right?"

Without saying a word, I reach into my bag, where I've been keeping the map. I hold it out to her, and she just stares down at it. I can't tell what she's thinking. She leans against the door behind her, like she's too tired to hold herself up.

Wes takes the map from my hand and holds it out to Gwen. Gwen looks so confused, confused and angry, but she takes the map from Wes and opens it in her lap. For a second, I see an image of Luke bent over it, spread out on the dining room table in the time between when we got out of school and my parents got home from work. I push it away.

"What is this?" Gwen asks, her eyes roving over the whole thing, her hands trembling.

"It's a map," Wes says, and Gwen shoots him a look that makes his eyes go wide.

"I can see that, Wesley. Where the hell did it come from?"

Wes looks at me, shrugs, his eyes still wide.

"It came from us," I say, and when Gwen looks at me, I realize how confusing that sounds. "I just mean, we're the ones who put all the marks on it, me, Wes, and Luke. Like three years ago. It was just something stupid we were doing, but I guess Luke kept it. He must have taken it with him when he left."

"You found it with his stuff?"

When she asks that, it's hard to get over how much we've kept from her, so many secrets, so much information that's just been piling up. "Someone sent it to me. I got it the day of Luke's funeral." At least, that's when I noticed it on my desk. I have no idea how long it sat there before I noticed. The world has been just a haze for so long.

I wait for her to say something, but she's still just looking down at the map, so I keep talking. "Someone sent it to me from an address in Michigan. That's where we're going. It's not really about where Luke died. I just want to know who sent me this map. Who had it."

"I can't believe you," she says, her words barely even there. "I can't believe you just weren't going to tell me."

My eyes shoot back to Wes, but he's not looking at me. His eyes are trained on the floor. "We meant to tell you earlier," he says. "Well, kind of. We weren't going to tell you at all. I was afraid you wouldn't come. I was afraid if you found out this trip was about Luke, you'd get angry. And then we decided we *were* going to tell you, but then we forgot and then we were here and—"

She clutches the map in both hands. "You had this with you the whole time," she says between her teeth. "And this isn't even—" She stops and folds the map up. "This doesn't even have anything to do with me. If the three of you made this map then you should have come alone. You shouldn't have brought Cade and me with you."

At that, Cade's head comes up, and he looks at me. He was never upset about being left out of the loop, but I guess it's completely different for him.

Gwen's eyes sweep over all three of us, and then she throws open her door and slams it shut behind her, and I scramble to follow her out. The slam of a car door behind me tells me that either Cade or Wes followed, too, but I don't stop.

"Gwen," I call to her, but she's walking down the side of the highway, like any second now she's going to put out her thumb and hitchhike back home.

When she turns to look at me, her eyes ablaze, I can tell she's not interested in what I have to say. "I never should have come on this trip," she says. "I've spent the last year trying to separate myself from all this shit, and you just yanked me back into it."

"We wanted it to be about the trip for you," I say. I feel like I'm begging, and maybe I am. "We're still going to see places, experience things outside of Eaton."

"I don't care about any of that," she shouts. "I never cared about getting out of Eaton."

"Then why did you come?" I don't mean for it to sound accusatory. I don't mean for it to sound like I don't want her here.

She throws up her hands. "Because I thought you wanted me to! Wes said both of you wanted me to come! I guess I was stupid to believe that, too."

"No," I say, pleading again. "I wanted you to come." It's not the whole truth, but it's the truth now.

When Gwen looks at me again, I realize she's crying, tears pressing into all the crevices between her eyes and her chin. "I missed you," she says, like it's painful to say it. "There were days I missed you more than I missed Luke. When I lost Luke, I lost you, too, and that was hard. You were important to me, and then you were both gone, and that was hard." She sucks in a breath and wipes at her face.

"I missed you, too," I say, even though I didn't, not really, until just now, but it's like at this moment, I'm feeling a whole year's worth of missing her.

She takes a deep breath and looks out at the highway. Cars are racing past, and I want to reach out and pull her close, away from any potential danger. But I know Gwen doesn't need me to protect her. She can handle herself. She didn't need it when I hid the map from her, either.

She finally sighs and crosses her arms, turning toward me but walking by like I don't exist to get in the car. She pulls the door shut, and then it's just me and Wes, standing outside in the sun. He taps once on the hood and then shrugs.

"Ann Arbor?"

Chapter Eleven

We get to Ann Arbor after sunset and immediately check into a hotel room. But Gwen doesn't get in the elevator with the rest of us. She stares at the open doors, her arms crossed, and we all exchange glances, even as the elevator chimes to let us know the doors are about to close.

"Let's go for a walk," Wes says, stepping back out of the elevator to join her. He reaches out to brush her bangs away from her forehead. It's probably the gentlest thing I've ever seen Wes do, and it makes pain spear through me. I know things will probably be hard for them now. The door slides closed behind them, and like he was waiting for that, Cade stands closer to me, our shoulders pressing together.

The elevator rocks as we race to the fifth floor, and I watch the numbers light up as we move up, up, up.

"Are you okay?" he asks. I can see his reflection in the mirrored elevator doors, watching me. I look down at where Wes left his bag at my feet.

"Gwen is really upset."

"What about you?" he whispers. "What about how you feel?"

I crane my neck to look up at him. "I don't feel anything," I say.

He clamps his lips shut and doesn't ask me anything else. As soon as we're inside our room, I collapse onto one of the beds. I hear Cade laugh from the other side of the room. It hasn't gotten past me that we're currently alone in a hotel room, with no end to our privacy in sight, so I carefully keep from making eye contact with him while I roll over and pull my duffel bag onto the bed with me.

"Want to order pizza? Watch a movie?" he asks.

"Sure," I say, taking out my phone. "I can find a place to order from." But when the screen is completely black, I remember that I turned it off in Louisiana, remember what happened the last time I turned it on. "Actually, you should probably do that part." I tuck my cell phone in the pocket of my bag with the map.

Cade orders pizza and then reaches for his bag. "I'm going to take a shower while we wait," he mutters, and I look up to find him standing at the end of my bed, a change of clothes in his arms. "I smell like Wes's car."

"Which means that you smell like fast food tacos and feet."

Cade grimaces, and I smile at him. He looks like maybe he wants to say something else, but he just turns and locks himself in the bathroom.

———

Gwen and Wes don't show up while we're eating pizza or while we're watching *The Breakfast Club*, and eventually, I'm too tired to wait any longer. I shower, holding my face under the hot water. If Cade smelled like tacos and feet then I probably do, too, so I scrub with the hotel soap until I smell fresh.

As I throw on a T-shirt and a pair of shorts, I listen for the door out in the room to open, for Wes and Gwen to come in, for signs that Cade won't be the only one in the room when I step out of the bathroom, but I don't hear anything. Except I do hear something, and when I open the door, I realize it's soft music, playing over the speaker of Cade's phone.

I don't recognize the song, but it's the kind of song that seems like it was written just to lull you to sleep.

"What is this?" I ask, tossing my dirty clothes on the floor by my duffel bag and watching as Cade turns away from the window. His eyes drop to my legs, and I'm self-conscious suddenly, standing in front of him, feeling naked. What is it about pajamas that make a person feel so unclothed? I have to remember that Cade has seen me in my pajamas before, not to mention my underwear just a few hours ago.

Cade is wearing a shirt, and I'm thankful for that. My nerves are alive enough already without having to also deal with so much of his skin. He's wearing a T-shirt and basketball shorts, and it's a second before he answers me.

"Sufjan Stevens," he says. "Thought it might help us sleep. I'm not used to all this city noise."

I laugh. In Eaton, the only sounds at night are the trains and the cicadas, but I can hear the sounds of sirens, of music, of nightlife outside our hotel room window. I walk to his phone and turn the volume up, trying to drown out the noise even more. I turn to his bed and see a book right in the middle of the mattress. I reach out to grab it. It's a book about Napoleon.

I'm still holding it in my hands, feeling the heavy weight of it, when Cade moves behind me. I feel him settle just a little too close, feel his breath on the back of my neck. I drop the book on the bed and turn around to face him.

I can sense his hesitation in the way his eyes move over my face, the uncertainty painting a line between his eyebrows.

"It was because of Luke," I say, even though he didn't ask.

"What?" he says, his voice a whisper.

"Luke was the reason there was never another date. He's the reason I couldn't face you after that night." I know it's not really the truth. Luke can be blamed for a lot of things, but he can't be blamed for the choice I made to let Cade go. But his leaving, it did something to me, and it was enough to make me feel like I wasn't living a life that Cade could be a part of anymore.

"The night we went to the drive-in, that's the night that Luke left. He went while I was gone, and when I came back, I don't know, it's like everything changed. I couldn't even imagine trying to be happy after . . ." I shake my head because it sounds so stupid when I say it out loud. Why was it so hard for me to go back to life after that? Why did I have such a hard time remembering who I was without Luke?

"I kept telling myself that if I hadn't stayed out so late that night that I might have been able to stop him. I know that's not true, though. But it was hard to look at you, to remember where I was that night and what Luke was doing, and I was blaming you for something, which is just idiotic. So, I'm sorry."

Cade's eyes are still moving over me, and he finally takes a deep breath and says, "I always kind of suspected that might have something to do with it." He shrugs. "I know you needed time, but I also knew that if I could reach you somehow, maybe I could show you that, I don't know, that I'm still here. That I'm fine with waiting. That you're still the girl I've always liked, the girl I asked out to the drive-in, and I still want to be with that girl." He points at me. "This girl."

I drop my face into my hands. I was someone else before Luke left, always chasing Wes and Luke around, always wanting what Luke wanted and doing what he did, just like Cade said in the treehouse. "I already told you, I don't think I'm that girl anymore."

He pulls my hands away from my face. "Of course you are, Ellie. You're still you. Things are just a little different. Things change, people change, that doesn't mean you're not still you."

"I never should have pulled you into my shit."

"I'm pretty sure I pulled *myself* into your shit." He still has a hold of my wrists, and he runs his thumbs back and forth across my skin. "I know things are weird right now, but I'm not going anywhere. I'm here."

I tug my wrists from his hold, put a hand behind his neck, and rise up to kiss him. I'm afraid he'll hesitate, afraid he's not ready for this, but he kisses me back, soft and gentle and just the way it should have been that night on my front doorstep, one last good thing before everything fell apart.

I sigh against his lips, and then he's kissing me so completely that I grab his face, just trying to catch up to him. I feel flames across my skin. I wish I could absorb this moment, let this feeling swallow up everything.

A sound outside the room breaks through, like a wall between us, and we pull apart just as the door swings open and Gwen and Wes come into the room, talking loudly. It's as if we don't exist as the door slams shut and Gwen and Wes continue laughing about something. I take advantage of their inattention, climbing into the bed I'll share with Gwen and hunkering down under the covers. Maybe I can even pretend I've been asleep this whole time. *Hear you come in? No, I was fast asleep as soon as we got to the hotel.*

I close my eyes, listening to the rustling of clothes and discussion over who will take the shower first, and then the bathroom door closes, the water running again, and I peek. Wes sits on the edge of the bed beside mine and looks down at the phone on the nightstand, still playing Sufjan Stevens.

"What the hell is this?" he asks, looking down at the screen.

From the other side of the bed, over by the window, as far from me as he can be, Cade says, "It's just some music to help us sleep. The city is loud."

"Whatever you say, man," Wes says and then I hear the blankets rustle, and the next time I peek, Wes and Cade are both in bed, the blanket up to their chins.

I listen for a long time, until I hear the soft sound of Wes's snoring and Cade's deep breaths. And then the bathroom door opens, and Gwen emerges in a cloud of steam. I don't pretend to be asleep anymore. I sit up and watch her as she puts her old clothes in her bag and unwraps the towel from around her hair. She meets my eye as she shakes out her wet hair, but she doesn't say anything. She gets into the bed, but she keeps her back turned toward me, and I can't help but wonder why Wes is back in her good graces but I'm not.

"I was going to forgive him," she says, still facing away from me, and it takes me a second to realize she's talking about Luke, not Wes. After a long pause, she looks at me over her shoulder. "But he didn't care if I forgave him."

I don't know what to say to that, can't even begin to understand how she's felt for the last year, something so akin to what I've felt but also somehow the complete opposite.

"What do you think we're going to find in Dexter?" she asks, and while her voice isn't exactly gentle, it's not full of anger, either.

"I have no idea."

She turns over and pulls the blanket up. I don't lie down beside her, just watch her from where I'm sitting at the end of the bed. "No more secrets," she says quietly, and I'm honestly so relieved to hear her say this—because it's obviously a truce and because I've been so tired of the secrets—that I smile and agree.

"No more secrets."

———————

I can't sleep. I slept so much this morning, so much on the drive, and again at the lake, and now that I'm in an actual bed, my eyes are wide open, my heart pounding, every cell in my body attuned to the fact that we're here.

We're in Ann Arbor.

We're in the same city Luke was two weeks ago, and even though I told Wes I don't *feel* Luke here in Michigan, maybe it wasn't true. Maybe I do feel him, or feel something, something that makes the hair on my arms stand up, something that makes the air seem heavier, something that is probably one hundred percent my imagination but still keeps me from being able to rest. I sit up and press my head to my knees, my skin clammy.

For the last year, Luke has been this person that I knew was out there, somewhere, like a planet in the galaxy that some scientist tells you about but you don't see with your own eyes, so it might as well not exist. For the first few weeks after he disappeared, I thought I saw him everywhere.

Every time I turned a corner at J-Mart or even at Eaton High, I thought I saw him. I sat at a red light on Main Street long after it turned green, my eyes fixed on someone the same height as him, with the same pale skin and dark hair.

And then, after a while, he became like a myth. Maybe he never existed at all. Memories started to feel like something I made up, like scenes in a movie instead of something we actually experienced in real life. Eventually, people stopped talking about him. He stopped being the name in everyone's mouth. He wasn't the one who could do the most shots without getting sick at all the parties anymore; he wasn't the one who was charming all the teachers; he wasn't the one who was winning all the track meets. He was disappearing from everyone's minds, and it felt like I was the only one who still remembered.

———

When we get home from the Nova concert, I get straight in the shower, the way I do every time we come home from a concert. Concerts make me feel like I stink and like I'm covered in other people's germs. Getting into my fresh pajamas after a hot shower after a concert is pure bliss.

But when I get back to my room, Luke is sitting on the edge of my bed, his fingers laced between his knees, his head hanging low.

"What's wrong?" I ask him, shutting the door behind me and tossing my towel onto my desk chair. I sit down beside him, but he doesn't answer my question. He sets his head on my shoulder, and we're quiet for a long time.

"You're scaring me," I say, quietly, and he just nods.

"Could I sleep in here tonight? I'll shower first." The way he looks at me

is so strange. It's not very often that Luke isn't one hundred percent confident in himself. Every step he takes always seems to be a bold one, a sure one. It's something I've always admired about him. But right now, his eyes shine, and he's looking at me like he's pleading with me.

"Sure," I say because I want him to stop looking at me like that. I want him to look like normal Luke again.

He smiles and leaves the room, and a second later, I hear him shut the bathroom door in the hallway and start the shower. I turn off the light overhead and just leave on the bedside lamp as I crawl into bed. I have a queen, so it's not like we can't both fit comfortably, but when Luke comes back, in an old undershirt and a pair of basketball shorts, his hair dripping, he doesn't lay down with the expanse of the bed between us. He lays right beside me, his shoulder pressing into mine, and we stare up at the ceiling.

"When you graduate from Tate, I want to take you to Italy."

I smile up at the ceiling. "That sounds nice."

"We can walk around Venice and eat our weight in pasta and go to all the museums."

My eyes drift closed, and I imagine it, Italy with my big brother, with Wes and Gwen, too, probably, because they're all attached at the hip.

"We can ride in one of those riverboats and hike around the countryside. And we can visit the vineyards and eat pastries, and it'll be so amazing."

His voice, deep and soft, sends me to sleep.

———

It's four a.m. when I finally climb out of bed, my heart racing. I stand in the dark room for a minute, watch the rain crash against the window, watch lightning flash in the distance. It feels like the entire city of Ann Arbor is shrinking, compacting around me until there's nothing but me in this hotel room, trapped.

I take Wes's car keys from the nightstand, stick Luke's map in my back pocket, and sneak out of the hotel room. It's raining outside, but despite the never-ending nightmares, the way my body turns immediately to fight or flight when thunder crashes, this doesn't feel scary. It feels like a companion tonight.

I stride out to the car, throwing myself into the front seat and slamming the door shut behind me. I can't see anything out the front windshield. All I can see is the water sliding down the glass, waves and waves of it, so much water that it's almost comical. I don't turn the car on, even though it's chilly, even though my hands are trembling and goose bumps have sprouted along my wet arms.

I put my key in the ignition and then stop. I don't know what I would do, where I would go. It's the middle of the night, but I don't know if I can stay here anymore. I reach into my back pocket and pull out the map. It didn't get wet in my mad dash to the car, but my wet hands make the paper go soggy in some places. The corners are already bent, one of them torn a little, and I wipe my hands on my pants to try and dry them, but that only makes them wetter.

I press the tip of my finger to the spot on the map where Eaton should be, our town so tiny that it's not even a word, not even a dot on the map. You wouldn't even know it was there, sandwiched halfway between Dallas and Austin. I follow the dark red line that Luke marked, from Texas over to Louisiana, up to Missouri and through Indiana to Michigan. From there, my finger starts to find other places, the spot where I put a star in New York because I've always wanted to see a Broadway show, the place where Wes circled a little island off the coast of Florida where he wanted to spend a week sunbathing, all the places that we marked because we never thought this would be real.

The passenger-side door opens, the rain is loud for a split-second, and then someone drops into the seat beside mine.

"Shit," I gasp. "You scared me."

Water drips down Cade's face. "What are you doing out here?" He looks from the keys in the ignition to the map in my hand. "What are you doing, Ellie?" he asks again because Cade always seems to know what's going on in my head, always seems to understand, even when I can't.

Cade's not wearing anything but a baggy T-shirt and a pair of wet sweatpants. I start the car, switching the heat on because he's shivering. It's not nearly as warm in Michigan as it is in Texas. But he doesn't seem overly concerned about the temperature. His eyes shoot from the map in my hand to my face.

"Are you okay?" he asks.

I look down at the map, my wet finger marks all over it, soaking through. The easy answer is to tell him that yes, I'm okay. The not-so-simple answer is that I have no fucking clue. I don't know if I'm okay. I don't know if I'll ever be okay.

My hands are shaking, and Cade reaches out to take the map from me. He holds it so gently, like it's going to crumble in his hands. I feel like I'm drowning. I watch him fold up the map, all the words disappearing while I watch, and I feel the beast in my chest start to wake up, start to creep around, start to whisper things in my ear.

"It was supposed to be all of us."

When the map is folded, Cade hands it back to me, and I hold it in my open palms for a second before dropping it into my lap. "What was supposed to be all of us?"

I shake my head. "All of *us*. Me, Wes, and Luke. We made this map together. We were all supposed to go on this trip. We were all supposed to go together. Just because we forgot about it didn't mean we didn't want to go. He—" I suck in a breath, trying to steady myself. I have to let it go. I have to just let it go.

Cade is shaking his head, and my hands quake on the steering wheel, so I grip it hard. "He was supposed to take you with him," he says, so gently, echoing the words I was thinking. "He left you behind."

I snap, slamming my hand on the console between us. "Stop it! If you think you're helping me, you're not. You didn't know him, Cade. You don't even know what you're talking about. Luke was—"

He cuts me off again. "He was human. He made a mistake. You can say that. It's okay."

My hands tremble with whatever is creeping along just under my skin. I feel like any second I'll burst, but I grit my teeth.

"I know he made a mistake. I know he was human," I say. Why is he talking like I don't know what Luke did?

"Ellie," he says, and when I look at him, he's looking down at my hands, where they're curled around the steering wheel, so tight that my skin has turned white around my knuckles. I pull my hands away, my skin sticking slightly to the vinyl, and drop them into my lap.

"I don't know what—" I can't even finish the sentence. There are a million words I could use. I don't know what to feel. I don't know how to deal with this. I don't know if it's *okay* to be . . . whatever I am. I take a deep breath, stamp down everything rising inside, just like I have for the last year, just like I have since the day Luke died, clamping it down inside until I can be unfeeling again.

But it's not so easy this time. This time, this thing I've been keeping inside just breaks through again, just demands attention. I gasp for breath. Why did he have to leave? Why couldn't he call me? How could he just leave us all behind? Who does that to their little sister? Who just abandons them? Who does that?

"I don't know," Cade says, and I realize I've said it all out loud. He's watching me, his body turned toward me, one hand fisted against the glovebox and the other holding onto the console between us,. "But it's okay to be mad."

I'm already shaking my head. "I can't be mad at Luke. I can't be. He's dead. I can't be mad." I keep saying it, over and over, like that'll make it true. Whatever was burning inside me seconds ago fizzles out, a low simmer in my stomach. "I just want him to come back."

"I'm sorry," Cade says, loud enough to be heard over the storm. "I'm sorry he left. I'm sorry he died. I'm sorry." His voice breaks. "But it's okay to be angry at him."

"He was my best friend," I say, the words hitting the windshield and coming back at me, lifeless and flat. "We were going to travel the world together. We were going to go to Tate and then move away from my parents together. He was always going to be there, always." I know I should stop talking, that I should force all my words back down inside myself where they belong.

But I can't stop. I can't stop moving, can't stop thinking, can't stop wanting the future he promised me. Wanting the life we were going to have. Wanting my brother back.

I cover my face with my hands. "Why didn't he want to be my brother anymore?" I say around the tears climbing up my throat. They won't be contained this time, and then they're everywhere. In my hands, on my shirt, coating my face and my chin and my neck. And when Cade reaches across the console to hold me, they cover him, too.

I'm so angry. I'm so fucking angry. And it's burning away everything in me until there's nothing left. And it's sadness that's gnawing at every piece of my exposed flesh. And I can't fucking breathe because I don't understand why.

Why he couldn't wait for me to finish school so we could go together. Why he couldn't call me from the road and tell me what was going on. Why we were best friends one minute and complete strangers the next. Why he moved to Ann Arbor and stayed and lived here instead of carrying on with the trip that took him away from me in the first place.

And against Cade's shirt, I start to scream. I don't know where the screams come from. They seem to be coming from my brain and my rib cage and my kneecaps. It's like my whole body is screaming, and I'm watching it happen from the outside, watching me squeeze my eyes shut and scream until my throat is raw and I can feel Cade's fingers leaving bruises where he's holding me too tight.

I go limp when I'm finally empty, like being asleep while also being awake. Cade still holds me, but he doesn't say anything, and I'm thankful for that. Nothing he could say would make it better, so he doesn't say anything.

And we sit there, the rain beating on the windows, harder and harder until the world around us disappears into an ocean.

——————————

I jerk awake when someone taps on the window. It's not raining any-more, and Cade and I have both dozed off in our seats, not touching. I'm facing him, watching him as his eyes open and his body stretches, but when I turn to look over my shoulder, I see Wes standing at my window, and I realize I can see him really well because it's bright out, the sun high in the sky. I reach over and roll down the window.

"You know, we paid for beds," Wes says, his mouth almost a smile but not quite.

"God, sorry," I say, straightening up in my seat and holding in a groan when my stiff muscles protest. "I guess we fell asleep."

"You know, if you guys wanted your own room, you could have just said so." His eyes shoot between Cade and me. He raises his eyebrows, and I groan. I roll up the window, until Wes is forced to remove his face or else be caught in it.

In the passenger seat, Cade rubs at his eyes. "Damn. I can't believe we fell asleep." He sighs and then he looks over at me, and I know he wants to ask me if I'm okay. I sense the words, lingering on the tip of his tongue. But instead, he says, "What was Wes talking about?"

"Nothing," I say quickly, taking the keys from the ignition and the map from where it's fallen between my seat and the console. I stick both of them in my pockets and push open the door.

Wes is sitting on the hood of the car, and when he stands up, there's a wet spot on his butt that makes me laugh.

"Gwen is worried," Wes says, all of his previous humor gone. We follow him back into the hotel, past people eating breakfast and the smiling man at the front desk, straight into the elevator.

"Where the hell were you?" Gwen asks when we open the hotel room door. It's almost eight, and both Gwen and Wes are packed and fully dressed, ready to go. Cade and I come in and sit down on the bed I shared with Gwen.

"We went for a drive," I say, glancing over at Cade. He sends me an I-won't-tell-if-you-don't look.

Wes looks like he still has something to say, but instead, he snatches up his duffel bag from where it sits on the desk, and I feel, immediately, what he's feeling: an agitated urgency. Keep moving, and you won't feel anything. I learned this morning that that doesn't work. I thought running away from Eaton would keep the monster inside me at bay, and it didn't.

Down in the lobby, we wait as Wes checks out of the room and then we file out the front door, without bothering to partake in the hotel's free breakfast. I trail behind, my eyes on the strange shapes that line the rug by the automatic sliding door. I'm having trouble focusing. Everything feels like a dream, like I stepped out of reality and into someone else's life. None of this makes sense anymore.

When we're all packed into the car, I think about sitting in the driver's seat before the sun came up, sleeping in it with Cade, holding the map in my hands with nothing but hysteria in my brain.

I'm not sure I'm ready for whatever is next.

Chapter Twelve

"Is this the place?" Gwen asks, looking out the window, but I don't answer her. I don't know if I could, even if I wanted to.

The address in Dexter is a little one-story house that doesn't fit in with the rest of the street. Every other house is two stories with add-ons and large carports. It's like the whole world was built around what was left of the previous one, and all that remains of the old world is this house, with mulberry branches sagging across the front yard.

Cade is beside me, like a bodyguard, ready to rescue me if I lose my nerve.

"Let's go," I tell everyone in the car, not even able to look at them. If I do, I won't be able to do what I came here to. I walk straight to the house, standing at the end of the path that leads up to the door. Gwen and Wes press in on either side of me.

I stare at the house for a long time. There's no car in the driveway, but there's also no FOR SALE sign in the yard. Did Luke live here? And if he did, did he have a roommate? Maybe his roommate sent the map. Maybe the person who sent me the map isn't even here. What if the house is empty, waiting for someone else to move in? Or worse, what if someone else already lives here? It can't take that long to find new renters for a house, right? What if I knock and someone who doesn't even know who Luke is answers the door?

Will I regret it if we came all this way and didn't knock?

Because it's all I have left. This is all I have left: these stupid stops he made on the way here and then something concrete, some person who knew Luke, who got a hold of that map, and knew that it should come to me when Luke died. Maybe that person is inside this house. And maybe they're not.

I'm still staring at the door when I notice the little white cross in the front window. It looks like a living room window from the outside, and the cross is so small, barely visible, just two white strips of paint no longer than the palm of my hand. Without thinking, I bend down and run my finger along the vertical line. I can feel the texture of the paint, and that tells me it was painted on from right where I'm standing. I straighten up and walk back to them, watching me. Gwen's eyes never leave the cross.

When I knock, it seems to echo around the entire neighborhood. There are no people out jogging or walking their dogs. No cars driving by. It's just this house and us, early in the morning.

We wait a long time, but nobody answers. I knock again, that same echo-y knock from before, and still, nothing. Whoever lives here is either not home or not answering. Maybe even still asleep.

"I guess that's it?" Wes asks, gesturing toward the front door. I turn to look at him and Gwen, and I can see in their desperate eyes that they're expecting me to give them an answer. They're waiting for me to make the next move, either to get back in Wes's car and drive on to Chicago or not. I can't let this trip be for nothing.

I walk along the side of the house, around to the back. There's a back door, with a screen in front of it. I open the screen door and knock.

Nothing.

I decide to take my chances.

"What are you doing?" Wes hisses at me when I check to see if the door is unlocked. "Are you fucking insane? We don't even know whose house this is."

I still don't answer him. If I open my mouth, I'm afraid I'll lose it like I did this morning in the car. That I'll start talking about what Luke did to us, and how we deserve better than the way he left us, than the way he moved on without looking back. So I keep my mouth closed and keep looking for a way to fix this.

The back door isn't unlocked, so I start looking for open windows. The window over the kitchen sink is locked and so is the window that looks into a dining room, which I can tell only because the curtains are wide open. I keep feeling around the house even as Gwen and Wes continue to ask hysterical questions.

"Who lives here?" Gwen hisses at me.

"Are you seriously about to break into someone's house?" Wes demands.

Cade stays quiet, following my every move.

When I find an open window, covered with plastic blinds from the inside, I look over at Cade while I push it open. "You're a bad influence on me," I tell him. His eyes are wary as he watches me. This isn't the same as what we did at that theater in Shreveport, and we both know it.

The window opens all the way, and I reach in and push the blinds aside before crawling into the room. Luckily, there's no furniture under the window, so I crawl into the room and turn to yank on the cord to pull up the blinds before Cade scrambles in behind me.

"Ellie," Gwen says from outside, and when I stick my head out the window, she and Wes are still standing there, their arms crossed. "Ellie, I don't think this is such a good idea."

Wes doesn't say anything. He has his jaw clenched tight.

I look down at them, and I know I can do this without them, but this doesn't just feel like mine anymore. I think whatever we find here belongs to them, too, just like this trip belongs to them, too. "Guys," I tell them. "I'm not going to make you climb through the window. But I need you with me. Please."

Gwen looks at Wes, and he looks back at her, and then she moves forward and throws her legs over the windowsill.

The window we come in is the living-room window. The house is bright from the sunlight flooding into it, and I glance around. There's no evidence of Luke here, just frilly throw pillows and tan furniture. The living room feeds right into the open kitchen, the dining area off to the side. It doesn't even look like Luke could have possibly decorated this place. The walls in the kitchen are bright red, and the dining table has a bowl of fruit in the middle. The furniture looks old, and I imagine a family living here, with antiques that have been passed down for generations.

"What the hell is this place?" Wes asks, and I walk back into the living room to join him.

"I don't know," I finally say, and I mean it this time because I'm pretty sure that Luke was never here. He couldn't have been. I'm ready to admit defeat, admit that someone else must have moved into this house recently and there's nothing of Luke here, and then my eyes catch on something sitting atop a shelf of the entertainment center.

It's a picture frame.

And inside is a picture of Luke and a girl I've never seen before, smiling at the camera, looking like they just won the lottery.

For a second, it's like everything inside me is frozen. But then I move toward the frame, my hands shaking as I take it off the shelf and look down at the glossy image. My eyes move over him first: his familiar smile, made straight by braces, the round nose he got from our dad, skin so white he burned outside in minutes. And then I look at the girl, their faces pressed together, their eyes shining, their happiness obvious.

My stomach turns, and I drop the frame onto the carpet. I can see the open bathroom door at the end of the hall, a pale blue bathroom with the rising sun shining in, and I rush for it, slamming the door in time to throw up in the toilet.

"Ellie?" Cade's voice filters in through the door. He tries the handle, and I press my back against it. I know he can open it if he wants to, but he stops trying. I almost feel like I can hear him breathing on the other side.

I take a deep breath, but the world is spinning. I open my eyes, and there he is, scattered all over the countertop. He's in the cologne on the counter, the bottle of aspirin by the sink, the tube of toothpaste, the same brand he always used.

I turn and open the door and suddenly, I'm on a rampage. Luke is everywhere I look, and I can't believe I didn't see it the second we came in through that window. He's in the guitar on a stand at the end of the hallway; he's in the Nova poster on the wall; he's in the way the carpet smells.

I can feel Cade's eyes on me as I move into the kitchen and throw open cabinets. His favorite cereal, his favorite brand of soda, his favorite flavor of chips.

I spin around to find that Cade is approaching me, slowly, like I'm a rabid animal, and honestly, at that moment, that's what I feel like—an animal in a cage, ready to bite if someone comes near. So, I rush around him, my eyes focused on the hallway. By process of elimination, I can guess which door opens to the master bedroom.

Inside, the room is dark, the curtains pulled closed. I don't turn on the light. I don't need to. I can make out everything in the room by the light of a nightlight beside the bed, and I head straight for the closet. When I open it, the scent of Luke is like a tidal wave, and it's so strong that I'm paralyzed.

"Ellie." It's Cade's voice. He's opened the curtains, sunlight flooding in, and when I turn to face him, I don't see him at all.

One wall is covered in Nova posters, pictures of Jack Olsen rocking out on stage, gripping his guitar for dear life. There's a desk with a computer on it, and I know it's his, recognize the stickers covering the top, band stickers that he collected at merch tables over the years.

I feel something crawl up my throat, but I try to ignore it as I turn to the wall by the desk. There are pictures there. Glossy photographs are taped to the wallpaper. No frames, just little squares of scotch tape on the four corners of every picture.

The pictures I see first are of Luke and the girl from the framed picture in the living room. Pictures of them lying in bed, smiling sleepily up at the camera. Pictures of them in the park, wherever that is. Pictures of them at some romantic restaurant.

But as I move to the outer pictures, the ones bracketing those photos, I see more familiar faces. Wes, smiling at the camera begrudgingly with a controller in his hand. My face, the three of us on the Ferris wheel at the carnival, when he whispered in my ear to keep me calm. The three of us laughing at some joke that I can't remember now as my mother snaps a picture. Luke and me at a Nova concert when I was thirteen.

The monster crawls around in my stomach, but I don't know what he's looking for anymore. My eyes flit from picture to picture, and only one thought goes through my head again and again.

"He had a whole life here." I can feel Cade watching me. I can feel him inching closer to me, but I don't move away. "He left us, and he came here, and he started a whole new life, like none of us even existed anymore." The words scrape their way out of my throat, painful and raspy.

My eyes catch on another photo. This one isn't taped to the wall. It's in a small black frame on the nightstand. It's a picture of Luke and me. It was the night he graduated, and everyone wanted him to go to their parties, all his friends and his fans. But we went bowling instead, me and him and Mom and Dad, and ate so much junk food that we made ourselves sick. I want to smash the picture. I want to watch the glass break into tiny pieces, but I fist my hands by my sides instead.

"He's not coming back," I say. I can't even explain why I say it. I can't explain why, in this moment, it feels real. For the first time, it's real. Luke isn't just gone. He's not in another state. He's not somewhere I can't see him. Luke is nowhere. Luke took his last year from us, and now I'll never get it back.

I'll never get *him* back.

And then my knees give out. All of the adrenaline that's been holding me upright for two weeks finally dissipates, and the only thing keeping me from collapsing is Cade's arms.

"Ellie." This time it's just a whisper in my ear, as he wraps his arms around me like a snake. But his arms are the only things keeping me breathing.

"Let's go," he says against my ear, his breath warm. I haven't noticed until now how deep his voice is, soothing. How tired I am. How hot my face is, like the sun is shining directly on it, and it takes a second to realize it's hot from the tears.

"Come on, Ellie." I let Cade usher me out of the bedroom, but in the hallway, Gwen is standing against the wall, one hand against her stomach and the other pressed to her mouth.

I stop in front of her, forgetting about the pictures in Luke's room and the scent of him in every inch of the house and the pain that's radiating all the way from the backs of my eyelids down to the balls of my feet.

The full force of what I've done hits me. I brought her into this house without any way to warn her of what would be inside. But I never, for even a second, thought there would be pictures on the walls of Luke and another girl. I never would have brought her here if I thought that was what we were going to find.

I open my mouth to apologize, Cade's arms still surrounding me, but the look on Gwen's face, horror and shock and sadness, makes me feel like I'll crumble. She has tears streaming down her face.

And when she finally speaks, I guess I'm waiting for understanding, for something that'll help us both survive, but she says, "I can't do this."

I try to imagine this scenario from her point of view. Her dead ex-boyfriend's little sister, who she didn't see for almost a year, drove her to Michigan and snuck her into a house that just happened to be the house that her dead ex-boyfriend shared with his new girlfriend.

"I'm sorry," I say, but she's already walking away. I watch her throw open the front door and rush out to the car. Wes watches her for a second, and I realize he's crying, too. The tears streak down his face, and he sniffs once, wiping his hand across his mouth, before taking off after her. And while I watch, the car pulls away.

"Where are they going?" Cade asks, his eyes on the open doorway.

But I don't know. And I don't know if it even really matters. I walk to the front door and shut it, leaning against it. The room is spinning, and I don't know how to make it stop.

"Come here," Cade says. He's gripping the kitchen counter, and I go to him because I don't know how else to steady myself. I don't know how else to process where I am, what I've seen here.

In the kitchen, Cade puts his arms around me, and I let my arms hang by my sides. I'm too exhausted even to try.

"I'm an awful person," I say, and Cade sighs.

"Ellie, you didn't know."

I squeeze my eyes shut for a minute and then open them, looking at the refrigerator, at all the things scrawled across it.

"Ellie," Cade says, but then I process what I'm looking at. I pull away from him, gently move him out of the way.

Luke's fridge is covered in magnets, holding up ticket stubs, pictures of him and the red-headed girl that are all over the house, and right in front of me, a black and white print out. A sonogram photo.

I'm still staring at it, my brain stuck on the little white lines, unable to formulate a response, when someone knocks on the door. Cade's hand rests on my arm, and I turn around to face him as someone knocks again, louder this time. Cade walks slowly and quietly to the front of the house and tries to look out through the blinds without touching them.

And then a voice through the door.

"Someone in there?"

Cade backs away from the door and looks at me over his shoulder. "It's the police."

Chapter Thirteen

We can't even try to make a run for it. Gwen and Wes took the car, and it's not like we're going to try to get away from the cops on foot when they have a car.

"Shit," I say because I don't know what to do.

Cade's eyes are flitting around, like he's trying to figure something out, and then there's another knock. This time at the back door.

"Shit," Cade says. We walk to the back door together. We'll just explain the situation, right? We can tell the cop that Luke used to live here, tell him . . . God, no. I can't tell him that Luke is dead. I don't even know that the words would make it all the way out of my mouth. And none of it matters anyway. We've been reported missing. He'll figure it out, and we'll be shipped back to Texas.

"Out of options," Cade says, and I nod, agreeing with him.

Cade opens the door, and standing in the doorway is a cop that looks completely unamused. He looks at us with a blank stare and his hands on his hips.

"I'm going to need you to step outside," he says, taking a step back from the door to give us space.

Cade lets me walk out first and then follows close behind me. My nerves are going haywire, sending messages to my brain to run, to get away from this any way I can.

"Is there a problem?" I ask in my smallest voice.

The cop scoffs. "The neighbors saw you and three other people sneaking in through a window."

I deflate when he says this. There's no getting out of it now. We're busted. We're going to get arrested, and they're going to call my parents, oh God, they're going to call Cade's grandmother, and she'll probably forbid him from seeing me ever again, which I guess is really a good thing, at least for him.

The cop looks over my shoulder, back into the house. "Where are the other two?" he says, hands still planted on his hips.

"They—" Cade starts, but I cut him off.

"It was just the two of us." I glance at Cade, trying to convey to him that he has to shut up about Gwen and Wes. I know the law. If we're minors, reported missing, Gwen and Wes could be accused of kidnapping us.

The cop sets his jaw. "The person who called said he saw four. *Where are the other two?*"

"You can search the house. I swear, it's just the two of us." I'm infinitely grateful that I'm able to tell the truth and that Gwen and Wes took off, even if the way it happened still sits heavy on me.

The cop eyes me distrustfully, and then footsteps sound on the dirt road on the side of the house, and someone appears. It's a small redheaded girl, with an apron tied around her middle, but it's not enough to hide the bulge of her stomach, and when she sees the three of us standing by her back door, her eyes go wide.

"What's going on?" she asks, her eyes moving over all of us, and I feel like someone just turned me into a concrete statue. I can't move, can't speak, can't blink. And when her eyes fall on me, I stop breathing, too. I don't know what to acknowledge first, the fact that the girl standing in front of me is the same girl from all the photos inside the house, the fact that she is very obviously pregnant, or the fact that she's looking at me like she knows exactly who I am.

"Ellie?"

When she says my name, I flinch. Even though I know she knows me, know immediately that she's the one who sent me Luke's map, I'm still not expecting her to say my name like this, like we've known each other for a long time.

The cop looks between us. "You know these people?" he asks. "Because your neighbor said—"

"It's fine," she says, looking away from me finally, and I feel like I can breathe again as soon as her pale eyes aren't on me anymore. "False alarm."

The cop scowls at her and then at me and then rolls his eyes. He doesn't say another word before walking around the side of the house that the girl came from. As soon as he's gone, she turns to me.

"I recognize you from the pictures," she says, which is weird because I, of course, recognize *her* from the pictures. I'm distracted by how unbelievably pretty she is in real life, with big blue eyes and freckles across her nose, and a glow that probably has something to do with the baby in her stomach.

When I still just stare at her, unable to fathom in my mind what's going on, she says, "I'm so sorry. I'm Chloe. God, of course you don't know who I am." She holds out her hand to me, and I'm not sure what to do, so I shake it, even though my entire arm is numb. She shakes Cade's hand, too, but I can't watch it.

"Do you want to come inside?" Chloe asks us.

Chloe.

Something about knowing her name makes me finally come awake, and suddenly the only thing I can see is her belly, protruding into the space between us.

"Is it his?"

Chloe's eyes shoot to me. She looks like she can't decide what she's going to say, how she's going to answer this question, and then, as if I never spoke, she asks, "Are you hungry? I can get us free food at the diner where I work." Without waiting for us to answer, she marches over to the back door, slams it closed, and locks it.

What do you say to your dead brother's pregnant girlfriend when you just met five minutes ago? I sit in Chloe's front seat, the air conditioner blowing directly on my sweaty face, wishing I was in the back with Cade.

I don't say anything. I don't say anything because I have a million questions sitting on the tip of my tongue, and absolutely none of them will come out. I can't even decide which one is the most important.

"Are you cool enough?" Chloe asks, reaching forward to adjust the blower level.

"Yes," I squeak out, the word high-pitched and unrecognizable. When I glance over my shoulder at Cade, he smiles reassuringly at me.

Sal's is a minuscule diner in Ann Arbor that smells like vanilla ice cream and coffee. We pick a booth against the front windows, the sunshine shining brightly in at us, almost blinding.

"Chloe," the waitress says when she makes it to our table. The diner is full of people ready for their pancakes and coffee, and I'm just ready to get out of here because I can't even process this life that I've stepped into. "I thought you went home."

Chloe waves the girl off. "I'm just hungry. Can you bring me some hash browns? And, um, this is Luke's sister, Ellie. And her, um . . ."

She motions at Cade, who smiles up at the waitress. "I'm Cade. It's nice to meet you." I'm in awe at how easy it is for him to push aside everything that's happened in the last hour in order to be polite to this stranger.

The waitress, whose name tag says "Charlotte," looks at us with wide eyes, and I really wish Chloe hadn't told her I was Luke's sister. It's like being back in Eaton the day he died all over again. My cheeks heat, and I avoid her eyes by pretending to examine the menu. I can't bring myself to smile at her the way Cade did, especially not now that I can feel sympathy coming off her in waves.

"Order whatever you want," Chloe says without looking at us, and I realize that the waitress is already pouring her a cup of coffee, the word *decaf* written on a strip of orange plastic on the carafe.

"Some toast?" Cade says, like a question, and it makes something go warm inside me. Everything in this world is strange and confusing, but Cade is something familiar, a little piece of home, and even though I know I probably shouldn't, I cling to that. Because somehow I have ended up adrift in Michigan, a place I don't know, with people I don't know, and I reach over and take Cade's hand. He looks at me, but then he just squeezes my hand under the tabletop.

"For you?" Charlotte asks. Charlotte looks like the kind of person who always covers your shift when you ask her to, the kind of person who always answers her phone, the kind of person who cries over other people's misfortunes.

"Just some orange juice, please." I don't actually want anything. The thought of eating just reminds me of my dinner coming back up in Chloe's toilet. Luke's toilet. My stomach roils again, but I also don't want to be rude, especially after Chloe drove us here, all the way from Dexter.

Charlotte tucks her pad back into her pocket, the pad that she didn't have to use because all we ordered was hash browns, toast, and orange juice, but she doesn't walk away. She puts her hand on the table, her fingers spread out against the Formica, and I look up at her, her head blocking the fluorescent light shining down on us.

"I'm very sorry for your loss," she says.

There are moments in my life I can remember that don't feel real: when I hit the brakes too hard on my bike and catapulted over the handlebars, when we got into Luke's car one morning before school to find it had been broken into and ransacked, when I walked into the kitchen one evening to find my parents arguing menacingly in hushed tones.

When I look back on those moments, they feel like they happened to someone else.

When Charlotte says this to me, it feels like it's happening to someone else, like I'm watching it happen from a stool by the bar, and it has nothing to do with me or my life.

She doesn't wait for a response, and I'm thankful because I have nothing to offer right now but vocal cords that won't budge. When she's gone, I realize that I'm clutching Cade's hand so hard that my palm is sweating, so I loosen my hold. Cade doesn't let me go.

"I'll tell you anything you want to know," Chloe says, her voice quiet. "I know this whole thing has probably been . . . shocking."

"I want to know everything," I say, steamrolling over the end of her sentence. I am at once eager and terrified. I *do* want to know everything, but I also want to hide myself from all of this. I want every detail, and I also want to go on knowing nothing. I want the truth, but I also want her to lie if the truth is something that's too hard to hear.

"I feel like I know everything about you, so it's only fair that you know everything, too. Where should I start?" Chloe asks, herself not us, looking down at the tabletop, spreading her hands out across it like she's about to explain to us a very elaborate math equation on its surface.

"Who are you?" I ask, and I almost look at Cade to confirm that the words even came out of my mouth because I can't remember making my mouth move, but it was definitely my voice.

Chloe's eyes shoot to me—finally—and she bites her lip. "Luke was my boyfriend. I, uh, I work here, at this diner. We worked here together."

"Luke worked here?"

She nods, and then she points to something over her shoulder, and there on the wall, right by the kitchen entrance, is a framed photograph that I never would have noticed if she hadn't pointed it out. Luke smiles out from the picture, looking proud, in a red T-shirt with a name tag pinned to it. *Employee of the Month*, the writing across the top of the frame says. It's so much the complete opposite of the photo they had on display at his funeral that my breath catches. He looks so happy, his cheeks all puffed out in a huge smile, and I find it startling how Luke seems to exist everywhere in this place just like he existed everywhere in

Eaton.

Charlotte returns with my orange juice, but I know if I try to swallow it now, I'll just choke. She leaves my glass and disappears again. A second later, she puts a plate of toast in front of Cade and hash browns in front of Chloe. The smell of the potatoes makes my stomach turn.

"Are you the one that sent me the map?" I already know the answer, but I want confirmation since it's the reason I'm here in the first place.

Chloe is sipping at her coffee, but she pulls it away from her mouth when I ask her this, like it burned her. "Oh, my God, yes. I forgot about the map. Yes, I sent that to you. I thought Luke would want you to have it. He told me all about that trip." The corners of her mouth turn up. I don't know why. "Luke was always talking about it. And, um, about you, Ellie." She gestures toward me, like I don't know who I am. Maybe I don't. "He told me about leaving Texas and going on this trip that he planned a long time ago—"

"That *we* planned."

Her eyes shoot to me, and whatever trace of a smile there was is gone now. "Right. I know. You and Luke and Luke's best friend . . ." She trails off like she's trying to remember.

"Wes," Cade says.

She nods. "Wes. Luke talked about him a lot, too."

I throw my hands up, waving them around, trying to get her to just stop for a second. She's moving too fast. "How did you even know Luke? None of this makes sense. Ann Arbor wasn't in the plan."

Chloe nods, and she laces her fingers together on the tabletop, like we're in a business meeting. "Luke said he came here because he wanted to see all the Great Lakes. He was on his way to Lake Huron. He stopped to get something to eat and . . ." She gestures again. I want words. Why are words so hard for her? As soon as I think it, I feel guilty. I'm pushing her to talk about this when it took me a whole year just to tell Cade about the night Luke left. Do I really have any right to hurry her along?

She sighs and fiddles with her coffee cup.

"I was working the night shift. We're a twenty-four-hour diner, and I always take the midnight to eight because I'm kind of an insomniac, and I sleep weird hours, so I don't mind taking the night shift." When she says this, I notice the bags under her eyes. She must have just worked that shift before she found us with a cop behind her house. "People always tip better because they assume you're being forced into working the crap shift."

She takes a sip of her coffee, and I feel that same urgency, like I want her to tell me the whole story without taking a breath.

"So I was working the night shift," she says when she's put her coffee cup back down. "And it's three in the morning, and this boy waltzes into the diner like he owns the whole world." She sighs again, and I notice she's smiling again, too, down at the table. "Mostly what you get at three in the morning is tired truck drivers who want too much coffee and too much bacon and people who just got off long overnight shifts. Cleaners, stockers, people like that. Sometimes people who just got in on a red-eye in Detroit, on their way home from business trips or whatever. I like to ask people where they came from, where they're going. But there was never anyone like Luke."

She stops, takes a deep breath. "I'm not much of a romantic. I don't believe in love at first sight or any of that but . . ." She shrugs. "It just happened. One minute I'm serving him waffles and scrambled eggs, and the next minute, it's the end of my shift, and I'm sitting across from him in that booth, telling him my whole life story. And he told me his, too. About how he left everything behind in Texas because he didn't want to live in the same place his whole life. He said he didn't want to be another Eaton High School cliché, working at the J-Mart at forty and sending his kids to the same schools he went to."

Fuck, she sounds just like Luke. All the same things he's been saying to me since we were kids, when we realized that all the adults we knew in town had lived there their whole lives, all Eaton High and Tate alumni. I believed every words she said before, but now that I've heard this, it feels real. It feels true. And that knot forms in my throat again.

"My parents moved us around a lot," Chloe says. "When I graduated high school, I moved here for a guy." She rolls her eyes. "That didn't really work out. And by then, my parents had just separated, so my dad moved out here with me. So I don't really know what it's like to want to leave like he did. I just wanted to stay somewhere."

I clear my throat, clear away the knot. "How old are you?"

She stops with such a surprised look on her face, like she forgot I was here. "Nineteen."

Nineteen.

I can't imagine being pregnant at nineteen. At nineteen, I fully intend to be at Tate, probably still working at Books and Things. But a mom? I don't really mean to, but I can't keep from looking over at Cade, and when I catch him looking back, I blush and focus on Chloe again, sending a little nod so she'll know to continue even though I feel, now, like everything is moving too fast. In his place, I would have been in a panic, and yet I think of all the pictures of the two of them in their house. They were so happy.

"He told me he decided to stay in Ann Arbor after that night. And he came in every night after that, always at three in the morning, staying until I got off work." She shrugs. "It was kind of a whirlwind after that. I found out about the baby, and we got the house, and . . ." She doesn't finish her sentence. Because she doesn't have to. I know what comes next in the story.

Luke dies, and Chloe is left here on her own.

"Who's going to help you take care of the baby?" Panic settles low in my stomach. There's a piece of Luke still on this planet, and I can't even believe it. Even with the evidence in front of me in the form of Chloe's swollen tummy, this is the part of the story that still doesn't feel real. How can Luke be having a baby when he's not even here? He's going to be a dad, and he won't even be alive to see it.

She shrugs. "My dad. It'll probably just be us." She rubs her stomach with so much fondness in her eyes that I have to look away.

"He wasn't going to tell me," is all I can say. I feel like shit as soon as I say it. This isn't about me. She's going to have a baby, by herself. But the only words going through my mind, over and over are the ones I've already said. "He wasn't going to tell me."

"He was," Chloe says. "He just didn't know how. But he was going to tell you. He talked about you all the time, I swear it. You were his favorite person in the world."

"Then why?" I say, my voice swallowed up by the sounds of plates smacking together and people all over the diner having loud conversations. "Why did he leave me behind? Why didn't he tell me he was leaving? Why didn't he ask me to come with him?"

"Because he knew you would."

Cade squeezes my hand hard, and I don't even realize that my hand has gone limp.

"Look, I'm not going to pretend I know everything about you or about you and Luke. I only know what he told me. That he really loved you, but that he had to make his own decisions without worrying about you. He knew you'd be fine with whatever you chose to do with your life."

"Are you saying he was never going to come back home?"

Chloe's mouth hangs open. Maybe because she thinks she's said too much, maybe because she thought I knew. Maybe because she doesn't even really know. And it isn't fair for me to expect Chloe to know. I know that talking to her, no matter how close she was to him, isn't going to give me answers. Chloe isn't Luke. And only Luke could understand why he did what he did.

"I don't know why I'm here," I finally say, and I guess it's the truth. Maybe I don't want it to be, but it is. I thought finding out who sent the map would solve everything, but it doesn't.

I hear a gasp, and when I look up, I see that Chloe is crying. She wraps her arms around her middle and catches her breath. When she speaks, the words are thick and broken apart by the tears in her throat. "We were so busy living in a world by ourselves that I guess I never really stopped to think that you might be hurting without him. He always made it sound like you were better off without him, like you all were. He was convinced you would be so happy, even if he was gone. I think he really believed that, so I guess I believed it, too."

I feel a lump rise in my throat, but I force it down. I will not cry in front of Chloe. And I won't cry *again* in front of Cade. He's been silent the whole time, and when I look up at him, his eyes aren't on me or on Chloe. They're on that framed photo on the wall of Luke. Employee of the month. That's not even surprising. Luke was always the hardest worker at every job he had: the four months he spent stocking shelves at J-Mart, the summer he spent mowing lawns, the year he spent waiting tables. Managers loved him; customers loved him. Luke was always everyone's favorite.

"Was he going home from work?"

Chloe's wet eyes find mine, and I see the confusion in them before it clears, and she understands what I'm asking. She nods, her red bangs bobbing as she does. "He worked the shift before mine. He stayed after to spend some time with me. We were both so busy all the time, trying to get everything ready for . . ." She rubs her stomach again. I can tell that it's become a habit for her, maybe even a nervous tick, a thing she does when she can't say what she needs to.

I don't know what else to say. I don't know what else I *can* say to Chloe. I don't have answers, either. The sounds of her sniffles eventually die away, until there are no sounds coming from our table. We sit in silence for a long time, and I realize that Cade hasn't eaten his toast. He looks just as lost as I feel, as I suspect Chloe feels, too. We're all just drifting along with no direction.

"We should probably find Gwen and Wes," Cade says, finally, after what feels like forever.

I feel a little guilty that I haven't been worried about them. For all I know, they might be halfway to Chicago by now. I look at Chloe's tear-stained face, and I can't help but remember the tears running down

Gwen's. I look away from her.

I reach into my pocket for my phone, planning to call Wes and beg them to come back for us, but I can't. My phone is still in the side pocket of my bag in Wes's back seat. I sigh. "Can you call Wes?"

Cade nods. He's pulling his phone out of his pocket when someone approaches the table. When I look up, I'm fully expecting Charlotte to have joined us at the table again, but instead, it's a man in a police uniform, the same cop as before, and I can tell from the way he's standing, his hands on his hips, his mouth turned down in a frown, that this isn't going to be good.

"I thought you two looked familiar," he says, crossing his arms, and I just stare at him. It takes me a second to process the situation, to put everything together, to understand what he means.

"What's going on?" Chloe asks. She doesn't seem too alarmed, doesn't seem to notice the police car outside the window with its lights on, flashing red and blue. I stare at the name on his uniform while he answers. OFFICER PHELPS.

He gestures at us but speaks to Chloe. "These two were reported missing in Texas a few days ago. Your cousin Bret sent the picture to me on a whim when it went out, but damn, I never thought I'd see them in Dexter." Her cousin? The way he says it confuses me, and I'm quickly losing the thread of this conversation.

Chloe's eyebrows slant down into a V. "Missing? But they're not missing."

Officer Phelps grumbles. "Their parents seem to think they are. I already made the call. An officer is on his way over from one of the Ann Arbor stations as we speak. He'll be here in a few minutes."

Cade's mouth falls open, and he stutters, but I'm strangely calm. Wasn't it always going to end this way, with my mother getting exactly what she wants? That's life.

"Can't we just go home?" Maybe if I come back on my own, my mother will leave me alone.

Officer Phelps grimaces. "Sorry. No."

The little bell over the door jingles, and then we're joined by another cop. And now everyone in Sal's is staring at us, including Charlotte, who's standing behind both cops with the decaf carafe in her hand.

"Nice to see you two," the other cop says, coming up to us. He looks a little like a cartoon character, with a baseball hat on and sunglasses perched on his nose. I think he's looking down at us by the tilt of his head, but I can't say for certain. "I'm going to need you to come with me."

I look at Cade, and I can see his pulse in the side of his neck, beating quick. But before I have a chance to say anything, Chloe pushes up from the table, until she's standing next to the first cop, her belly almost touching him.

"What are you going to do with them?" Chloe asks the new cop.

He shrugs. He doesn't seem to be particularly concerned about anything. "They'll be held in a detention center until a relative can come and get them."

Chloe's eyes go wide. "A detention center? They're not guilty of anything."

The cop puts up his hands in a helpless gesture. "That's the law. There's nothing I can do. They can't be left alone, and I don't have any officers who are going to be interested in babysitting them until a parent gets here."

I'm surprised he's telling Chloe all of this so casually, like they know each other. He's barely even glanced at us.

Chloe puts a hand on Officer Phelps's arm. "Can't you take them to the station back in Dexter?" I look at the hand on his arm. She seems to have a little influence in this situation, and it makes me wonder if there's any way we'll be able to wiggle out of this, to keep moving to Chicago and the rest of the trip, to get back to Gwen and Wes, wherever they care.

The Ann Arbor cop makes a noise of protest. "They're in my jurisdiction. This is Ann Arbor, not Dexter."

But Chloe doesn't seem interested in what he has to say. She turns pleading eyes on Officer Phelps and says, "Please, Dad."

I feel a jolt at hearing her call Officer Phelps this, and I look over at Cade, who glances over at me before looking back where Chloe is still clutching her father's wrist.

Officer Phelps, Chloe's father, looks down at the floor and shakes his head. "I can request they be transferred, but it could take some time." He shuffles his feet and then looks up at the Ann Arbor cop, who's pushing up his baseball cap to wipe sweat off his forehead.

When the cop realizes we're all looking at him, he puts his hands on his hips, lifts his chin, and says, "Hope the joy ride was worth it."

Chapter Fourteen

"This isn't exactly how I saw this trip going," Cade says, and I nudge him with my elbow. We're in the back seat of a police cruiser, parked outside a police station in Ann Arbor, watching out the window as Officer Phelps and the cop from Ann Arbor have a heated discussion.

"They're going to send us back, aren't they?" I pull my feet up onto the seat and wrap my arms around my legs, tucking my face against them so I don't have to look anymore. I was calm before, in the diner, probably because it didn't feel like any of this could possibly be really happening to me. But now that we're here, waiting for them to decide our fate, my whole body shudders. I don't know what happens next. I don't know what they're going to do with us.

"I think they have to," Cade finally says. "We're minors. They can't just let us go."

I snort. "Right. Minors. I'll be eighteen in six months. Maybe I'll just run away again then. Luke did it, and there was nothing anybody could do."

Cade just looks at me, probably because he knows it's an empty threat. I don't want to run away like Luke did. I don't have the energy to, even if I wanted to. I didn't want the trip to end this way, but I'm also kind of ready to go home, back to my own bed and my own stuff and my own town in Texas. This was Luke's dream, not mine.

"I haven't studied for my SATs."

Cade's eyebrows turn in. "What?"

I press my forehead to my knee and turn to look at him. "I know I'm supposed to be taking my SATs soon, but I haven't even started studying for them. My grades dropped last year, my GPA took a big hit, I haven't even started looking at colleges, and I don't even know if that matters because I'm probably going to go to Tate anyway, and not because anyone expects me to, and not because I'm scared to leave Eaton, and not even because I'll get a tuition break because my mom works there. I like Tate. I like Eaton." All the words come spilling out of me, and I have to take a big breath once they're out.

Cade doesn't say anything, but the corners of his mouth are turned up slightly. He reaches over and takes my hand. I feel like I've been fighting for too long and now my body is sore and worn out.

"I'm scared," I say. I convinced myself when Luke died that nothing would change now that he's gone forever. He was gone for so long before he died, so what could possibly be different? But I can already feel it. Before, there was still that chance, lingering under everything every single day, that Luke might come back. But now, that's not even there anymore. Now, there's just a red-headed girl in Michigan with a cop for a father and a baby on the way. Whose life is this?

Cade runs his hand through my hair, brushing it away from the side of my face. "You're going to be okay."

"I guess you'd know." If anyone can assure me that I'll eventually be okay, it's Cade.

He smiles a little, and then the driver's side door flies open, and Chloe's father drops down behind the steering wheel. "Buckle up," he says.

"Gwen and Wes," I say to Cade, remembering when I look at Officer Phelps what we were doing right before he showed up. Cade's eyes go wide. Time and time again we've forgotten about them. It's been over two hours since they drove away from Luke's house, and we haven't told them where we are.

"Shit," he says, glancing up through the window at Officer Phelps. He takes out his phone and tries to turn it on, but the screen stays black. His eyes shoot to me. "Must be dead," he says, holding down the power button, but nothing happens.

"What can we do?"

In the front seat, Chloe's father turns the car on, puts it in gear, and we roll away from the police station. Cade looks at me, his eyes wary, and then shrugs. "Maybe we can call them when we get back to Dexter."

"Maybe."

It feels like hours before anything happens. The police department in Dexter is also the fire department in Dexter, and it's still the quietest place I've been in days. People walk through every few minutes, speaking quietly among themselves, but it's like a library in here.

"What happens next?" I ask Officer Phelps. Chloe's been sitting with us this whole time, the four of us crammed around Officer Phelps's desk at the precinct, and she seems to perk up when I ask her father this.

Officer Phelps, bent over a stack of paperwork, slides his glasses down his nose. "Both your families have been notified that you're here. Miss

Johnston, one of your parents is currently on a plane from Texas. Mr. Matthews, your grandmother asked your aunt and uncle from Indiana to come and get you."

At this, Cade's head comes up, and he looks back and forth between all of us. "Really? My aunt and uncle are coming?"

Officer Phelps shrugs. "Far as I know." He goes back to scribbling on a form.

Chloe bites her lip and rubs her stomach. "I'm so sorry for getting you into this, guys."

Cade sends her a confused look, and I imagine the same look is mirrored on my face. "This is definitely not your fault." I tell her. "You didn't even do anything. This is my fault."

Cade sends me the same look. "It's nobody's fault. Everybody made their own choices."

At that, Chloe and I both shut up. Cade is probably right.

The sun is already starting to set, blaring orange outside the large windows, when Officer Phelps gets a phone call. When he replaces the receiver, he gestures at Cade. "Time to go."

Cade sighs, and I can see the relief in his eyes. Maybe he's feeling the same way I do, that this sucks and we're ready for it to be over. But Cade probably isn't even going back to Eaton. He's probably going to Indiana. The knowledge stirs inside me. Indiana is so far from Texas.

We both stand, and through an open door at the front of the room, I can see Sam and James and Laney, all waiting for Cade at the reception desk. They look tired, and I can't help but think that if James had just sent us back to Texas when we got to Indianapolis, none of this would be happening. We've made everyone's lives that much harder.

Cade takes my hand, but when I move to follow him out of the room, Officer Phelps puts a hand on my arm. "I'm sorry, Ellie, but you have to stay here."

Cade whips around, and I see realization dawn on his face, the same realization I had moments ago. We're not leaving Ann Arbor together. He shakes his head anyway, his eyes set on mine. "I can't leave her here."

Officer Phelps sighs, but it's a gentle sigh. I get the feeling that Officer Phelps does everything gently. "I understand this is difficult, but that's the way it has to be. Once everyone is accounted for, I'm sure you'll figure it out."

I nod, trying to pull my hand away from Cade's, but he clutches at me. "We can wait. I'll ask them to stay until your parents come." There's a strange kind of desperation in his eyes, and I glance at Chloe and her father before pulling Cade away from them, off to an empty corner of the room. We're still in eyesight, but I'm pretty certain they won't be able to hear us. I take his face in my hands, and I can see the defeat written all over his face before I've said anything.

"I'll be fine," I say. "Don't worry about me."

Cade leans in close to me, his voice quiet. "Ellie, a few hours ago, I had to carry you out of Luke's room. I don't want to leave you."

He has a point. But whatever rose to the surface back at Luke's house is simmering deep down now. I'm too exhausted to feel anything, too unsure of where I'm supposed to go from here.

I let my hands slide to the collar of his shirt, and I tug at it. "I promise

I'll be okay. My parents won't be long. I have Chloe." I don't really know if having Chloe with me is reassuring or not. She's been mostly quiet the whole time we've been here, and I can only imagine that she'll just get quieter when Cade leaves, seeing as he's the one who always manages to find something to say when no one else will.

Cade purses his lips, sighs, drops his hands away from me. "Okay. I'll go." He says it like I'm about to go to my execution, and he's being set free. I grip his shirt tighter, pulling him down to me, until his mouth is on mine.

For a second, I forget about the police station and Chloe and her father and Cade's family. I push up onto my toes and kiss him the way I wanted to that night at the drive-in, wrapping a hand around the back of his neck. When I drop back down onto my heels, he presses his forehead to mine and then pulls back.

He reaches out and brushes some of my hair out of my eyes. "I'll see you soon, Eloise." And with that, he walks away.

I feel a different kind of emptiness when he's gone. Before, the emptiness was almost comforting, a vacant sunkenness, but now, it's a clawing kind of emptiness, like shadows and sharp corners. I watch Cade hug Sam and Laney, say something to James, before the three of them walk through the glass front door without looking back.

"I'm sure your parents will be here soon enough," Officer Phelps says. When I turn, I find that he's watching me with sympathy in his eyes, and I go back to my little wooden chair beside his desk.

"That's what I'm worried about," I say, and Chloe snorts.

I look over at her, at the sun shining through her red hair, and I get why Luke liked her so much. It's hard not to.

"Should I tell my parents about the baby?" I ask her. "When we get back to Texas, I mean."

Chloe looks at me for a long moment, her eyebrow puckered, and then her skin seems to smooth as the confusion is wiped away. "Your parents already know."

I should understand the words that just came out of her mouth, but they seem like gibberish, like she spoke them in extreme slow-motion, the words distorted and indecipherable. "They know?"

She nods, and I can tell by the sadness in her eyes what she's just done, revealing one more lie, one more secret on a list already so long that I've lost track. Of course, she doesn't know about all the other lies. But she knows that this one hurts. That much is clear.

"Chloe," Officer Phelps breaks in. "I think you should go home and get some rest. You've been going since last night. You can't push it." He glances down at her stomach, and she reaches up to press her hand there.

"Yeah," she says, looking at me. The sadness is still there, and how she can bear to have sympathy for me after all she's been through, I'm not sure. She reaches over and plucks something from her father's desk, a business card, and flips it over on the desktop. "Can I borrow that?" she asks Officer Phelps, motioning at his pen, and he hands it over. She scribbles something on the card and then hands it to me.

Her phone number.

While I'm still looking at the card, she bends my way slightly and puts her hand over mine. I meet her eyes, so blue and so kind. "Call me if you want to talk," is all she says, and then Officer Phelps helps her to her feet.

"I'll walk you out," he says, taking her by the arm and leading her to the door like she's injured. I watch them go and feel a weird pull toward them, something that makes me want to beg them not to go.

Because now I'm completely alone.

———————

Officer Phelps has been filling out paperwork for what seems like hours when I look up and see two faces pressed to the door beside the reception desk, looking in on me. My heart leaps into my throat, and I glance at Officer Phelps quickly, waiting to see if he's noticed. I can see through the window that Gwen's and Wes's faces are pressed to that the reception desk is empty.

"I need to use the bathroom," I tell Officer Phelps.

He doesn't even stop writing. "Out the double doors, hang a right. It's at the end of the hall. Be quick."

I hurry away from his desk and as soon as I'm in the lobby, I grab both Gwen and Wes and pull them into the hallway where Officer Phelps said the bathroom was. I can see the sign for it at the end of the hall.

"You can't let anyone see you," I say, panicked at all the many ways this could possibly go wrong, but Gwen has already moved toward me, wrapping her arms around me.

"We were so worried," she says, squeezing me. "We went back to the house and there was no one there, and then Cade told us you guys got picked up by the police." She steps back and looks at my face, examining me like I might be injured. I try to erase the image in my head of her crying and running from Chloe's house.

"It wasn't quite as scary as it sounds," I tell her. I don't want her to give me any more credit that I deserve. "Gwen, I'm so sorry," I say, feeling like it's the most important thing that needs to be said right now, but she waves me off.

"It's fine," she says in a way that tells me it's really not but that she's going to pretend it is. "Just tell us what to do."

I shake my head and glance behind them, watching to make sure the receptionist isn't coming back. "Nothing. Just go home, okay? Go back to Eaton."

Gwen's eyebrows turn in. "Without you?"

I shrug. "It's kind of our only option. My parents are on their way anyway. You guys should go back home. Or um . . ." I stop, the words catching in my throat. "Or you can finish the trip without us." The thought makes my stomach ache.

Gwen reaches out and squeezes my arm. "Absolutely not. We'll go back to Eaton, wait for you there."

I just nod, feeling, irrationally, like I'm going to cry again. "And don't tell anyone you were with us. I don't want you to get in trouble."

"Yeah," she says, and then she's hugging me again, and I wish I could beg her to stay. I wish I could ask her to wait for me, to stay until my parents come, but I know I can't. So I pull away and look at Wes.

Wes looks just as tired and sad as Gwen does. "We'll see you in Eaton," he says, tapping me gently on the shoulder before the two of them disappear out the front door. I stand at the end of the hallway and watch them drive away for the second time today.

It's just Officer Phelps and me in the room when he gets a call to tell me that my father is here for me. He doesn't mention my mother, and I have to assume that's because she's not here. I meet my father at the reception desk, and he signs some kind of papers, but I can't even watch him do it, so I just wait by the front door until he's done.

We don't say a word to each other as we walk out to the parking lot and get in a car that I've never seen before: black and shiny. A rental.

We drive to the airport, where my father buys two tickets back to DFW airport, and by the time we're on the plane, my skin is clammy from the anxiety of no words passing between us. I feel like I need to say something, but I feel even more like I need to wait for him to ask me something, to ask why I'm here or how I knew where to go or who I was with, *anything*. But he doesn't, and it's been so long that I feel like my lips are permanently attached together, that I couldn't get my mouth and jaw and vocal cords to work, no matter how hard I try.

So I turn away from my dad on the plane. I don't have anything to do, don't even have my phone, since it's all in Wes's car. So I stare out the window, and I wait for something to make sense.

———

The display on the seat in front of me says we're somewhere over Kansas when my father puts something in my lap. I have no clue what to expect when I see the long, white envelope. I stare at it for a long time and then glance at my dad, but he's not looking at me. He presses his face into his hand, so I reach for the envelope.

There's a stack of papers inside. I turn the flap down and look at the front of the envelope, and that's when I see the addresses on it. It's addressed to my father's building at work, but that's not what gets me.

It's the return address.

From an address in Ann Arbor.

Ann fucking Arbor.

I close my eyes, bracing myself, telling myself that maybe it's nothing. Maybe it's from a long time ago. From someone my father used to know. A business acquaintance. A friend from college. It's definitely not from Luke.

I try to make myself believe it. I take a deep breath. And then I open my eyes and reach inside the envelope. I pull out a stack of papers. They've been unfolded and refolded multiple times, until they have more than one crease down the middle, the papers bisected in half in a dozen different spots.

The first thing I see is Luke's signature, on a line with two others, stacked one on top of the other. I can't make out the printed words above them. Not because they're illegible, but because my hands are shaking so fiercely that the words are a blur on the paper.

When I can finally read it, when I get everything in my body to settle enough, when I get my blood to stop quivering, I look at the papers. It's some sort of legal paperwork. It's some kind of paperwork for a house. And it has Luke's signature on it. And my dad's. I skim over it, trying to make sense of it, when I see the address, printed clearly on the very last page.

26 E Cole St Dexter MI 48130. The house that Luke lived in with Chloe. There's a ton of papers, some kind of lease, but then the legal paperwork ends and there's just a letter. I recognize Luke's handwriting immediately. It's always been slanted chicken scratch, since we were kids, so small and almost unintelligible. But it's there.

Dad,

 Thanks for doing this. I'll fax a copy to your office as soon as everything is taken care of. We're moving in next week. Talk soon.

 Luke

There's a lot to wade through, so much information and so many questions in just three sentences. But my eyes get stuck on those last two words. *Talk soon.* Talk soon. Like they were talking all the time. Like they were in constant contact.

But that's not possible. It's not possible because Luke was on the road. He didn't leave us anything. His social media accounts were deleted. His phone always went to voice mail.

But here it is, a piece of mail from him like it's nothing. Like we didn't lose him in every way, like this isn't a tiny piece of him that's so goddamn huge that it could be hidden away until this very moment.

There's still one more piece of paper, and when I look at it, and see that it's a US map with Luke's exact route penciled in, it's almost more than I can take.

"I don't understand what this is." I almost choke over the words. My hands have started shaking again, so hard that my father reaches over and takes the papers out of them. He puts them back in the bag that I just realized he has.

"I helped Luke get out of Eaton."

I finally look over at him. I watch his mouth move, but everything sounds fuzzy. How long did he know? How long did he know that Luke was going to leave? How long were they planning it? How long were they keeping this a secret from everyone? And how many times did my father look at me across the dinner table, knowing that Luke was going to leave and maybe never come back? How long did the two of them smile knowingly, while I sat there like a clueless idiot?

"He came to me a while ago, said he had this trip all planned out. He said he couldn't take it anymore, and that he needed to leave."

I scrub my hands over my face. I'm so angry at him, I could scream. But I want answers. That's all I've ever wanted. "But why? Why did he need to leave? Why couldn't he just wait?"

My father presses his lips together, and I'm afraid that his words have dried up. He's barely spoken a word to me since Luke died, wasn't much of a talker before that, and I'm certain that any second now, the words will stop flowing, and he'll go back to being the ghost he's been for the last month, for the last year, floating around on the edge of our lives.

But after a minute, he says, "I think that's a story for another day."

"No," I say, my voice too loud. I lower it when the person in the seat in front of me sends me an angry glance. "No, you don't get to just *not* answer my questions."

He puts up a hand to stop me. "That's not my side of the story to tell, Ellie. All I can tell you is my side. I helped Luke, got him a credit card that your mom didn't know about, helped him get a house, kept his secret."

"I can't believe you knew all of this and didn't tell me." Anger is a monster I don't have to invite in anymore. It always lives inside me, so it takes close to nothing for it to make an appearance, to butt its head into any situation.

"He asked me not to tell you."

"I'm pretty sure that promises like that expire when the person with the secret *dies*, Dad."

"How was I supposed to tell you this, Ellie? How could I possibly put this on your shoulders after everything? How could I know that you would be able to handle it?"

"It's not your job to worry about what I can and can't handle. I deserved to know."

His shoulders slump. "I know. I wanted to. But I thought maybe it would be easier for you not to know." He pauses. "Sometimes I wish I didn't."

"Why?"

He pauses, looks like he's measuring his words, treading carefully. "It's hard being left behind. Right?" He looks at me expectantly, but I don't think I can agree with him. Not because I don't know what it feels like to be left behind, but because I'm not so certain that *he* was left behind.

I resist the urge to reach into his bag and rip the letter back out of it. I think again about those last words: *Talk soon.* "But you got to talk to him all the time. You knew where he was. How can you even—"

"We didn't talk all the time. He needed my help. He asked me for help when he needed it, and the rest of the time I didn't exist. You know how Luke was."

My stomach clenches. It was hard enough for me to admit to myself that I was mad at Luke, that he did something wrong by me, but hearing my father talk about Luke this way, after being so disconnected for so long, is too much for me. "I don't know what you're talking about."

His eyes turn to me, slits that seem accusatory. "Yes, you do. You knew better than anyone. Luke kept people around when he needed them, but at the end of the day, it was only Luke. He looked out for himself; he did what he wanted. Hell, he took off and forgot we existed." He's starting to raise his voice, and I'm afraid we're going to get kicked off this plane.

He seems to realize this. He looks around, ducking his head a little like no one will realize he's there if he just makes himself small enough. Finally, he speaks again. My face is hot with rage, my heart pounding hard.

Even though I know he's right.

I want to put an ocean between us.

His face is as blank as the day he told me Luke was dead. I wonder if there'll ever be life in his eyes again.

"I didn't do any of this to hurt you. Luke asked for help. He was my son. I would have done anything he asked me to. If roles were reversed, you would have done the same thing."

On this point, I know for certain that he's wrong. Just like Luke thought, I would have been selfish. I would have begged him not to leave. I would have begged him to take me with him. I would have given anything to keep him.

"If it was *your* secret," he goes on, "I wouldn't tell, either."

I look him in the eye for the first time in months. They're ice blue. Luke's eyes. I was always jealous of that, of the way Luke and my dad had interesting eyes, the kind of eyes that people comment on when they meet you, while my eyes were plain: brown and simple like my mother's.

"I've never had secrets," I say, and this much is true. Until the moment I got that map and kept it from Gwen and Cade, I've never kept secrets. Not from my parents, and certainly not from Luke.

My father just nods. "That's something I've always admired about you."

Once the moment has passed, and I'm pretty sure my father isn't going to pick up the thread of the conversation, I say, "What about Chloe?"

My father grimaces. "I didn't know about the baby, not until we got there." He shudders. "We found out we were going to be grandparents the same day we went to pick Luke up. It almost destroyed your mother."

I try to imagine it from my mother's point of view, but it's tainted. All I can think about are all the words they screamed at each other, all the ways she found to sabotage Luke, over and over again. I scrub at my face. I can't bring myself to think about my mother's role in all of this right now. I'm ready to be done with this conversation, to be done with all of it. But my father isn't ready to let go.

"Why'd you go to Michigan, Ellie?"

It's a question with a million different answers—to find Chloe, because we planned the trip with Luke, because Luke did it, to get away from my mother, to get away from Eaton—but I don't know which one will be the most satisfying for my father. I shrug. "I don't really know."

He frowns but doesn't say anything.

"If I'm being honest," I say, "I guess I thought maybe you'd be glad to be rid of me. It's not like Mom really wants me around."

I try to read my father's expression, but he's still a blank page. "This is still our family, and that's not going to change."

A hot tear slides down my cheek, and I brush it away quick. "I don't know if I can do this without him," I say, so quiet that I'm not positive he heard me at all.

———————

When I open the door, I hear voices in the living room, and I know immediately it's not some movie that my parents decided to watch. I know these voices, know the cadence of their arguments because it seems to be their consistent state: Mom and Luke.

"I can't believe you did this," Luke says, his voice like acid. "I get it, you want to control everyone's lives. You think you know what's best for us, but this is crossing a line."

I tiptoe up to the wall that separates the living room from the kitchen and as subtly as I can, I peek around the pillar I'm hiding behind. Luke has an envelope in his hand, and he's waving it in my mother's face as my father looks on from the couch. I recognize it. I know it because I watched Luke discover it sitting on top of his desk this afternoon when we got home from school. I watched the way his entire body deflated when he opened it. An acceptance letter from Tate.

At first, I thought he was overreacting. Luke does that. A lot. I thought maybe he was looking at that acceptance letter as something so much worse than it was, like it was the final straw, like it was the sound of the chains behind attached to his wrists, the door to any other kind of life finally closing.

But now, watching the two of them, I know it's more than that.

"You want to go on adventures and see the world, that's fine, Luke. But when that's over, and when you still need a future to look forward to, Tate will be here. All I did was secure this for you so that you would have something to come back to."

Luke slams the envelope down on the table beside the sofa and rushes off, and I stay where I am, hidden behind this pillar, certain I'll never move again.

———————

The house has never been as quiet or as still as it is when we get back home, like the only thing to touch the air for days has been the specks of dust that float though the patches of light coming in through the entryway window. I don't know if this house is ever really going to feel like home again, but it feels emptier now, with just the two of us.

"Where's Mom?"

My father sets his duffle bag down beside the front door. I've somehow come away from Michigan completely empty-handed. "She went to stay with your aunt for a few days."

I snort. "Guess she wasn't really that worried about me. Why did she did bother with the missing persons report?" I'm already halfway to the stairs when I hear my father's voice behind me.

"Actually, I'm the one that filed the report."

I spin around and see that he's still standing by the front door, his hands tucked into his pockets. For just a second, he looks more like the father I remember: starched jeans, button-down shirt, brown shoes, always brown shoes, even if they don't match his clothes. There's some color in his skin, and for the first time in a year, I feel like he's looking *at* me instead of *through* me.

"Why?"

He shrugs. "I was worried. Luke left, and look what happened. I didn't want it to happen to you, too."

My parents aren't affectionate. They're not the kind of parents that insist on saying *I love you* anytime one of us leaves the house or demands hugs and kisses or anything like that. This, right here, may be the first time my father has said anything that gave away that he cares. I'm so unpracticed for such an occasion that I have no idea how to respond.

I know he wants to say more, but I'm exhausted, so I turn for the stairs again and go up to my room. Inside, I shut the door and take a deep breath. I missed the smell of my own room. It's late, so I don't feel bad about turning out the light and immediately crawling into bed. I missed my bed.

I'm drifting off, somewhere between reality and Dexter, Michigan, when I think about the day Luke brought the map home, how excited he was, how he promised we were going to go, how he became so obsessed, so one-track-minded about it. That's what he did, becoming obsessed with things. Everything was his favorite thing until it wasn't anymore: his favorite restaurant, his favorite video game, his favorite outfit . . . his favorite person.

That's when something starts to claw at my throat. His favorite person. Sometimes it was Wes, or Gwen, or that teacher that let him get away with something, or someone on the track team, or the new kid. But underneath it all, I always thought it was me. I was his favorite person, his real favorite.

Maybe I was wrong.

I reach into my back pocket for the map. But there's nothing there. I check my other pocket. Also empty. I sit up in bed and feel around in my sheets, hoping maybe it just fell out while I was drifting off.

But it's not here. I flip on my bedside light and scan the floor, but it's nowhere. The house is completely silent, and when I go out into the hallway, it's totally dark, too. I retrace all of my steps, all the way down the stairs and out to my father's car. I check the front seat, the back seat, the entire driveway. Nothing.

Which means it's gone. It could have fallen out of my pocket any-where, Sal's, the police station, the airport. I can't believe I've been so distracted that I didn't notice it was gone earlier, and now there's no way I'm ever getting it back.

I go back upstairs and curl up in my bed, but my whole body is trem-bling. That was the only real thing of Luke's I had left. Chloe gave it to me because she trusted me. And I lost it.

I cry until my eyes are crusty, memories flashing through my mind so fast I can't catch hold of them.

Luke, bent over the map, a grin on his face and a marker in his hand. Luke, stuffing the map into his bag when one of our parents came into the room. Luke, taking the map with him when he left that night. When he moved on. When he found a new favorite.

Chapter Fifteen

When I wake up, the sun is shining bright, and there's someone standing in my doorway. I rub my eyes, stinging from the sunshine—I didn't close my curtains last night—and then realize it's my mother in the doorway.

Her hair is down, like it almost never is, her arms crossed, leaning against the doorjamb. She looks different, but I can't explain how, and I wonder if maybe I'm making her up. Maybe she's not even really here, and this is just the way I remember her from before. But before what, I don't know. Before she turned into our mother who hovered over us, held the puppet strings, or at least tried to, until Luke had enough. There had to be a time before, right? Has she always been like this? Why can't I remember?

"I thought you were at Aunt Linda's."

She presses into the carpet with toe of her shoe. Tennis shoes. I didn't even know she had tennis shoes.

"I wanted to come see you. Make sure you're okay. Your father says he told you everything."

Not everything, I think. There's still a detail that's missing. I think I have a pretty good idea of the truth, but I want to hear her say it. "What did you do to him?"

She sighs. "I didn't want him to lose any time. I figured he would go through his phase, take his time off, whatever, and then he would go to Tate, and then he'd be happy that I applied for him. He always talked about leaving, but I thought he meant a year off. Maybe a semester. Not *this*."

I pull my legs up against me, tucking my knees under my chin. "You wrote his application essay and everything?"

"No. He had to write one for one of his classes. I just did a little editing before I sent it."

It was ballsy, that's for sure. Applying for your son to a school you want him to go to without his permission, knowing that there was a fifty percent shot it might all go up in flames.

But I can see it from Luke's point of view. My mother, exerting her control in any way that she could.

There's a long silence, and then she says, "I just wanted him to choose *us*."

The tears threaten to take over again, and I push them down. I can't take any more of that. I cried until I felt sick to my stomach, and now my eyes are crusty, my cheeks, too. "What happens now?"

For once, I'm okay with my mother being in control here. I want her to tell me what to do. I want her to plan out the next five years of my life. I want her to leave things on my desk for me to do because moving forward on my own seems impossible, making decisions, figuring out what I want. Wouldn't it just be easier if she did it all for me?

"I don't know if I can ever forgive your father. Or myself. I'm going to stay with your aunt for a little while. Just until . . ." She never finishes the sentence. "Your father will be here with you."

I don't know if she means for that to be comforting, or if she's just

looking for something else to say. Either way, she doesn't seem to know
how to follow up. She stands in the doorway for a long time, and then
finally, she says, "I should go. I'm glad you're home."

"Mom." I don't even know what I want to say, why I called her back.
I just don't want her to leave yet. She turns and looks at me, her hands
clutching the doorjamb giving away the tension she won't let show in
her face. "Please don't go."

She sighs. "I can stay for a little while, but—"

"Don't go to Aunt Linda's." I think I shock us both when I say the
words. I've never known how to feel about my mother. I still don't. But
she's my mother. That has to count for something.

She bites her lip, but her eyes still turn red, watery, her nose going
pink. "I don't think I can stay, Ellie. It hurts."

"What about me?" I don't know if I can bear to watch someone else
walk out of my life, even my mother, who I've always wanted to get away
from, always hated having hovering around. My dad said we were still a
family, but will we still be a family if she gives up on us now?

Her chin puckers, and a tear finally escapes, sliding down her skin. "I
can't fix it."

Nobody can fix it. We're broken, and there's no going back. "You don't
have to fix anything. Just—just stay." I'm choking my words out now,
pleading. "Please, please don't go."

She presses her forehead to the doorjamb and squeezes her eyes shut.
"Okay," she finally says and then gasps for a breath. "Okay. I'll stay." She
lets go of the doorway and takes a deep breath. "Are you hungry?"

She doesn't wait for me to answer. She turns and disappears into the
hallway, and I feel a strange contentment. It doesn't make things better,

but at least it doesn't make them worse.

———————

The next time something wakes me up, it's voices and the scent of cinnamon. I turn over and see Gwen and Wes in the light of my desk lamp, quietly arguing about something as they hover in the corner of the room. Gwen glances over at me, and her eyes go wide when she sees that I'm awake.

"Oh God, I'm so sorry. We didn't mean to wake you up." She holds up something, and I realize it's my bag. "We just wanted to bring this to you. It has your phone in it. Your mom let us in."

I rush over and take it from her, collapsing back on my bed as I rifle through the pockets. "Is the map in here?"

Gwen comes to sit on the bed beside me, her hands pressed into my blanket. "I thought you had the map with you."

I sigh and shove my bag to the floor. "I did, but it must have fallen out of my pocket somewhere." I feel the tears threatening again, and I clamp them down. "Sorry we had to abandon you guys in Michigan."

Gwen waves me off. "It wasn't your fault."

I send her a disbelieving look. "It was literally *all* my fault. Well, and my dad's, I guess."

Wes, leaning against my desk with his arms crossed, makes a tired noise. "Yeah, he told us everything. And your mom is like, cooking enough food for twenty people. I feel a little upside down right now."

Gwen nods, agreeing. "Yeah. I can't believe all that stuff was going on behind your back, Ellie. I'm so sorry."

"What about what was going on behind *your* back?" I ask her. I think about all the girls Luke was with over the years, the way he kept them around for a few weeks and then discarded them. I never thought he would do that with Gwen, but isn't that exactly what happened?

Gwen looks down at her hands in her lap. "Don't worry about me, Ellie. I can handle my own stuff."

"Do you think Luke used people?"

Wes comes to stand beside me, towering over me. "What are you talking about?"

I shrug. I can't look at either of them. I almost feel ashamed that I've let my father get to me like this, but I can't help but think that maybe he's right. Maybe Luke used people. Maybe he got what he needed from them and then pushed them away, and I just didn't notice because he'd never done it to me, because I thought he never would.

Gwen glances up at Wes, and I see them have a silent conversation the way they do sometimes. Finally, Gwen reaches over and takes my hand. She laces our fingers together, and I look down at them before meeting her eye. "I think it doesn't matter anymore," she says. "It's okay if you need to be mad at him, but I think it's okay if you just want to miss him, too. You can love people even if they're not perfect."

I think of my mother, hovering in my doorway, of my father, watching them fight in the living room that day and saying nothing. Of my own faults, the way I've hurt people.

I set my head on Gwen's shoulder and try not to cry. Part of me wishes for the numbness I felt before. Now, everything hurts, an ache that travels along my veins, sinking into my bloodstream. Feeling nothing has to be better than feeling this.

Gwen runs a hand down my arm. "Want to come hang out with us tomorrow night at Wes's? Video games? Pizza? Maybe a horror movie or two?"

I nod. That sounds so good. My chest feels lighter knowing that they're not just going to leave again. We're not all just going to go our separate ways like we did before. "Okay, but I swear if the only thing Wes gives us to drink is diet root beer, I'm leaving."

Wes's mouth falls open, but Gwen presses her face against my shoulder and laughs.

"Diet root beer is delicious!" Wes says, but then he sighs and reaches a hand out for Gwen. "Hey, I gotta get home. My mom is kind of freaking out about all this. My neighbor sent her that stupid missing kid thing, and she had a cow. Fucking Eaton. But call us if you need anything."

Gwen takes his hand and follows him over to the door, turning to send me a sad smile over her shoulder before she leaves.

———

I go back to work at Books and Things on Monday. It's the last week before the end of summer break, so I need to get as many hours in as I can. The shop is busy, thanks to people coming in last minute for their school books. Mine are stashed under the register so I can make sure to get them before we sell out.

"Doing okay?" Laurie asks, and I just roll my eyes at her. She's asked me this about twenty times since I came in. But I guess I should be grateful that she let me come back in at all, seeing as how I just disappeared and didn't tell her I was going to be gone. But according to her, everyone in Eaton was pretty freaked out when my face showed up on flyers with HAVE YOU SEEN ME? written above it, so she forgave me when I showed up for my shift this morning.

"I'm fine," I tell her. "I'm just a little tired." I've been back in Eaton for a few days now, but I still feel that bone-deep exhaustion every day. At least now it's not accompanied by the brain fog and the tears.

She reaches out and tugs on a strand of my hair. "Okay. Well, in that case, get back to work. What are you just standing around for?" She winks at me and goes to help a girl look for a copy of *Frankenstein*.

I ring up copies of *Romeo and Juliet* and *The Crucible* and *The Scarlet Letter*, one person after another without ever really making eye contact with anyone.

And then someone sets a package of Oreos down on the counter. The thin kind. When I look up and see Cade's eyes, shining down at me, it feels like the whole world lights up. He smiles and pushes the cookies across the counter to me.

"I couldn't bring myself to buy the peanut butter ones. It felt a little like blasphemy."

I'm halfway around the counter before I have the good sense to stop myself. Over by the Required Reading display, Laurie is watching me, even as she hands a slim book to a customer.

"Laurie, could I go on break?"

She doesn't even say anything, just waves me in the direction of the door, a grin on her face. I grab Cade's hand and pull us both out into the parking lot. As soon as we're out of eyesight of any of the customers in the shop, I throw my arms around Cade.

He presses his face into my neck, breathes in and then lets me go.

"You should have told me you were on your way back."

He smiles and shrugs his shoulders, and there's something about the way he does it, his eyes on the ground, his face spread in a grin, the heel of one foot pressing nervously into the toe of the other, that makes him look so unbelievably adorable.

I sigh and press my back to the side of the building, a furniture shop that sits between Books and Things and Cade's garage. The air between us feels different. We haven't seen each other since he left me at the police station in Dexter, and between him dealing with his family in Indiana and me dealing with my family here, we haven't spoken, haven't sent so much as a text message. So, where does that leave us now?

"How was Indiana?"

Cade's chin wrinkles in a thoughtful expression. "It was good. There was, uh, a lot to talk through. It's weird, hearing so much about my own past that I didn't know."

"I know the feeling."

He doesn't look sad necessarily, but his eyebrows curve in, and his mouth is pulled into a line. He looks so serious, the complete opposite of the person he was just seconds ago. I don't know if he wants me to, but I reach out and take his hand, run my thumb along his palm, press my fingers between his.

"Are you okay?" I ask him. A lot happened in Michigan, in Indiana, on that trip. Sometimes, it feels like I was dreaming, and that the next time I wake up, the next time I try to think about all the things that happened, they won't have been real. They'll be a faded memory.

But Cade, he's here. He's real and concrete, and he remembers. He went through it all, too. He went to Indiana and faced his fears.

"Are you?" he asks back.

"Maybe," I say because I don't have a clear enough answer. More okay than I was when I got home. Less okay than I was before Luke left. Maybe I'm a new kind of okay. This is the new normal, not quite all the way okay. "Better now." I mean now that he's here, back where he's supposed to be, and I hope he knows it.

"I missed you," I say even though I don't know if it's an okay thing to say. I look down at our feet, and I see the space between our shoes, just enough space that if he took one more step forward, his toes would press up against mine.

"I missed you, too." I'm still staring down at our shoes. His shoes move closer to mine. I crane my neck to look up at him, and the weird thing I felt in the air just moments ago shifts, becomes nonexistent.

I meet his eyes, and I'm so surprised, as I always am, by how soft they are, how he looks right at me with nothing but tenderness. I hold his gaze, and when I press my hand against the back of his neck, I get this feeling, something low in my stomach, like I just stumbled onto buried treasure.

I pull him down to me, and when his mouth is inches from mine, I say, "Be careful. I might get the impression that you have a crush on me."

He smiles, and then he eliminates those inches, and his mouth melts against mine. I let him press me against the building and kiss me, deep and hungry and delicious.

I guess, all this time, and especially after Luke left, I thought maybe I was just like my mother. I thought maybe I was made of stone, too. Because that's what it feels like to be empty inside, to be numb, like you're made of marble.

But I'm not made of stone anymore. I'm made of this feeling I get when Cade kisses me, when Gwen smiles at me, when Wes calls me his sister, like I have light shooting out of my fingertips, and I want it. I want it all.

———————————

When I get home that night, my father is on the couch. The TV is on, and he's asleep, sprawled across the cushions, snoring. I shut off the TV, but I don't wake him up. My mother must already be asleep in the guest room, where she's been living since she decided not to move out completely.

I go up to my room, ready to go straight to sleep. I worked open to close at the shop, and even though it's really nice to be back in my old routine, back at work, back to feeling like myself, I'm exhausted.

I pull the stack of books I bought for English lit out of my bag to put them on my desk and freeze.

There's an envelope on my desk. Shock slips through me, like somehow I've gone back in time to the day of Luke's funeral and here's the envelope that put the whole thing in motion.

But when I reach out to pick it up, instead of just a return address, this time, there's a name. Chloe's name, in the top left-hand corner of the envelope.

And just like that day, when I first opened the envelope Chloe sent me, when I open this one, there's a map inside. I pull it out and unfold it, and it's Luke's map. I don't know how Chloe got it, whether I lost it in her house or in the police station, but it doesn't matter, because it's here again, in my hands, like it was never gone.

Looking down at it, I wonder if I'm the right person for Chloe to have sent it to. Surely, she deserves to hold onto it more than I do. Chloe and Luke belonged to each other in those last months. They started a family together. So why does she want me to have the map, when she has just as much claim to it?

But I know. Because no one else saw Luke's face when he brought home that map and spread it across the dining room table. Because of all the times Luke came into my room in the middle of the night with an idea of one more place we could stop once we finally took to the road. Because it was my idea, as soon as I saw the map again, to go to Michigan, to tell Wes, to do all of it.

I flatten the map out on my comforter and look at it for a long time. It feels different than it did before. I run my finger along the line that Luke traced, stopping at each circled spot, feeling a fondness for each place. I take the map and tack it to the wall above my desk, stepping back to look at it when it's fixed in place, and even though it's not Luke, it's a tiny piece of him, and for now, it's enough.

Acknowledgments

First, always, I have to thank my God, for blessings that I could never deserve, for this experience, and for this book, which is my heart on a platter.

Jean Feiwel, thank you for giving me the chance to keep writing for Swoon Reads and letting me be part of this family. Lauren Scobell, thank you for your ever-constant kindness and support. Kat Brzozowski—I could never thank you enough for all you've done for me. You help me turn messes into books I can be proud of, and for that I'm forever grateful. A million thank you's for everything. Emily Settle, thank you for all of the hard work you do for me and for all the authors at Swoon Reads. Thank you, Connie Gabbert, for my dreamy cover and Liz Dresner for the design. Special thanks to Dejavis Bosket and Ruqayyah Daud for your comments and suggestions, some of which completely changed the course of this novel. Thank you to Raymond Colon, Ilana Worrell, and Kelsey Marrujo for all you do. And thank you to the rest of the team at Swoon Reads for working tirelessly to keep us all moving forward.

When I became a part of Swoon Reads, I never could have imagined that I would become part of the squad that dreams are made of. When we talk about Swoon Reads being a family, we mean it. Swoon Squad, you are my family now and forever. Thank you for all of your support and your kind words. I wouldn't have made it out of this with my sanity if I didn't have you guys to lean on. I would love to name each and every one of you, but there are so many of us now, so I'll refrain. You all have such big hearts, it amazes me. To my other group, the Electric Eighteens. I am so, so honored to have debuted with all of you. So many talented authors with bright futures and endless enthusiasm. Thank you, all of you. And my lovely friend, Kathy Berla. I'll never reach the end of my appreciation for you. Thank you for taking the time to read this book when it was still a baby.

Thank you, Diane Gonzalez, for your expertise on exactly what would happen with two teenagers who were reported missing and then showed up on the other side of the country; Mady and Micah Lacefield, for helping with all my inquiries about Indiana, but you guys should really move back to Texas; and Lillie Vale, for assuring me that they do, in fact, have fried pickles in Indiana.

This book is the product of a very, very hard year and the years of heartache that followed. And without my friends, who are closer than my own blood, I'm certain I wouldn't have survived those years. Because of that, no thank you will ever be enough, but I can try: Yoon Kang, for taking care of me, feeding me, painting my nails, letting me rant, staying up late into the night making bouquets and centerpieces, and a million other things I don't have room to list. You're the most selfless person I know, and I don't know how I got lucky enough to call you my best friend. Jayma Richmond, for putting a roof over my head and for many, many hours spent playing Call of Duty. Katie Thomson, for hurting with me then and for hurting with me now. You understand in a way no one else can. Meghan Logan, for crying with me, for listening to me, and for never speaking to me with even an ounce of judgement. You are an excellent friend. A huge thank you to my second family, The Fluitts. I'm not sure any of you realize how you've kept my head above water in the last few years. Chris, thank you for always making me laugh, even on my worst days. Sarah, thank you for always being strong and optimistic and kind, even when life throws you hardball after hardball. William, thank you for sharing your imagination, your heart of gold, and your fearlessness with me. Hudson, thank you for always being hilarious and adventurous. And Joshua, thank you for cuddles and smiles and endless hours of cartoons. I love you all dearly.

And my real flesh and blood family: Kathy, thank you for going on this adventure with us and for making me watch Sherlock. How could I survive edits without Sherlock and John? Mom, thank you for literally everything. You are generous beyond measure. Thank you for always being up for a trip to the bookstore, thank you for always getting it when I quote The Office, thank you for always being there when I need help. You mean the whole world to me. And Jeremy, my favorite person of all. Thank you for incredible road trips, hours of Brooklyn 99, a fortune spent on pizza, and for being the best husband I could have ever asked for.